Skating Over
the Line

ALSO BY JOELLE CHARBONNEAU

Skating Around the Law

Skating Over the Line

Joelle Charbonneau

Minotaur Books

A Thomas Dunne Book ⚏ New York

This is a work of fiction. All of the characters, organizations, and events
portrayed in this novel are either products of the author's
imagination or are used fictitiously.

A THOMAS DUNNE BOOK FOR MINOTAUR BOOKS.
An imprint of St. Martin's Publishing Group.

www.thomasdunnebooks.com

www.stmartins.com

Library of Congress Cataloging-in-Publication Data

Charbonneau, Joelle.
    Skating over the line : a mystery / Joelle Charbonneau.
        p. cm.
    ISBN 978-0-312-60662-6 (hardback)
    1. Roller-skating rinks—Fiction.   2. Automobile thieves—Fiction.   3. Murder—
Investigation—Fiction.   I. Title.
    PS3603.H3763S55   2010
    813'.6—dc22   2011018784

First Edition: October 2011

10   9   8   7   6   5   4   3   2   1

for my father, Tony

Acknowledgments

There are so many people who have helped with the creation of this book. Countless thanks are owed to my husband, Andy, who reads every word that I write and pushes me to be better; to my son, Max, who makes every day an adventure; and to my entire family, which never fails to support me no matter what I do. I also want to thank the Chicago-North RWA chapter for cheering me on and the fabulous ladies of the Broken Writers group, who pick me up whenever I am down.

To the Thomas Dunne team—thank you for making me and Rebecca a part of the Minotaur family. My thanks to the wonderful Andy Martin, who inspires and champions us all. I owe huge amounts of applause to my fabulous editor, Toni Plummer, who never fails to find ways to improve the story. Also to PR extraordinaire, Bridget Hartlzer, thank you for working so tirelessly to get the word out about the Indian Falls gang.

There are no words to express how grateful I am to work with the amazing Stacia Decker. Her belief in me and my work helps me believe in myself. Also thanks to all of Team Decker and the entire group at the Donald Maass Literary Agency for your support. You are incredible.

Last, but not least, I would like to say thank you to all the readers, booksellers, and librarians who pick up this book. Without you, none of this would be possible.

Skating Over
the Line

One

I hate men. Okay, maybe hate is an overstatement. There are perfectly nice men in the world who brake for squirrels, are loyal like Lassie, and didn't drop unwanted surprises in a girl's lap. Too bad I didn't know many of them.

Brushing a wayward red curl out of my face, I stared down at the letter in my hands. A combination of terror, outrage, and a weird kind of hope coursed through my body.

"Hey, Rebecca?"

I jumped at the sound of my name. Tearing my eyes away from the paper, I gave what I hoped was a welcoming smile to the teenage girl peering through my office doorway. "Do you need something, Brittany?"

If my voice sounded a bit breathy and strained, Brittany didn't seem to notice. She just shook her Goth black mane and said, "Nope, but Deputy Sean is looking for you." Her accompanying eye roll spoke volumes on her opinions of the local law department. "He's in the parking lot."

Great. A normal visit from Deputy Sean involved being chastised once again for the time I'd poked my overcurious nose into police business. On a typical day, I went to great lengths to avoid Sean Holmes. However, today was anything but typical.

I let the letter fall from my fingers onto the desk, ignoring the temptation to read the message one more time. "Great," I said, giving a hundred-watt smile. "Let's go see what he wants."

I headed out of the office, away from the unwanted letter, and into the roller rink my mother had adored.

Lights flashed. The Village People blared over the loudspeaker as people young and old skated in a counterclockwise circle. The smell of popcorn mixed with wood polish and sweat created an aroma that was distinctly the Toe Stop Roller Rink. This was my livelihood. At least it was until I could sell it and get back to the life I'd left in Chicago.

Dodging a teenage boy on Rollerblades, I pushed open the front doors and stepped into a heat wave. I squinted into the August sunshine in a search for Indian Falls's finest. *Aha!* The former Indian Falls High football hero was lounging on his squad car, eating an ice-cream cone. A perfect example of our tax dollars at work.

I trotted across the parking lot to him. He did a once-over of me in my black shorts and fitted white tank top.

I shook my head. "I can't believe I'm actually coming outside in this heat to talk to you. Couldn't you be obnoxious in the air conditioning?"

Sean leered over his sugar cone. "What can I say? I like seeing you sweat."

I fought the urge to stick out my tongue. Sean brought out the juvenile in me. Unhurried, Sean finished the last bite of his cone.

He crumpled the paper wrapping and tucked it neatly in the front pocket of his jeans. No littering. He placed his hands on his hips, and his eyes narrowed. "Have you seen Jimmy Bakersfield's car?"

"You mean the magenta Volkswagen with the big orange rust spots and the 'Nixon '72' bumper sticker?" I laughed. Jimmy went everywhere in it. He'd bought the thing when it was new, decades ago. He even boasted the car still had the original paint—or what was left of it. "Sean, everyone has seen that car."

Sean frowned. "Have you seen the car today?"

Sean was serious. He wasn't poking fun at me or saying something sarcastic. All of a sudden, I didn't feel like laughing. "Why?" I asked. "Did something happen to Jimmy? Is he . . . you know . . . okay?"

I swallowed hard, waiting for the answer. Two months ago, I'd come back to my hometown to sell my inherited rink and stumbled across the body of the town's handyman—in the girls bathroom. Murdered. Two weeks after that, I'd ended up at the wrong end of a gun while tracking down the killer. Whoever said small-town life was peaceful hadn't visited Indian Falls.

Sean gave me a superior look. "Of course he's okay. I can't say the same for his car. Jimmy says it's gone missing."

"Missing?" I blinked. "As in stolen?" Whoever had stolen that car had to be hard up. The car was a train wreck.

"More likely, he left the keys in the car and some kids took it for a joyride. Either that or Jimmy got tanked and forgot where he parked it." Sean pulled a notebook from his back pocket. "So you didn't see the car parked in your lot today? He told me that's where he last saw it."

I shook my head. "I didn't even know Jimmy was at the rink."

"He wasn't."

3

Sean and I turned at the sound of my grandfather's voice. Smiling, Pop shuffled slowly down the sidewalk toward us.

I shook my head, wishing it was arthritis or old age inhibiting my grandfather's movements. Pop's black jeans were skintight. They made his white satin shirt look almost normal. It was unbuttoned to mid-chest, allowing tufts of steel gray hair to peep at unsuspecting passersby. These days, Pop moonlighted as an Elvis impersonator. Much to my dismay, he believed in living the job.

"Jimmy was at the Senior Center all morning." Pop wiped a wrinkled hand over his sweaty brow. "He went back there to call the cops when he saw his car was missing."

Sean was flipping though his notebook, doing his thorough cop thing, so I forged ahead. "What was he doing parked here? The Senior Center is two blocks away."

"Which is why he parked here." Pop gave me a Polygrip ad–worthy smile. "Jimmy is kind of a ladies' man. He needs exercise to stay in shape. Walking to the center helps him stay fit, and it keeps the car out of sight. Both score dates."

Sean read from his notebook. "Jimmy said he parked his car at that end of the lot this morning."

Sean pointed toward the narrow parking area directly beside the rink, next to an empty gravel-filled lot. Two dark green Dumpsters were the only things sitting there now. Most people, including me, tend to park in the front. No wonder I hadn't spotted Jimmy's Technicolor ride.

Continuing in his best policeman's voice, Sean said, "Jimmy walked to the center at nine o'clock this morning, where he played cards and watched *The Price Is Right*. After lunch, he came back to collect his car and discovered it was gone."

"Lunch was later than normal," Pop offered. "The center usually serves it at noon, but Eleanor and Marjorie got into an argument about a guy on one of those daytime dramas. Nobody wanted to go to lunch before the fight was over, in case there was bloodshed. Marjorie lunging for her knitting needles was the most exciting thing to happen at the center in ages."

Sean and I gaped at Pop.

Sean recovered first. He turned to me. "Are you sure you didn't see anything, Rebecca? His car was in your lot."

So were twenty other cars. Including my own. Still, I didn't think it was smart to point out that detail. Sean wasn't in the mood. Not a surprise. When it came to needing information from me, Sean was never in the mood.

Instead, I said, "I was inside the office most of the day, but I can ask around the rink to see if anyone else did."

"That's a good idea." Pop bobbed his head up and down. "Rebecca here is great at getting people to talk. People think of her as part cop anyway after solving— Ouch!"

I'd elbowed Pop in time to stop him from finishing the sentence. Too bad Sean had heard enough. His eyes bugged out, then narrowed as he turned two shades of red.

"Rebecca is not a member of the Indian Falls Sheriff's Department." Sean's voice sounded as if he'd taken a hit of helium. "I'll talk to the witnesses, and the two of you will stay out of it. Otherwise, I'll arrest you myself."

With that announcement, Deputy Sean hitched up his gun belt and stalked across the parking lot toward my roller rink.

The minute he disappeared inside, I turned to my grandfather and demanded, "Why did you have to say that? Now Sean's going to start giving me jaywalking tickets while I'm standing on the sidewalk."

Pop shrugged while struggling to pull a handkerchief out of his front pocket. "I wouldn't worry. The sheriff will rip up the tickets. He likes you. Besides, I wasn't saying anything that wasn't true. People think of you as a local private detective. That's why I walked down here. Jimmy wants to hire you."

"For what?"

The handkerchief came free from Pop's pants pocket. The momentum sent him staggering back against Sean's squad car. I moved to help him, but Pop waved me off.

"Jimmy wants you to find his car," he explained while lounging on Sean's cruiser. "He doesn't trust the sheriff or Deputy Sean to track it down. I can't say I blame him. The cops couldn't catch a killer. What chance do they have of finding Jimmy's car?"

"A better chance than I do, since they're looking and I'm not."

"You can't turn Jimmy down." Pop wagged his finger at me. "I promised him you'd find his car. Everyone at the Senior Center is expecting it. If you don't help find it, I'll never be able to hold my head up at the center. Then what will I do?"

My foray into criminal investigation had been a fluke, and a self-serving one at that. Solving the last crime had been the only way I could sell the rink and get my life back on track. Too bad the rink hadn't sold right away. If it had, I wouldn't have been having this conversation. I wouldn't have had to disappoint my grandfather, whose shoulders had just slumped in a dejected manner. And was that sweat running down Pop's cheek, or was it a tear?

Damn!

"Okay."

Pop almost gave himself a hernia doing a victory dance in his painted-on pants.

"But," I added, "I'm not promising anything. I'll just ask a couple of questions and see what I can learn."

Besides, Sean was probably right about kids taking the thing for a joyride. With any luck, the car would turn up later today, abandoned in a cornfield. Pop would be able to strut around the center, and I'd be off the hook. What was the harm?

"I'm going back to the center to tell Jimmy. He'll be relieved." Pop patted my cheek.

I nodded while walking with Pop to the sidewalk, but in my mind I was back in my office, holding the letter. "Hey, Pop," I said. "I got a note today from my father."

"What's that sorry excuse for a man want?" Pop asked.

I took a deep breath and said, "Stan is coming back here, to Indian Falls."

I don't know what reaction I expected, but it wasn't my grandfather fainting.

Two

Sprawled on the ground, Pop blinked up at me. "What happened?"

I helped him get into a sitting position while taking deep breaths to calm my panic. "You fainted."

"Fainted?" Pop snorted. "I've never fainted in my life."

The cantankerous sound of my grandfather's voice did my heart good. Pop was okay. Knowing that, I was able to smile.

"Then what are you doing lying on the asphalt?" I asked, trying to hide my amusement.

Pop sputtered for a moment, then announced, "It's because of these damn pants."

Pop struggled to get to his feet, and I helped haul him upright. Indignant, he said, "The women at the center told me I had to wear tight pants in my Elvis act. Well, now I know why Elvis died so young. He probably hit his head after losing circulation in his . . . you know."

I did know, and I would have been a lot happier if I didn't.

Thinking about my grandfather's . . . well, it made me a whole lot more uncomfortable than the sweltering heat.

"Pop," I said, deliberately averting my eyes as he adjusted the crotch of his pants. "While I would love nothing more than to blame your pants, they aren't the reason you passed out."

Pop blinked at me. "They're not? Huh? You think it was the heat."

"I think it was my saying my father is coming to town." Pop's face went white. I took a step closer in case he went down again. "Look, Pop, it's no wonder you're upset. You and Stan don't have the best relationship."

Neither did I. Maybe it was genetic.

Pop shook his gnarled fist. "I want to kill the hairy little wart. The man deserves it for breaking your and your mother's hearts. Heck, his coming to town is a good thing. Gives me a chance to get some of my friends together and rough him up."

Something told me the septuagenarian Untouchables weren't going to scare Stanley Robbins, but what did I know. My father might have a fear of disgruntled old guys.

Smiling at the bizarre image of Pop in a zoot suit, I said, "You're not going to rough up Stan."

"Why? You want to do it?"

Tempting. Too bad I had to take the moral high ground.

"No," I said with regret. My absentee father kind of deserved roughing up. "No one is going to touch him. In fact," I added, hoping for once my father's faithless personality hadn't changed, "I doubt we even see him. When was the last time Stan actually did what he said he was going to do?"

Pop squinted into the sunlight, thinking about my words. "You're right," he said with a frown. "That man ain't never going to set foot in this town. Too bad. I was starting to like the idea of giving him a good butt whopping. A couple of kicks to the keister would knock some much-needed sense into him."

He straightened his shoulders and took a shuffling step down the sidewalk, content to leave the topic of my wayward father behind. Come to think of it, I was, too. It was easier than dealing with the disappointment that always came along with Stan Robbins.

Looking back, Pop asked, "Are you coming?"

"Where?"

"To see Jimmy. I'd think you'd want to talk to him." Pop smiled. "Seeing as how you're the detective on his case."

The Senior Center was a large yellow-and-white brick structure two blocks down the street from my roller rink. At one time, it had been the town's high school. By the time I reached the age of pimples and hormonal angst, a larger high school had been built on the outskirts of town. This building had sat empty for years, until the town's senior citizens commandeered it for bingo and bake sales. Now the place was a hotbed of activity for the over-seventy crowd.

Pop and I walked into the blissfully air-conditioned building, each scarfing down a large cookies-and-cream Blizzard. The Dairy Queen was conveniently located between the rink and the center. This was the real reason I'd agreed to talk to Jimmy.

The minute Pop stepped from the red carpet of the foyer into the beige-colored lobby, women appeared from every direction. A robust gray-haired woman in a yellow tank top came barreling down the blue linoleum-tiled hallway and skidded to a stop in front of my grandfather. My grandfather smiled at her, staring at her breasts. Not the most gentlemanly move. However, the woman wasn't wearing a bra, which made them kind of hard to ignore.

Two white-haired ladies came scurrying from another linoleum-tiled hallway to the right. One lady was tall and thin, the other short and squat. Together, they stopped on the other side of Pop and glared at the lady in yellow. Then, as if on cue, all three women began to speak, vying for my grandfather's attention.

"Arthur, did you hear about poor Jimmy's car?" cooed the bouncing boob lady.

Not to be outdone, the short woman sighed and ran her fingers down Pop's arm. "I can't believe the crime in this town. First the murder, now this."

Pop's eyes looked a little wild as the tall woman began to gush. "Single women like me," she said, with a pointed glare at the bra-less lady, "have to be careful. I'm going to be scared to walk home on my own, unless a man like you would be willing to escort me."

Pop's look of horror made me choke on my Blizzard. I coughed, trying to clear a piece of Oreo cookie from my throat, and four pairs of eyes swung in my direction.

Ditching his admirers, Pop shuffled over and gave me an enthusiastic thwack on the back with his ice cream–less hand. The jolt cleared my windpipe and sent me careening forward. Thank goodness the wall was there to break my fall. The fact that the women were more interested in Pop's heroics than my antics made the episode embarrassing but bearable.

I straightened a skewed painting of a flowering cactus and said, "Pop" above the din of feminine voices. "Isn't Jimmy expecting us?"

Pop flashed me a grateful dentured grin. "Sorry, ladies," he said, removing the short lady's hand from his arm. "My grand-daughter and I have important business with Jimmy. Since she proved to be such a crackerjack detective when solving the murder, Jimmy wants her to take over the investigation of the theft of his car."

Rolling my eyes, I grabbed Pop's arm and marched him toward the hallway to our left. Before we could reach it, Pop turned around and said, "Don't forget to come to the show on Friday night. I'm going to be singing 'Love Me Tender.'"

I rolled my eyes again as a tittering of oohs and sighs followed us down the hall.

"Why did you have to say that?" I asked, letting go of Pop's arm.

Pop shrugged. "I need a big audience on Friday. I have an important agent from the Quad Cities coming to see my act. If things go well, I might get some casino bookings. Those pay good money."

"I wasn't referring to your commercial. Why did you tell them I'm taking over Jimmy's investigation? Couldn't you have told them we were going to play cards or something?"

Pop looked shocked. "I couldn't lie to them." I gave him my best "You have to be kidding" look. Pop was a champion fibber. His lips spread into an unapologetic grin. "Okay, I could have lied to them, but I didn't think of it. Sue me. Those three are big fans of my Elvis act and they can get a little aggressive. Twice now they've tried to tear off my clothing. I didn't think you'd want to see that."

Okay, I couldn't fault him for that. Still, the Senior Center was the hub of Indian Falls gossip. An hour from now, everyone in town would have heard that I was butting into police business. Including Deputy Sean. I'd be behind bars by dinnertime.

Pop, however, didn't seem concerned. "Besides, they would have gotten the information out of Jimmy the minute we left. Jimmy doesn't have my willpower. He's a sucker for a pretty face."

We pitched our Dairy Queen cups in an empty trash can and kept walking. Pop led me past the dining room and the workout facilities before leading me into a small room with a television and a couple of worn armchairs. Slumped deep in one of the chairs, sleeping through a CNN report, was Jimmy Bakersfield.

The minute we walked through the door, his eyes sprang open and his head turned toward us. Jimmy smiled at me, and I couldn't help smiling back. Everyone smiled at Jimmy. His eyes twinkled with laughter while surrounded by drooping, tanned skin weathered by age.

He stretched and pulled his large body upright. The movement caused his gray-and-brown-streaked comb-over to flop up and down. That combined with his tube socks, Bermuda shorts, and ragged flannel shirt suddenly helped me understand why the AARP women of Indian Falls considered my grandfather the catch of the county.

"Hi, Mr. Bakersfield." I waved. "I'm sorry to hear about your car."

"Me, too. And call me Jimmy." Jimmy's comb-over bobbed up and down. "You could've knocked me over with a feather when I saw my car wasn't where I'd left it. I've had that car for thirty-nine years, and someone up and stole it. How's that for rotten luck?"

I agreed it was very bad luck. "Pop and I saw Deputy Holmes in the rink parking lot. He seems determined to find your car as soon as possible."

"Bah!" Jimmy waved away my reassuring words. "Sean Holmes wouldn't be able to find his own ass with a map and a flashlight."

Pop cleared his throat and gave Jimmy a fierce look. Then he glanced at me, sending a red flush climbing up Jimmy's tanned face.

Jimmy hung his head. "Sorry. I don't normally use language like that in front of a young lady, but this thing with my car has me on edge."

I nodded sagely, trying not to laugh. Jimmy's wizened old face looked so contrite, and for no reason. When it came to Sean Holmes, Jimmy and I were of like minds.

"Don't worry about it, Jimmy." Pop patted his friend on the arm and sat in a faded pink armchair. "Why don't you tell Rebecca here about your car. With her on the case, you'll be back driving it around town again in no time."

Sighing, I perched on the chair next to Pop and listened as Jimmy gave me the same information he'd given Deputy Sean.

"So, what do you think, Rebecca?" My grandfather's eyes gleamed with pride. I could tell he was waiting for me to have a psychic moment and crack the case wide open. If only I hadn't left my crystal ball in my other purse. "Do you have any other questions for Jimmy?" he asked.

No. But a truthful answer would have made my grandfather pout, so I improvised. I stood up and walked around the room. Pop and Jimmy probably thought I was pacing in order to think. Truth was, my foot had fallen asleep.

"Did you leave your key under the floor mat?" I asked. My grandfather did this all the time. He said it was a typical Indian Falls practice. I thought it was a passive-aggressive way of scoring a new car.

Jimmy dug into his pocket and pulled out three keys attached to a beer-opener key chain. "Can't do that with a car like mine. It's a classic, you know. That's why it costs so much for insurance."

Sure. That's the reason.

But at least now I had a useful, if not crime-stopping, question to ask. "Jimmy, have you called your insurance company yet? They'll need to know about your car."

Jimmy nodded. "I called Dean right after Sean Holmes blew out of here. Dean Gross handles all my insurance. He has for years. Got me a lower rate last year based on my age and spotless driving record." He ran a hand through his thinning hair, dislodging the hairspray hold. "Dean's normally a crackerjack insurance guy, but I think hearing that my car's been stolen really unhinged him."

"Why? Did he say your insurance has lapsed or that theft isn't part of your coverage?" I'd had that happen two years ago, when I was living in Chicago. It had taken me months to convince the insurance company that I had paid my premium. Going after Jimmy's insurance guy was a task I could throw my energies into.

My enthusiasm was deflated when Jimmy replied, "No. Nothing like that. I hate to admit it, but I told him I was a little fuzzy on whether I'd paid my last bill. The minute I said that, Dean got all quiet. It was like we'd gotten disconnected. I was about ready to hang up, when Dean said I'd called him last week and asked the same question."

Pop gave Jimmy an understanding pat. "That kind of thing can happen. I bought two tubes of denture glue last week because I forgot I'd bought the first one."

Jimmy's eyes narrowed and his face flushed. "I know I didn't call Dean. I said he must have gotten me mixed up with someone else, but he insisted I called. Said I asked all sorts of questions about my coverage. Even claimed I might not remember because of my age. Can you believe that? Telling me I'm losing my mind ain't no way to keep my business. Once my car turns up, I'm going shopping for a new insurance agent."

I vaguely heard Pop voice outrage in defense of his friend. But while the two issued insults about the bias of insurance companies toward old people, my mind was stuck on Dean Gross's mysterious conversation with Jimmy.

Interrupting Pop's particularly colorful description of Dean's sexual prowess, I asked, "Did Mr. Gross say what day of the week you called?"

"Tuesday." Red-faced, Jimmy pulled up a drooping tube sock. "That's how I know I didn't make the call. My grandkids were here visiting on Tuesday. Spent the whole day in the barn with them. If you ask me, Dean is going a little funny in the head."

Pop slapped the arm of his chair. "Well, my granddaughter here will get to the bottom of everything. Won't you, Rebecca?"

I opened my mouth to say no. No matter how much I didn't want to disappoint Pop, the truth was, I had no idea how to find Jimmy's stolen car. The cops were on their own. Deputy Sean would be thrilled.

But before I could get out the words, my pocket began to vibrate. I pulled out my cell phone and flipped it open to answer it.

"Rebecca," I heard the husky voice of my Realtor, Doreen, say, "you'll never believe it, but I think I just sold your rink."

Three

Light-headed, I raced back to the Toe Stop. Doreen was waiting for me at my office door. She followed me inside, her eyes gleaming behind a pair of rhinestone-bespeckled glasses.

"I did it," she crowed, waving a bunch of papers in the air. "I found someone who wants to buy this rink. He's even willing to pay your asking price."

Goose bumps sprouted up and down my arms while my heart tightened inside my chest. I sat down hard on the old wooden chair behind the desk. Happiness does strange things to me, I thought as I grabbed the papers Doreen held out.

Abba's "Dancing Queen" serenaded me from the rink loudspeaker as my eyes skimmed the documents. Sure enough, someone had made an offer for the rink. A good offer. The one that I'd been cooling my heels in Indian Falls for. This deal would cut me loose from my responsibilities here and allow me to go back to the life I'd started to build in Chicago.

"They know I want the place to remain a roller rink?" I asked.

This condition had killed several other potential sales. As much as I wanted to sell, I owed it to my mother to be true to her dream. I couldn't bring myself to live permanently in Indian Falls and run the rink, but I could make sure the place survived.

Doreen preened. "They do."

I blew a strand of hair out of my face. "So, when do we close the deal?"

"The end of the month. Of course, that's if the rink passes a formal inspection and—" Doreen gave another *tsk*.

"And what?"

"And you find a manager. I told them you were going back to Chicago. Trouble is, they won't be living in town. They want someone who already knows the business in place by the time they take over; otherwise, the deal is off." She shifted her glasses to the tip of her long nose and peered over them at me. "You can find someone, right?"

I gave Doreen an overconfident smile. "Sure thing."

If only finding a rink manager was as easy as lying.

Doreen left wielding a signed contract, and I headed to the rental counter to give the kid working there a break. I hoped work would help alleviate the sick, gnawing sensation in my stomach. If only the job hadn't consisted of exchanging smelly shoes for pairs of almost equally smelly roller skates, my plan might have worked. After two hours, I allowed two teenage employees to take over the task and went back to my office to ponder my nonexistent enthusiasm for finally leaving town.

Maybe it was the lack of living arrangements in the city that bothered me. Two months ago, my best friend and roommate,

Jasmine, had packed up my things and sublet my room to her cousin to help me avoid bankruptcy. Getting the storage locker key in the mail had provoked a similar stomach reaction. That had to be it. Right?

Or maybe it was the thought of leaving behind my sometime boyfriend, Lionel, the town's incredibly sexy vet. He wanted me to pull the listing on the rink so we could try our hand at a real relationship. Only, I wasn't sure I was ready for that kind of commitment.

Determined to ignore the problem, I grabbed my phone and checked for messages. Pop's voice boomed into my ear. "Rebecca, I know you haven't had much time to run down leads, but Jimmy wants to know if you've found his car yet. Give me a call or come down to the center. Tonight is meat-loaf night."

I slapped my forehead.

Somehow in the haze after Doreen's phone call, I'd actually agreed to take Jimmy's case. I was an idiot.

Then again, asking questions around town would keep my mind occupied. In the process, I might even uncover someone willing to become the Toe Stop's manager. Can I multitask or what? I thought.

I tooled out of the office, gave a wave to the kids manning the rental counter, and headed out to the packed parking lot. Sweat ran down my back as I cranked my yellow Honda Civic to life. I had only one lead in Jimmy's missing-car case. It was time to pay insurance agent and longtime Indian Falls resident Dean Gross a visit.

Cars streamed into the rink's parking lot as I steered mine onto the road. The sun was heading down, but the temperature hadn't followed suit. Somehow, that didn't deter the town's enthusiasm for roller skating. I guess sweating in air conditioning beat doing it outside. A good thing for my balance sheet and for the potential new owners.

Twenty minutes later, I pulled into the driveway of a rambling Victorian farmhouse painted a vivid lime green. A large turquoise sign with green lettering announced the presence of Gross Insurance. Thank God Dean Gross has a successful agency, I thought. The world wasn't ready for his taste as an interior designer.

I climbed out of the almost cooled-off inner sanctum of my car and climbed onto the blue-trimmed porch. Truth be told, I didn't expect to learn anything from this visit—except perhaps that Jimmy was in the beginning stages of mental decline. Still, there was no harm in satisfying my curiosity about the phantom phone call.

Pushing a sweaty stray curl behind my ear, I pressed the doorbell. The guy must have been standing behind the front door, because it immediately swung open and Dean Gross flashed a gap-tooth smile through the screen door.

I grinned back at the slightly rotund man. "Hi, Mr. Gross." Not my best opening, but I had to start somewhere. "I don't know if you remember me. My name is Rebecca Robbins."

"Kay Robbins's little girl? Why, I haven't seen you since your mother's funeral." He opened the screen door and motioned for me to come in out of the heat. I was more than happy to oblige as he added, "Your mother was a real nice lady, Rebecca. The whole town lost someone special when she passed."

My throat tightened and the back of my eyes began to itch. My mother had died over a year ago. Aside from Pop, she'd been the only person I'd ever been able to count on to be there for me.

"Thanks," I said, before changing the subject. Crying in front of an insurance agent sounded like zero fun. "Hey, I hope you don't mind my dropping by so late, but I had a couple of questions for you."

Dean smiled and took a seat in the lipstick red rocking chair, leaving me with the orange slipcovered sofa. "Did you want to talk about getting insurance for the rink?" Dean asked, rubbing his hands together with thinly veiled excitement.

Oops. I'd forgotten the rink's policy was through another agent. With a small smile, I replied, "No, but the rink might need a new policy soon. Actually, I came to talk to you about Jimmy Bakersfield."

Dean's face clouded.

"He's very concerned about the phone call you got last week," I quickly explained. "You see, Jimmy doesn't remember making that call. He's worried that he might have done other things he can't remember now. I'm sure you understand how nervous that would make someone getting up in years."

The middle-aged insurance agent scratched his chin and agreed yes, that would make him nervous.

"So would you tell me about that phone call?" I asked. "Jimmy would feel better if he understood exactly what he said and when he said it."

Shrugging, he told me the same story Jimmy had already repeated to me.

"And you're sure it was Jimmy's voice on the other end of the phone?"

Dean's head started to bob downward. Then it stopped. He pursed his lips together and his forehead crinkled with thought, giving him a startling resemblance to a bulldog. "Funny, but I remember thinking that Jimmy sounded like he had a cold. His voice was lower, and he sniffled a lot. You don't think that's important, do you?"

The sky was dark when I hopped back in my car and steered it onto the road. My talk with Dean hadn't yielded any breakthroughs aside from the fact that Jimmy'd had a cold last week. The cops would have to do the rest. My investigation was officially over. It was time to get busy finding a rink manager so I could get back to my real life in Chicago.

My car hummed as I drove down a dark country road. Stars winked back at me from the sky, and my throat tightened. I would miss looking at the stars. Chicago nights were a little too bright and more than a little polluted. But nightclubs, a variety of potential jobs, and my best friend, Jasmine, were there, too. All in all, it was a fair trade.

Kaboom!

I jumped in my seat and whacked my head on the roof of the car. My ears rang and the hair on my arms stood on end as the night vibrated around me. Jamming my foot down on the brake, I looked around for the source of the explosion. Far in the distance, red flames lit up the night.

Spinning my car toward the fire, I hit the gas and headed toward the yellowish beacon. My heart raced as I zipped down the country roads, hoping no one was hurt. From this distance, I couldn't tell what was on fire, only that the fire was spreading.

Four turns and fifty miles an hour later, I could see the fire was in the middle of what looked like a field. I pulled to the side of the road and leaped out of the driver's seat. Racing toward the fire, I flipped open my phone and started dialing.

A chain-smoking female voice answered as I skidded to a stop twenty feet in front of the source of the fire.

"Indian Falls Sheriff's Department. How can I direct your call?"

I squinted at the engulfed object and choked back a scream.

"Are you there?"

Pressing a hand against my chest, I choked out, "Jimmy Bakersfield's car is on fire, and someone is still inside."

Four

"*Miss, help is on the way*. Please get back in your car and wait for the police and the fire department to arrive."

There was no way I was going to wait around for the cavalry to arrive while someone was trapped in a bonfire. Flipping my phone shut, I tried to ignore the panic bubbling through my esophagus and forced my feet toward the flames.

Waves of heat licked at my neck. The voice of sanity in the back of my brain instructed me to turn back. It was probably a smart idea, but when did I ever do the smart thing? Brushing a stream of sweat from my nose, I inched forward, hoping to see signs of life.

Only there weren't any. I inched closer. The person inside the car wasn't moving at all. This was very bad.

A tire exploded, sending me to the ground and pieces of hot rubber flying like fireworks. Scrambling to a safe distance, I contemplated the wisdom of another rescue attempt as the Indian Falls fire truck and ambulance arrived.

By the time they got the hose hooked up and the water running, the other three tires had burst. I watched them put out the rest of the fire before it could run rampant in the field. Then I saw the paramedic race in. I knew before he started shaking his head that the news wasn't good.

Eyes misting, I couldn't help being thankful that I hadn't had time to attempt any more heroics. Those last three tires would have gotten me for sure. I just wished the person inside had been as lucky.

"Why is it that whenever there's a disaster, I find you standing near it?"

The masculine voice raised goose bumps up and down my arm. Turning, I looked into Dr. Lionel Franklin's handsome face. Despite the lighthearted tone he'd used, I could see concern deep in his green eyes. Sadly, Lionel was right. My time in Indian Falls had been filled with disasters both big and small. Tonight's had a body count.

"What are you doing here?" I asked. Lionel's veterinary practice and his home were located a good twenty minutes away.

"Being a volunteer fireman doesn't do much for my bank account, but it's a good way to keep up with the news." Lionel reached out and brushed my cheek. The contact made me shiver. Lionel's touch always had an effect on me, and right now it took every impulse control I owned to keep from flinging myself into the comfort of his arms.

Since I'd come back to town, we'd been doing a bizarre dance between friendship and dating. It'd involved a couple of movies, a ride on his retired circus camel, and some serious make-out sessions.

But no sex.

Lionel had great lips and very gentle hands. My body's reaction to his kisses told me, no question, doing the deed with him would have a serious impact on me and tip the delicate balance of our relationship. I wasn't sure I was ready for either. Especially now that I'd seen a burned body. My equilibrium was shot.

"I've also just been appointed the backup coroner. Doc Truman is out of town, so they called me when you said a body was in the car." Lionel's mouth tightened. His fingers closed around mine. "Now, would you please tell me what the hell you're doing out here?"

All tingles of sexual interest vanished. I took a step back and pulled my hand away as if I'd burned it. "You make it sound as if Jimmy's car going up in smoke is my fault."

He sighed. "Becky, with you I wouldn't be so sure it's not. You seem to attract trouble."

"Look," I yelled while jabbing a finger in his direction. "This is not my fault. My grandfather wanted me to help get Jimmy's car back. That's what I was doing when I stumbled across this bonfire. If I had only gotten here a little sooner, I might have been able to rescue—" My throat tightened at the memory of the burned figure. I tried to finish my sentence, but nothing came out. I sniffled hard and choked back a sob. I wasn't going to cry. At least not right now. So I raised my voice and changed the subject. "When did you get to be the backup coroner? You never told me that. Don't you have to be a people doctor to qualify for the job?"

"I took a class and a certification test," Lionel shouted back. "Animals and people aren't all that different."

Everyone turned at the sound of Lionel's very loud, very angry voice. I couldn't help but notice that no one ever seemed to care when it was me doing the shouting. Redheads are expected to be a trifle dramatic, but hearing the trusted vet screeching like a banshee was a bit out of everyone's comfort range.

To his credit, Lionel didn't bother to look embarrassed. He just shook his head and lowered his voice. "Look, I was worried about you. Less than two months ago you were stalked and then held at gunpoint by a murderer. Can you blame me for being concerned? I don't want you involved in another dangerous investigation. I don't think I can handle it."

With that, my anger, like Jimmy's car, was extinguished. I found it hard to stay mad at someone I cared about. Besides, I kind of understood how he felt. For most Indian Falls residents, coming across dead bodies and exploding cars wasn't part of the normal routine. Truth was, I'd been so shocked at the sight of a flaming car that I'd gone kind of numb. Now that my mind was working again, my legs jiggled like Jell-O.

I took a steadying breath. "Okay, I think it's safe to say we were both a little upset by Jimmy's barbecued car. Truce?"

The crooked smile he gave me made my heart dive into my stomach. His hand latched onto my arm and gave me a tug toward him. A moment later, his lips brushed mine. I sighed. My legs were still a little wobbly, but at least now I could blame their instability on Lionel's kiss instead of on the explosion.

"Ms. Robbins."

I cringed at the sound of that voice. Turning, I spotted Deputy Sean Holmes standing five feet behind me. He looked as though he'd been sucking on a less than ripe lemon.

"Hi, Sean." I gave him my best smile and a little finger wave, hoping to improve his disposition. No such luck.

"If you can tear yourself away, I would like to have a word with you."

"Go ahead," Lionel said, abandoning me to the wolf in cop's clothing. "I'm going to see if I can help the guys stow the fire hose. Someone will let me know when I need to look at the body." With that, he headed for the flashing lights. I couldn't blame him for not seeking out his deceased patient immediately. I didn't want to think about the person in that car, let alone examine him.

Mustering a pleasant expression, I strolled up to Deputy Sean. "What can I do for you?"

Sean gave me his best stern-cop expression. A flip of his notebook and he went into his cop routine. "You're the one who reported Jimmy's car on fire?"

I was certain the dispatcher, Roxy, had already told him that. Still, I replied, "Yes," then waited for Sean to jump all over me.

In a very professional voice, he continued. "The report says no one besides yourself was here when you arrived at the scene. Did any cars pass you on the road on the way to the Schmitts' farm?"

For the first time, I realized where I was. This was Alan Schmitt's field. When I was in grade school, Mom and I would come here to get corn stalks for Halloween.

"No. I think the roads were deserted, but I wasn't really paying attention. I was just trying to get here fast. The person in the car . . ." I said in a quiet voice. "Is the person . . ." *Dead.* I couldn't say it, but Sean's softening expression told me he understood.

"I shouldn't tell you this, but I know you'll find out from your boyfriend." The annoyed, almost jealous tone Sean used when saying the word *boyfriend* made me almost miss hearing him say, "The body wasn't real."

Huh? I blinked. The words made no sense. I'd seen the body.

"What do you mean, it wasn't real?"

Sean gave me a look that said he suspected I was hard of hearing. "It was a mannequin. One of those life-size dolls people use in store displays."

"I know what a mannequin is. Why was it there?"

He shrugged. "That will be one of the first questions I ask when I arrest the person who did this. You're sure you didn't see any other cars?"

"No. I didn't notice any other headlights, but I guess I could have missed someone who was driving without their headlights on." Driving without headlights in the country was dangerous, but so was blowing up cars. Although they would have had to have driven in the opposite direction; otherwise, in my extreme haste to get here, I would have hit them. Somehow I didn't think mentioning to a cop that I'd been breaking the speed limit was a good idea. So instead, I added, "I'm guessing the person who did this was on foot."

The book snapped shut. "Guessing doesn't solve crimes. Police work based on evidence and well-developed deductive reasoning does."

My back stiffened at the condescending tone in Sean's voice.

"Amateurs like you rely on luck. The truth is, your attempts to help only get in the way of people like me who are trained and actually know what we're doing."

His words waved a red cape in my head.

"Got it?" he demanded.

Sure, I got it. Sean Holmes didn't want me anywhere near this case. Well, something told me Sean was going to be disappointed.

Sure enough, early the next morning I found myself delegating work so I could head back to the scene of the explosion. I couldn't shake the fact I had missed something important at the scene. Sean would have a fit if he found me there, but curiosity beat out my fear of being arrested any day.

Parking in the same spot as last night, I hopped out and looked around. Jimmy's car was gone, which wasn't going to help my investigation. Still, on an up note, so was Deputy Sean. Aside from two guys in a neighboring field, the place was deserted. No one was here to notice me as I stepped around the police tape and poked around.

Aside from a lot of wet, trampled hay, there wasn't much to look at. Black scorch marks from the fire darkened the ground, making a good outline of where Jimmy's car had once sat. Now it was resting in car heaven. Meanwhile, I was shoe-deep in mud, trying to decide why.

I walked around the scene, waiting for a psychic moment to hit and tell me who'd done it. Ten minutes later, there was no word from the great beyond. I decided to pack it in. Walking back through the field of hay, I once again realized how lucky the farmer who owned this place was. The fire last night had burned really hot. I'd been able to feel the heat coming off the car sitting in the middle of the field as I stood on the road. A fire like that should have torched everything in its path.

So why hadn't it?

What would prevent fire from spreading through a hay field?

Hand on my car, I pondered the question. Rain? No rain had fallen recently. The farmers eating at the diner had been complaining about the lack of moisture for the past two weeks. Besides, the heat wave would have kept the fields dry no matter how advanced the irrigation system. The unburned, very dry hay all around me made no sense.

Unless someone had intentionally saved the field. Maybe the same someone who'd checked whether Jimmy had insurance before destroying his car? Of course, if that was the case, this was the most considerate criminal I'd ever heard of.

Not sure what else to do, I steered my car toward the nearest farmhouse. Who knows, I thought, maybe the farmer who owns the place knows something. It was worth checking out. Besides, it was the only lead I had.

Five

Several hours later, I'd learned that Mr. Toberman kept a loaded shotgun next to him while driving his tractor, that Mrs. Moore wanted to give the pyromaniac a medal for removing a town eyesore, and that Alan Schmitt thought aliens had landed in his field and caused the explosion. A truly productive afternoon.

Back in town, I steered my car into a parking spot outside Something's Brewing, Indian Falls's answer to Starbucks. The store was located around the corner from the sheriff's office, but my need for a pick-me-up outweighed my sense of self-preservation.

Something's Brewing was run by a guy named Sinbad Smith. Sinbad was a big Egyptian man who'd set up shop here just after I'd hightailed it to the big city. Unlike many outsiders' business ventures, Sinbad's store was an instant success. I was guessing it was due more to the high-octane nature of his coffee than to Sinbad's personality. The man was kind of pushy, but his coffeemaker was first-rate. When a person needed a caffeine fix, that was all that mattered.

I stepped into Something's Brewing and inhaled deeply. There's nothing like the smell of fresh coffee, especially in a homey environment. Sinbad's shop was decorated a lot like a hunting lodge. Three small wooden tables with chairs were situated around the small storefront window, and a brown leather sofa and two chairs were arranged around an unlit fireplace. Over the fireplace hung a large deer head. The deer head made my flesh creep, but not enough to keep me away. The two teenagers standing in line probably felt the same way.

The girls said hello while waiting for their iced lattes. The two were regulars at the rink. Once they got their drinks, they beat it out the door, leaving me to ponder whether to get an iced mocha or a cinnamon latte.

Sinbad's lightly accented voice called to me from behind the large wooden counter. "Hey, Rebecca. I heard you found Jimmy's car."

"Oh, I didn't really do anything."

"Don't be so modest. I am sure the sheriff would not have found the car for days if you had not been on the case. Everyone is saying how Jimmy was smart to hire you."

I tried not to cringe. Sinbad's coffee shop was one of the first stops in the Indian Falls gossip train. It was only a matter of time before Deputy Sean heard the town's opinion of my abilities. If I were smart, I'd take a vacation.

"I'll have a caramel-cinnamon latte with an extra shot." I was going to need it.

"This town is lucky to have you helping the sheriff. I am sure this must take away from time at your business."

That was one of the perks, but I could tell by Sinbad's expression that he considered this a great sacrifice on my part. "It does," I said with my best solemn expression.

"But you must worry when you are not there to be in charge. Who do you trust to make the decisions when you are away?"

The coffee machine began to hiss.

"My staff is pretty good, and when they have a problem, they ask me about it." Luckily, there weren't many problems. As long as the music played and the skate counter was manned, things ran smoothly.

"So you have not hired a manager yet? I remember you were looking, yes?" Sinbad poured an extra shot of coffee into a large cup, one eye under a raised eyebrow focused on me.

Weird. Why would the vacant position of rink manager interest the owner of a coffee shop? Perhaps he was looking to hire his own manager. There were only so many people in town willing and able to fill management positions. Maybe he was sizing up the competition.

I waited for him to add the foamed milk before saying, "Rink managers aren't easy to come by in Indian Falls. But I'll find one eventually."

Sinbad handed my drink across the counter with a wide smile. "I have the perfect manager for you."

I blinked. "What?"

The twinkling chime rang in the shop as the door opened. Sinbad looked toward the door and proudly announced, "Rebecca Robbins, meet your new manager. My son, Max."

I turned toward the door. Sure enough, there was a tall young man with glasses and curly dark hair, and he didn't look happy. In fact, I recognized that look. This guy was ready to blow.

Max barked out a couple of words in a language I didn't understand. Sinbad's face turned crimson as he came out from behind the counter and yelled back. I didn't need to be a linguist to understand. Max didn't want the rink job, and his father was trying to shove him kicking and screaming into it.

"You know," I said, taking a step toward the exit, "I should really get back to the rink. We can talk about the job opening another time."

My feet rushed to make an escape.

"We must talk about Max's job now." Sinbad stepped between me and the door. Unless I threw my hot latte on him, I was trapped. I looked down at my coffee and sighed. My body needed the caffeine. I was stuck.

"Max is a good boy. He will be a good business manager. You will not be sorry you hired him."

"I don't think—" Thank goodness I was cut off by Max, since I hadn't a clue what I was thinking.

"Father, stop this, now. You know I am not meant to be a business manager." Max took a step toward his father, allowing me to creep closer to the door.

Sinbad set his shoulders. There was steel in his voice as he said, "You went to college. You are a smart boy. You can run any business."

"But I don't want to. You know that. I'm going to direct movies. I already have a script, Father. It's going to be really great. Once I have a movie in the can, I can show it to investors. Then I will start my own studio. If you ever watched any of my movies, you'd know I was serious. I have several at home you could see. . . ."

Sinbad's body went still the minute Max said the word *movies*. He sucked in a loud stream of air at his son's prediction of greatness, and his hands clenched at his sides. That's when I noticed the vein on the side of Sinbad's neck begin to pulsate like that guy's stomach in the movie *Alien*.

It was really time to leave.

"Hey, guys, I have to get back to work. Max, good luck on your movie."

I scooted my body around the two angry men and bolted out the door, thankful to escape. Watching two men pummel each other was only fun if they were on TV, wearing spandex and funny costumes. Wrestling allowed a girl to munch popcorn while admiring a guy's butt. Sinbad didn't have an ass I wanted to spend time staring at, even if it scored me a rink manager and a guaranteed sale.

A few minutes later, I polished off my coffee and walked through the double doors into the rink. A blast of classical music hit me. Mornings at the rink were reserved for private lessons, which meant Tchaikovsky or Mozart instead of the Village People and Three Dog Night. Currently, my primary private instructor, George, was busy shouting instructions to Danielle Martinez, the Lutheran church's secretary and a good friend of mine.

I watched Danielle finish her program with a well-executed spin. She had only been taking lessons for two months, and her progress was amazing. George was hoping to have Danielle ready to compete in another six months.

The fact that Danielle was graceful and athletic shouldn't have been a surprise, considering her past profession. Before moving to Indian Falls, she'd worked in Chicago as an exotic dancer— something only Lionel and I knew. Smiling, I thought about the strange turns life often takes.

Danielle wiped sweat from her forehead and spotted me. With a wave, she called out, "Tomorrow is going to be fun. Seven o'clock, right?"

Damn, I thought while my head nodded. I'd forgotten about

our bi-monthly get-together. "See you tomorrow at seven," I yelled back. "Don't forget you have to bring dessert."

Danielle smiled as her music started again, sending her rolling to the center of the floor. I headed to my office, where the message light on the answering machine was blinking.

Pressing the button, I plopped down in the chair. Pop's voice bellowing out of the machine made me sit straight up.

"Rebecca, you need to come down to the Senior Center at once. Another car has been stolen, and you'll never believe who it belongs to."

Grabbing my purse, I flew out of my chair and through the office door before the machine stopped playing. I couldn't help myself. I was curious.

The responsible part of me stopped to talk to George before leaving. Like it or not, the rink was my business until the contracts were signed and the new owners took over. And to do that, I would need a manager. So I took the opportunity to ask George if he wanted the position—again.

The man stood six feet two inches tall. The skates added another two inches, which meant I had to crane my neck to look at him shake his platinum blond head and sweetly say, "No, but thanks for asking. Go ahead and run your errands. I'll take care of everything here."

With that, he zoomed off to yell instructions at Danielle. She had just wiped out and was sprawled face-first in the middle of the rink floor.

Exiting the building, I shook my head at George's attitude. The man had been a fixture at the rink for over twenty years. He'd been my mother's best student. Then he became her best teacher. Now he was mine, and for some funny reason he refused to take over managing the rink. George was happy being unofficially in charge. I only hoped he wouldn't run off to join the Ice Capades before I found someone willing to let me pay him to do the job.

The sun beat down, and I began sweating immediately as I walked from the rink to the Senior Center. I could have driven my car the two and a half blocks. Problem was, my Honda Civic was one of the only yellow cars in town. I didn't want Deputy Sean to spot it sitting outside the center. I was in enough trouble with him as it was.

Beads of sweat dripped between my breasts as I walked through the center's front doors. Sean's squad car wasn't parked at the curb, so I wouldn't have to duck into the steam room to avoid him. I'd had to do that once to avoid a fight between Pop's menagerie of hysterical fans. Seeing that much wrinkled flesh scarred me more than the menagerie's acrylic nails.

Pop was waiting for me in the lobby. His eyes were bright, his lips curled in a triumphant smile.

"What's going on?" I asked. "You said on the machine another car was stolen."

Pop's smile widened. "Yep. Someone took the car this morning from the retirement home's parking lot."

My grandfather's unconcealed glee bothered me. No one deserved to have their car stolen. Not even Deputy Sean. "Why are you so happy?" I demanded. "Your message sounded like the car belonged to someone we know."

"It does."

"Who?"

Pop looked down the hallway as the sound of footsteps approached. He hooked a thumb toward the doorway and said, "Him."

On cue, a man walked into the lobby, and my heart tightened in my chest. The man was wearing dark brown suit pants and a yellow silk shirt with its sleeves rolled up to the elbows. His slicked-back auburn hair was touched with gray at the temples. His eyes widened as they spotted me and Pop. With a toothy snake-oil salesman's smile plastered on his face, he held out his arms and said, "Hey, baby. How about a hug for your daddy?"

I was wrong, I thought as anger and resentment bubbled through my veins. This man *did* deserve to have his car stolen. It was just too bad he hadn't been in it when it happened.

Six

Running away wasn't an option. My feet were frozen to the floor as I looked into blue eyes the same shape and color as my own.

"What's wrong, honey?" My father's arms lowered an inch as confusion and unhappiness marched across his face. "Aren't you glad to see your dad?"

I resisted the unwanted tug at my heart. An unsuspecting soul might have believed Stan's hurt expression was real. Heck, I used to. That was until I learned my father was the king of deception and misdirection. Those skills were necessary for a good salesman, but they made for a lousy father.

"What are you doing here, Stan?" I asked, trying to keep years of anger, disappointment, and frustration out of my voice. My grandfather's widening smile told me I'd failed to.

"What do you mean?" Stan had the nerve to look confused. "I mailed you a letter telling you I was coming to town. Didn't you get it?"

"Yes, I got it," I admitted. "But what I meant was, what are you doing *here*, at the Senior Center? Are you peddling Polygrip now?"

Stan flashed his pearly whites. "Not at the moment, but I might look into it after I'm finished with my current business venture."

"What unsuspecting people are you swindling now?" Pop demanded, poking one wrinkled finger at my father's chest.

Stan slid a hand into his pants pocket and leaned back on his heels. It irked me to realize the man looked good. Relaxed and rested. Like he just stepped out of the editorial pages of the "Fifty and Over" edition of *GQ*.

"I'm not swindling anyone. I work in the music industry right now," he said with a charming, self-depreciating tone. "But I should tell you that I'm thinking about getting out. Life on the road isn't what it used to be."

"Especially when you don't have a car," Pop quipped. The laughter in his voice rang throughout the lobby. My father was getting a kick in the butt from Karma, and Pop was going to savor every minute of it. Still chuckling, Pop said, "Why don't you skip the small talk and tell Rebecca what happened to your car? She deserves a laugh."

Stan should have looked upset, right? Rebuffed? Unsettled? Any normal person would have been at least one of those. Nope. He just shrugged. "I got into town last night. When I woke up this morning, I went to find my car, but it was gone. Crime didn't used to be a problem in this town."

"A lot of things change in twenty years," I shot back.

Pop nodded. "Yeah, kind of like your father's choice of hotels. I didn't know the retirement home was renting rooms by the night."

"Yes . . . well—" my father stammered as he tugged at the

collar of his shirt. A crimson flush crept up his neck. For the first time today, he looked uncomfortable. "You see—"

"Stan, honey, I was wondering where you snuck off to."

We all turned toward the source of the husky feminine voice. Standing in the entrance doorway was my Realtor, Doreen.

Her eyelashes batted behind her rhinestone-studded glasses. "Stan, Deputy Holmes wanted to ask a few more questions about your missing car. He was worried when he couldn't find you, but I told him I knew you'd be back. After all, your suitcase *is* in my room."

My jaw and stomach plummeted. My eyes traveled from my father to Doreen and back to my father. "You stayed with Doreen last night?"

My father didn't answer me. Apparently, he'd developed a sudden interest in his loafers.

Doreen was far less interested in footwear. In an excited voice, she said, "Oh, I didn't see you there, Rebecca. Sorry. I hope I wasn't being indiscreet. Your father and I ran into each other last night at the diner, and he told me he needed a place to stay. You weren't home, and he had nowhere to go. Poor man." She peered at me over her glasses.

The muscles in my neck stiffened and my fingers curled into fists.

"Now, Doreen," Stan said in a low voice that made my nails dig into my sweaty palms. "I told you Rebecca didn't know when I was getting into town. I'm sure she would have made me welcome had she known I was here."

When pigs fly.

My father's defense made my eyebrows twitch. Doreen's eyes

swung toward me, as if she was waiting for me to say my father was welcome at my place. Only I wasn't going to say it. He'd given up his rights to playing the father card when he'd skulked off like the skunk he was almost two decades ago. If he thought differently, he had another think coming.

I crossed my arms over my chest.

My father looked at me with his big blue eyes. His mouth was curled in a gentle smile as he waited for me to say the words of welcome. The discount-store clock on the wall ticked off the passing seconds. Stan's feet shifted on the blue-and-gray linoleum floor. Pop's bushy eyebrows knit together in concern. A soft *tsk* escaped Doreen's mouth, underscored by the faint sounds of *The Price Is Right*.

Still I said nothing.

My father's eyes grew sad as his shoulders slumped in defeat. A knife twisted in my chest. My father jammed his hands into his pockets as his head drooped with a sigh. My stomach did a summersault. He really did look sad. Of course, I'd said that the last time he'd swept into my life, then sneaked back out.

I bit my bottom lip as I watched him standing there looking defeated. He could have changed, right? Stranger things had happened. Besides, he was my father. No matter how many times I might have wished differently.

Opening my mouth, I said, "Well, I guess—"

"You're not going to stay with Rebecca. You're staying with me, Stan."

My head snapped toward my grandfather. His hands were planted on his bony hips, and his eyes dared anyone to question him. I'd seen him set his jaw like that before, and I knew he meant what he said. My father was going to bunk with my grandfather. If either one of them came out of it alive, it would be a miracle.

"Pop, what are you doing? You don't want Stan staying in your house."

Pop just shrugged. My father and Doreen had gone back to the retirement home to answer Deputy Sean's questions, leaving Pop and me alone in the center's lobby.

"Look," I said, "Stan can stay at the rink. It's no big deal. Really. I'm never there anyway." Only to sleep and change clothes. I would be unconscious most of the time. That wouldn't be so bad, right?

"Nope," Pop barked. "That man is not moving into the rink. He lost all rights to that place when he left you and your mother high and dry." His eyes lost their steely quality. "Besides, I don't want to give him another chance to hurt you."

A lump filled my throat. "He can't hurt me, Pop."

My grandfather's grumble spoke volumes. He didn't believe me. I wasn't sure whether I was annoyed at his lack of faith or proud of his intuition. At seventy-six, Pop was sharp as a tack—albeit a slightly rusty one. And he loved me.

Swallowing hard, I changed the subject to something safer. "So what, exactly, happened to Stan's car?"

The mention of Stan's MIA automobile made Pop grin. "Someone nicked it. It was last seen in the retirement home's parking lot around midnight. Then poof." Pop snapped his fingers. "It was gone. You think it would be in bad taste to give the culprit a medal?"

Pop should talk to Mrs. Moore.

"I think the Sheriff's Department and the mayor might have a problem with that. Unless you came up with a *really* good reason."

Pop scratched his unshaven chin. "You know, our thief doesn't have very good taste in cars. First Jimmy's beat-up Bug and now your father's ancient Buick Skyhawk. Maybe we could make the thief an honorary member of the Indian Falls beautification committee. The new motto could be Cleaning Up the Town One Junker at a Time."

Pop slapped his knee and cackled.

"So how did the thief swipe the car?" I asked, half curious, half trying to distract myself from unwanted thoughts about my nonexistent relationship with my dad. "Did Stan leave the key under the visor?" I seemed to remember that he'd done this when I was a kid.

"Not that I can tell. He had his keys with him. Someone must have hot-wired the car." His eyes glazed into a sad, faraway look. "I always wanted to learn how to do that."

"Maybe the center will hold a class."

Pop brightened. "I'll have to tell the planning committee. I bet that would be a bigger draw than the Easter art class. Last time, the instructor ran out of pink paint and we had to use Pepto-Bismol."

While the artistic stylings of our town's senior citizens were riveting, my mind was busy trying to decide how the thief had targeted my father's car. Jimmy was a local. He had a set routine: Drive car to town. Park car in a remote section of the rink's parking lot. Walk down to the Senior Center and stay there until after lunch. The thief would have had an easy time boosting Jimmy's car without being caught. Stan's was a different story.

I left Pop in the center and went outside to look at the adjoining retirement home's parking lot.

The lot was surrounded by large fluorescent outdoor lamps. I remembered how Mom had complained when they went in. She said the lights were on all night and were so bright, she could see them at the rink. Mom hadn't complained to the center, but she did buy new blinds for her apartment. Since coming home, I'd noticed the lights but hadn't been too bothered by them. After all, until this summer, I'd been living in the city. Bright lights were expected there.

Still, the parking lot's lights made this a risky place to steal a car—even if the thief knew the mark's schedule. My father was a complete unknown. He didn't live in town. The thief wouldn't have known that he'd intended to stay the night. My father could have come out at any time and caught the thief in the act.

So why his car?

I didn't have any answers, but I was going to get them.

The side door of the retirement home opened, and Deputy Sean and my father stepped into the sunlight. Without missing a beat, I bolted down the sidewalk toward the rink. I wasn't sure I was ready to tackle either of them on his own. Both of them together were more than my nerves could take.

Two birthday parties were in full swing when I walked through the door to the rink. I groaned. Not that I begrudged the kids a great party. In fact, birthday parties were my favorite events at the rink. Just not today. A dull headache had been building in the back of my brain since I first set eyes on my father. I needed aspirin and a quiet place to regroup. Rocking music and screaming kids didn't fall into either category.

Thank goodness George seemed to have the chaos under control. I found him by the guardrail, watching the kids with a practiced eye. Before I could ask him to fly solo, George assured me he could handle things. Then he blew his whistle and skated off to the middle of the polished wooden floor.

46

George really like using his whistle. I hated it, but I wasn't about to stop him. I figured if it gave him a sense of control in this crazy world, then what harm could it do. Huh . . . maybe if I got him an engraved gold whistle, he'd accept the manager's job. I'd have to think about that.

I was feeling neglectful of my business duties, so I made a point of seeking out the mothers of our two birthday celebrants. Both were thrilled with the party. One even said, "I can't believe what a wonderful time everyone is having. You know, I was worried about the party when I heard . . . you know. But you seem to be handling everything just fine. I guess after solving that murder, this whole thing with your father isn't so bad."

That's when my mind shut down.

I know I said something. The women both laughed at whatever it was and thanked me again for keeping the rink operating. I said my farewells, plastered a painful smile onto my face, and dodged zooming kids all the way to my office.

The minute my foot crossed the threshold, I found myself yanked into a pair of strong arms. I opened my mouth to protest, but I was cut off by a very sexy, very hot kiss. My mind kick-started into gear and then promptly shut off as my blood began to race. When the kiss ended, I leaned back and looked up into Dr. Lionel Franklin's impossibly green eyes.

"Wow," I said as my heart skipped several beats. Lionel's kisses packed a heck of a wallop.

His lips twitched into a smile. "Articulate today, aren't you?"

I smiled back. "You took me by surprise. Give me a minute and I'll come up with a better response."

"My ego can handle 'Wow,'" he said, reaching out to tuck a stray curl behind my ear. "Besides, I'm not here to rack up compliments."

47

I took a step back and frowned. "Come to think of it, why are you here? It's the middle of the day. Shouldn't you be fondling a sheep instead of me?"

"Turns out I can do both." Lionel's fingers curled against my arm, sending tiny shivers up my spine. "Actually, I stopped by the diner and heard your father was in town. I wanted to see how you were holding up."

His eyes were filled with concern as they searched mine for answers. Too bad I didn't have any.

"I have a headache," I said as I slipped my arm out of his grasp and headed to the desk. Rummaging through the drawers, I could feel Lionel's eyes on me. It made it hard to concentrate. Still, a few seconds later I held a bottle of Excedrin aloft like a trophy.

I plopped down in my wheeled computer chair, took three pills, and left the bottle on the desk for next time. Something told me there would be a lot of next times in the days to come.

I looked back at Lionel. He hadn't moved.

"What's wrong?" I asked.

His left eyebrow twitched upward. "Becky, you haven't seen your father in years. You can't pretend it doesn't bother you."

Actually, I thought I could give the pretending thing a valiant attempt. Only no one would let me.

"Why should it bother me?" I asked, shifting my concentration to rearranging the clutter on my desk. "Stan disappeared from my life when I was in middle school. He popped up after I graduated from college to borrow money and then disappeared again. That's the extent of our relationship."

Lionel took the seat on the other side of the desk with an exasperated sigh. "Your dad hurt you, and now he's back. That has to mean something."

"It means if I'm lucky, I might get him to pay me the money he borrowed." I picked up three pencils and slid them into a kid-size roller skate. No one could find the left skate, so I used the right one as a pen holder. Was I creative or what?

"Rebecca!"

My head snapped up. Lionel only called me Rebecca in that tone of voice when he was at the end of his rope. Well, that made two of us.

"Look," I said. "My father is back in town and everyone in town knew about it before I did, which really sucks. So yeah, I'm not having a great day. But I'm fine. This is not an Oprah show in the making. I'm just going to throw myself into work. People always say that's what a person should do, right?"

Lionel had the nerve to laugh. "Do you really think handing out roller skates and serving nachos is going to make you forget your problems?"

Okay, maybe not. The pain in my head began throbbing in earnest. There had to be a better way of distracting myself than listening to the Village People sing "YMCA."

I smiled at Lionel. "I'm going to throw myself into finding a rink manager. Doreen has a buyer for the rink, but one of the conditions is having a rink manager who understands the business and is running the show when the new owner takes over."

Lionel looked like I'd hit him over the head with a wet fish. "You sold the rink?"

Oops. "I must have forgotten to mention it last night," I said. "The burning car distracted me. Doreen called yesterday and told me about the buyer. If everything works out, the rink will be sold by the end of the month."

I waited for Lionel to congratulate me.

He didn't.

"I thought you said you were starting to like living here."

The low, subdued tone of Lionel's voice sent my radar spinning. "I did say that," I agreed. "And I meant it."

Lionel's eyes narrowed. "But?"

My radar was shrieking now. For a second, I considered fainting—except that Lionel would probably wait around for me to regain consciousness so he could continue his interrogation. He wanted me to give up Chicago and live in Indian Falls. He'd pushed me on the subject more than once. Only, my heart wasn't sure how it felt about Lionel. He was incredibly attractive, great in a crisis, wonderful with children and animals, and he made me almost consider keeping the rink.

Almost.

The problem was, I didn't like being pushed into anything. Right now, Lionel was being pushy, and it made me want to push right back.

"But I came back here to sell the rink, and until I decide otherwise, that is what I am going to do." I raised an eyebrow of my own and stared at Lionel. "Got it?"

His eyes widened for a moment. Then he shrugged out of his chair and crossed to my side of the desk. Before I could see what was coming, I was snatched out of my chair and crushed against Lionel's chest.

"I got it, but I think it is time you understood something. For some crazy reason, I care about you. A lot. The two of us have something going. You don't want to define it, and I'm okay with that for now. That being said, I'm not going to just let you waltz out of town without a fight."

He barked out the last word and crushed his mouth against

mine. My knees trembled as white-hot shivers traveled from my lips down to my toes. His lips slanted over mine with a passion that left me dizzy, and I grabbed his arms to steady myself. His tongue touched mine, sending my heartbeat into overdrive.

And then it was over. Lionel pulled away, leaving me breathless and wanting more. I took a step toward him, but Lionel took two back.

"Think about that kiss. Then ask yourself if selling this place and leaving town is something you really want to do."

Before I could find my voice, Lionel turned on his heel and disappeared.

I sagged against my desk with a sigh. Great. As if I didn't have enough problems right now.

Grabbing my purse and the bottle of Excedrin, I headed for the door. I was pretty sure my attempt at finding a rink manager wasn't going to keep my mind off of both my father *and* Lionel. Maybe tracking down a pyromaniac car thief would.

Seven

The lunch crowd had already left by the time I steered my car to the Hunger Paynes Diner. Sammy and Mabel Pezzolpayne had owned and operated this Indian Falls establishment ever since I could remember. The whitewashed exterior was due for another coat of paint, and the menus were streaked with grease. Still, the Indian Falls faithful came in droves for fluffy flapjacks, ice-cream confections, juicy burgers, and, of course, the inevitable heartburn.

I was here for information on my father's visit and maybe a snack. My stomach was decidedly unhappy to have missed lunch. I took a seat on one of the faded red stools at the counter and looked around the room.

Only three of the diner's scarred Formica tables were occupied. Two back booths were packed with teenagers. Closer to the door sat four older ladies. One of them waved. Inwardly, I groaned, but I waved back. The four women were fans of Pop. The waver had dreams of becoming Priscilla to my grandfather's

Elvis. Thank goodness Pop wasn't prepared to share his Grace-land permanently.

I picked up a menu and scanned the lunch specials. My grand intentions of eating a salad went out the window as I spotted the meat-loaf sandwich. No one made meat loaf like Sammy.

As if on cue, Sammy shuffled behind the counter with a wide, gap-toothed smile. "If it isn't Miss Rebecca Robbins. What can I get for you today?"

"Hey, Sammy." I smiled back at him. When my dad left, Sammy was of the few people in Indian Falls who never treated me and Mom any differently. That meant something. "I'll have a diet Coke and the meat-loaf special."

Sammy hollered my order back to Mabel in the kitchen and came back to the counter with my soda. I took a sip and looked at Sammy over my straw. "I hear you had a big crowd here last night."

"Every Tuesday, Mabel makes stew. Her lamb stew always brings the customers in."

I smiled at the pride in Sammy's voice before asking, "Did you see my father in here?"

Sammy dropped his gaze and suddenly decided the counter wasn't clean. He grabbed a rag and attacked a phantom spot with a vengeance. "He was here. Hadn't darkened this doorway in a long time, but I recognized him. Stan hasn't changed much."

"No, he hasn't." I was doing my best to ignore the icky sensation growing in the pit of my stomach. "Did he come in alone?"

A scarlet flush crept up Sammy's neck.

"Yeah," he said in a low voice. "Stan was alone when he got here."

I took pity on the guy. "Sammy, I know my father wasn't alone for very long. I saw him and Doreen together this morning."

Sammy's eyes lifted from the counter. "You saw them?"

I nodded.

"I didn't want to be the one to tell you." He rubbed at his forehead with the back of his hand. "You father was a nincompoop for leaving you and your mamma. Then he comes here years after and makes a bigger horse's behind of himself. I wanted to serve him day-old bread and wilted lettuce, but Mabel wouldn't let me. Said it would be bad for business." Sammy lowered his voice to conspiracy level. "But I made sure to skimp him on the fries, and he never got a refill on his coffee."

I gave Sammy's weathered hand a grateful pat and told him, "You're not the only one to get revenge. Someone nicked Stan's car from the retirement home's parking lot."

Sammy's face broke into a brilliant smile. "Hadn't heard that. Good. The man deserves to be taken down a couple of pegs."

I gave a noncommittal shrug. It felt wrong to condemn my father in a public forum. After all these years, I still couldn't shake the bonds of family loyalty. Let's face it: I was an easy mark.

"Hey, Sammy, could you do me a favor? Could you tell me who else was here in the diner last night while my father was?"

"I guess so." Sammy refilled my half-empty diet Coke and came around the counter to sit on the stool next to me. "The Lutheran Women's Guild was here. They ignored Agnes and Eleanor, who were seated at the next table. Poor Agnes. After what her nephew did, you would think those church ladies would be nicer to her."

Agnes had been a suspect in the Indian Falls murder that I solved. Turned out her nephew was actually the culprit. To his credit, the killing of his friend had been an accident. He'd only intended to make the guy sick and frame his aunt for it. Because of my inept interference, the guy was going to get twenty to life instead of Agnes's money. Despite her nephew's nasty intentions toward her, Agnes visited her nephew at least twice a month. He was the only family she had left.

I was so busy feeling sorry for her that I almost missed Sammy's next list of people.

"Zach was here after the garage closed, and most of the Indian Falls football team came in after they finished practice. Some of them left early, but a lot of them stayed for a couple hours."

A bunch of rowdy guys were good suspects for car thefts and explosions. I was betting the thief had come into the diner last night during the time good old Dad blew into town. It was the only way I could think of to explain how the thief had picked Stan's car. Could someone have felt like Sammy and decided to take Stan down a peg? That didn't explain Jimmy's car, but maybe it was an angry customer playing copycat. Somehow, I found that hard to believe, but anything was possible.

"Anyone else?"

"The pastor and his secretary were here for a few minutes to pick up some sandwiches. Reginald and Bryan stopped in and talked to a few of the firemen about the car explosion. There might have been a few others, but I was doing kitchen duty. Mabel was working the front. If you want, I can ask her what she remembers."

As if on cue, Mabel popped her head of curly gray hair out from the kitchen. "Food's getting cold." She saw me and broke into a smile. "Hi, Rebecca. Gossip says you might be selling the rink soon and moving back to the city."

"That's the plan."

Mabel's smile faded. "Well, we will sure miss you. Having you living here in town is almost like having your mother back."

Sammy scooted behind the counter and followed his wife into

the kitchen. A minute later, he placed a steaming plate of meat loaf in front of me, then shuffled off to fill coffee cups and take orders for pie.

The smell of my meal was mouthwatering. Three large slabs of meat loaf sat on top of toasted bread. Next to it was a bed of creamy mashed potatoes. A generous amount of gravy covered both. Too bad Mabel's kind words had sunk to the bottom of my stomach like lead. Feeling like I was letting the town, my mother, and maybe myself down had ruined my appetite. I'd just have to take it to go.

Armed with a large take-home container of food, I snagged a promise from Mabel to call me if she thought of any other diners in attendance last night, then hit the road. First stop on my list was the local mechanic and all-around nice guy, Zach Zettle.

The minute Sammy mentioned that Zach was in the diner, my ears had pricked up. Zach was the kind of guy who looked tough but had a heart as mushy as a marshmallow. He was also a walking encyclopedia of automotive knowledge—an area in which I needed a crash course, literally.

Ten minutes later, almost time enough for the air conditioning in my Civic to take effect, I pulled into the parking lot of Zach's business. A red pickup, a shiny black Ford Taurus, and a sleek white BMW sat in the lot, waiting for Zach's attention.

I peeled the back of my shorts-clad legs from my leather seats and strolled toward the garage. A blue truck was up on the lift when I peered into the building. Garth Brooks bellowed from the radio, and Zach was nowhere in sight.

"Hello?" I yelled, competing with Garth. No one answered. Score one for Garth.

Stepping into the garage, I tiptoed around a puddle of some oily substance and crossed toward the car. "Hello," I called again.

Nothing.

I leaned against the truck and decided to wait. Now Garth Brooks was singing all low and soft and sultry. I tapped my toe to his growly music and swayed my hips against the car, enjoying the solitude.

Something slithered against my ankle. "Hey," I yelled. My eyes snapped downward while I said a little prayer to God that it wasn't a snake.

Five fingers were clamped around my left ankle. Unless reptiles had developed opposable thumbs, I was safe from fang bites.

Giving my ankle a yank, I took a step backward and stooped down to peer under the car. There was Zach, lying on his back under the truck. At least I thought it was Zach under all that grease. A second later, he rolled out from under the car and blinked up at me.

I waved. "Hi. Did I catch you at a bad time?"

The obvious answer was yes, but Zach didn't blow me off. He just shrugged and climbed to his feet.

His six-foot-something frame was draped in clothes worthy of a Wes Craven horror movie. Streaks of gooey black, rusty orange, and colors I'd never seen in the Crayola box decorated what probably had once been a blue coverall. Picasso would have declared Zach a work of art. I declared him a mess.

Zach ran an oily hand through his shaggy brown hair and smiled. "I'm glad you swung by. I need a break." He walked past me to a scarred workbench. With a flip of Zach's grease-corroded fingers, Garth stopped singing. Grabbing a sparkling-clean bottle of water, he asked, "What brings you out here? Does your car need some work?"

"Nope. Car runs great." I leaned back against the truck. Normally, I would have looked for a place to sit, but the truck was the cleanest thing in the garage. For the sake of my laundry, I'd stand. "I'm looking into the car-theft thing and thought I should ask you a few questions."

"You think I stole Jimmy's rusted VW?" A smile twitched under the grime.

I arched an eyebrow. "I trust you have better taste in automobiles."

Zach saluted me with the water bottle, chugged half of the liquid, and screwed the cap back on. The bottle took on the same soot color as the rest of the joint. "So, what kind of questions do you need me to answer?"

"You were in the diner last night. Do you remember who else was there?" His confused expression made me smile. "I know it sounds weird, but I have a theory. Humor me."

He looked up at the ceiling with his mouth open. This was Zach's "I'm concentrating" look. I'd watched him use it twice a month at Lionel's poker game. Every so often, I decided to take target practice. So far, I'd managed to land three pieces of popcorn and two pretzels in his mouth. Right now I was kind of sad I'd left the popcorn at home. Zach had never given me a better target.

"Okay," he said. "I was reading a magazine while I ate dinner, but I remember the football team being there. Agnes was there with Doc's secretary. Your dad came in next, and not too long behind him was Doreen and her band of bingo buddies. Once all the guys from the firehouse arrived, the place got a little loud. Did you really find Jimmy's car already in flames, or did you do the town a service and light it yourself?"

"Sorry to ruin your theory, but the bonfire was already going when I arrived."

Zach looked disappointed, then shrugged. "That car wouldn't

have lived much longer anyway. The transmission was shot. Jimmy should have bought a new one years ago."

I steered the conversation back to the previous night. "Do you remember anyone else coming into the diner?"

Zach's eyes searched the ceiling again before he shook his head. "Sorry. I was up early working on Sheriff Jackson's tractor yesterday and was a little foggy by the time I got to eat last night. Speaking of food, I haven't gotten around to having lunch. Do you mind if we go to the diner and talk?"

As if on cue, Zach's stomach gave a low rumble.

"I have a better idea," I said. I sprinted out to my car, leaving Zach gaping after me. Snagging the still-warm Styrofoam container of meat loaf, I trotted back to the garage. With a flip of the lid, I asked, "Would this do?"

The man looked as if he was going to cry. Mabel's meat loaf was known to have that effect. Zach reached for the food with his greasy hands, and I pulled the container back.

"Wash first," I said. "Then you eat."

Zach didn't argue. He bolted for the nearest sink and returned in a hurry with his face and hands scrubbed.

While Zach shoveled meat loaf into his mouth, I asked, "So how hard is it to boost a car?"

Zach considered the question while scooping up some mashed potatoes. "Hot-wiring a car can be tricky nowadays. Most new cars have computers and protective systems built in. Stealing a car used to be easy when we were kids. With all the new technology, boosting a car today takes a lot more skill."

I thought about that as he chewed. "So stealing older cars like Jimmy's VW and my father's Skyhawk would be easier than lifting one of the cars in your parking lot."

59

He nodded.

Okay, the thing about old cars sort of made sense to me now. But why torch the car after you'd boosted it? Didn't that defeat the purpose?

I was about ready to leave, when I had another thought. "Hey, did you overhear my father talking about anything last night?"

Zach's shoulders tensed. "Hard to miss. No offense, but your dad is loud."

"He likes the sound of his own voice," I explained. Or at least he used to. I wasn't exactly an expert on the subject.

"That was the impression I got. He was busy talking to the bingo ladies about his really successful business. When the firemen came in, your dad looked annoyed that he'd lost center stage. Then he got even louder, telling everyone how he needed to get a new car, only he never had time to shop for one. Too busy being successful, I guess."

I shook my head. "That it?"

"Nope." Zach grinned over his fork. "After someone mentioned the car on fire had been stolen, your father said he wished the thief would come and take his car. Then he'd be forced to get a new one. I guess he got his wish."

Huh. "I guess he did."

I left Zach to devour the rest of the meat-loaf special and steered my car toward town and Agnes Piraino's house. Agnes lived in a residential section of Indian Falls located three blocks from the bustle—such as it was—of downtown. I parked the car and stepped onto the porch. Four cats eyed me from their patches of sunlight.

One large yellow longhaired cat got up and sauntered toward me. I leaned down and gave the cat a scratch.

"How are you doing, Precious?" I asked. The cat nuzzled my hand.

I took that as a good sign. Precious took large doses of antipsychotic meds. When the meds were taken away, Precious was kind of like a werewolf—and not the wise Harry Potter teacher kind. Precious has been known to hiss, growl, scratch, and sink her pointy teeth into an outstretched hand. Right now, Precious was flopped at my feet, with all four paws pointing to the sky. In the right situation, drugs can be a very good thing.

"Rebecca, dear. It's so good to see you." The diminutive Agnes Piraino appeared behind the screen door. With her immaculately permed white hair, she looked the picture of the perfect grandmother. Except for the sad smile. Agnes still hadn't gotten over her nephew's betrayal. "How nice of you to come for a visit."

"Sammy told me you and Eleanor were at the diner last night."

Agnes's face brightened slightly. "Eleanor and I went to the movies. That Will Smith is so cute, don't you think?"

I agreed that Will Smith was very cute, then asked, "After the movie, you went to the diner?"

"Yes, we did," Agnes said in a proud voice. "We each ordered banana splits with extra nuts. Eleanor says that all women need nuts. I didn't know that, but she's a nurse, so she should know."

My blood curdled. I was pretty sure Eleanor hadn't been talking about the peanut butter kind of nut.

"Could you tell me who you saw at the diner last night? It might be important to the car thefts that have been going on the last couple days."

61

Agnes stepped out from behind the screen, allowing two more cats to escape into the great outdoors. "Anything for you, dear."

She took a seat on one of the porch's wicker chairs. Immediately, a cat hopped into her lap and went to sleep. "Eleanor and I got there about nine o'clock. Not too long after Doreen and all her friends came in."

Judging by Agnes's tone, she was unhappy with my Realtor. Before she could tell me about Doreen's slight, I prompted her along. Only problem was, she didn't have anything new for me.

Finally, I thanked her and turned to leave. When I was halfway down the stairs, she called, "Oh, there was one guy I've never seen before. He was only there for a few minutes, but Eleanor noticed him right away. He was kind of tall, with dark hair, and I think he had a tan. I said I thought he had nice brown eyes, but Eleanor said he had a great butt and that's far more important." Excitement flared in Agnes's eyes, and her voice got a little breathless. "I had no idea that a man's butt is so important, but Eleanor swears that it is. She said she's going to take me to a club next week where we can look at some really nice butts so I'll know the difference."

Something told me hanging with Eleanor was going to teach retired librarian Agnes more than she'd ever learned from a book.

Visions of old women ogling male flesh haunted me all the way back to the rink. While it gave me hope for my later years, I had no idea how anything she'd told me was going to help identify my newest suspect. What I needed was an eyewitness who was more interested in faces than in behinds. A person with an eye for detail and the ability to size up someone in the blink of an eye.

Taking a deep breath, I did a U-turn and tried to calm the icky sensation growing in my chest. There was only one person I knew who fit that description. Like it or not, I needed a con man.

I needed my father.

Five minutes had passed since I'd pulled into Pop's driveway, eyes glued on the blue-and-white-trimmed house. My estranged father was inside that house. My mind told me to get out of the car and talk to the man, but my body wasn't cooperating.

My fingers started to turn the ignition key when a clang of metal and the sound of my grandfather's very angry voice jolted me into action. I bolted out of the car and raced up the walk to the side door.

Another clash of metal rang through the neighborhood as I flung open the door and ran into the kitchen. The scene that greeted me made me stop cold. Pop was standing with his back to me in the middle of the kitchen, wearing red-white-and-blue boxer shorts, a white undershirt, and black tube socks. He was waving a large metal skillet above his head with one hand and the lid of a copper pot with the other. Crouched between the red Formica kitchen table and the back wall was my father, and he was looking more than a little freaked.

Stan's eyes flew to me. "Help me," he shouted. "Your grandfather has gone over the edge."

Pop took a step toward the kitchen table. He crashed the lid of the copper pot against the skillet, sending tremors of sound dancing through my skull.

"Pop, what are you doing?" I asked in what I hoped was a reasonable-sounding voice.

My grandfather glared at my father and waved the pot lid at him. "Ya fauh ole my eech."

I blinked.

"What?"

"Ya fauh ole my eech! I eed my eech."

A giggle bubbled up inside me and hiccupped out. My father glared in my direction, as if daring me to laugh. I clenched my hands at my sides and bit my tongue, but it didn't help. A glance at my tube-socked grandfather and my wild-eyed father burst the dam of hilarity.

My grandfather turned and looked at me with hurt-filled eyes. My father stood upright and crossed his arms. He shook his head and gave a loud sigh, which made me laugh even harder.

I knew I shouldn't have been laughing. My grandfather was upset. I should have been helping him. Only, I couldn't stop myself. My father was pinned against faded floral wallpaper with a geriatric version of Apollo Creed shouting nonsense while waving a pan at him. Call me crazy, but it was funny.

The two men stared at me until my stomach ached, but finally the giggles were gone.

"Okay," I said, a little breathless from my laughing jag. "Let's sort this out before someone around here hears the noise and calls the cops."

I could only imagine Sean Holmes's reaction to this scene. Just the thought that he might show up made any trace of amusement subside.

"Stan, tell me what you did that made Pop so upset."

My father squared his shoulders and said, "I think you should call me 'Dad.' 'Stan' sounds so formal."

He smiled.

I glared and shook my head. We were not going to discuss our lack of father-daughter understanding while my grandfather paced in his underwear. I just wasn't going to do it.

Stan gave me a forlorn look and sighed. "I didn't do anything. One minute I was unpacking my things and the next your grandfather was yelling and throwing pots at my head. Are you sure he should be living alone, Rebecca? Doreen says there are some vacant rooms at the home."

The mention of the home sent the pot lid and the frying pan crashing together. "Cahm hur sho I cun peddle youah ash."

"Stop it, Pop," I yelled above the kitchen cymbals. "No one is going to paddle anyone's ass." At least that's what I think Pop said.

Pop turned to look at me. He grinned. I winced. Pop looked like he'd lost a bet with a drunken dentist. This could mean only one thing.

"Stan," I said, turning toward my father. "What did you do with my grandfather's teeth?"

"Nothin' . . ." My father's voice trailed off. His eyes widened as he asked, "Were they in that glass upstairs?"

Pop waved his pan.

I nodded.

A trail of red crept up Stan's neck. "Oh. Well, you see, I was putting my stuff in the bathroom and saw someone had left a glass up there. I wanted to be a good roommate, so I brought it downstairs to be washed."

He gave us a smile bright enough to power Springfield.

Pop wasn't impressed. "Whe-ah ah mah eech?"

Stan looked at me for translation.

"Where are Pop's teeth?" I was becoming fluent in Gummish.

My father flipped open the dishwasher. Pop's eyes narrowed as Stan rummaged through the dishes. Several agonizing seconds later, my father stood up with Pop's dentures in his palm.

Pop dropped the pot lid on the counter, snatched the fake teeth out of Stan's hand, and stormed away, still clutching the frying pan. I wasn't sure what he planned to do with it, but then again, I wasn't sure I wanted to know.

Pulling out a chair, my father dropped into it with a loud sigh. "Thanks for helping me out. I thought the old coot was going to take my head off with that pan. He always did have a temper."

"Pop's always been nice to me."

My father flashed me his game-show host smile. "I'll bet everyone is nice to you." When I didn't smile back, he asked, "So what brings you to see your old man?"

It took me a minute to realize he meant himself and not Pop. "I've been asking around about your stolen car."

My father's smile widened. "It's good to know you still care about your old man. Even if you don't want me staying with you."

A tiny knot of guilt burrowed in my throat. I swallowed hard and continued. "Do you remember who you talked to in the diner last night? I think it might be important."

"Well . . ." My father leaned back in his chair with his hands clasped behind his head. "You know about Doreen. She was with a bunch of those church types. Bingo is still big excitement around these parts." He shot me a conspiratorial wink. "I think Doreen said the pastor was there with the attractive dark-haired woman with the great . . . eyes." I shook my head, knowing that Danielle's eyes were the last thing Stan was interested in.

My father didn't seem to notice my reaction. Wrapped up in his story, he continued. "I was going to introduce myself to the lady, but the firefighters came in about then. I'm sure I'll meet her around town. Other than that, there were some boys in the back throwing some napkins around, a guy in coveralls reading a magazine, and a gay couple. Funny, but I didn't expect Indian Falls to have changed quite that much. Not that I have anything against it."

"Sure, Stan," I said without any trace of sarcasm, which wasn't easy. The gay couple, Reginald and Bryan, were my friends. "Agnes Piraino mentioned seeing another man there who came in later and left pretty quickly." I omitted the cute butt detail, figuring my father wasn't into male anatomy. Unless, of course, it was attached to him.

"I think I know who she was talking about." My father stretched and stood up. "There was some guy who came in to pick up his takeout. The place was so crazy, with everyone talking about that exploding car, the poor guy had a hard time getting someone to wait on him."

My heart skipped. This had to be Agnes's mystery guy. "Do you happen to remember what he looked like?"

"He had dark hair, was wearing a red T-shirt, and was kind of tall. Older than the high school kids. Younger than me. His back was to me most of the time, so I didn't get all that good a look."

Disappointed, I asked, "Is there anyone who might be trying to get even with you by stealing your car?"

My father's shoulders stiffened. "Why would you ask that? Do you think I go around the country making enemies?"

"No." I gave myself a mental kick for not phrasing my question more carefully. "I mean, when you left town all those years ago, a lot of people weren't happy about it. Maybe there's someone holding a grudge or something."

My father shrugged. "I can't imagine anyone around here being that upset. It's not like I blew town with one of their wives or any of their money." Stan's voice trailed off as a horn began honking outside. He glanced at his watch and smiled. "Hey, kitten, I've got to run. Big plans, you know. Let's get together tomorrow." He gave my cheek a pat as he headed toward the door. "I've missed my little girl."

With that, my father strolled out the door, leaving me alone. You would think I'd have been used to it.

Ignoring the tiny ache in my heart, I contemplated the information Stan had given me about my suspect.

"Where is my boneheaded bunk mate?" Pop appeared in the doorway, wearing a stretchy black T-shirt and blue jeans. The Rocky impersonation had been replaced by John Travolta from *Grease*. "My teeth taste like bubble bath."

"Stan went out," I said, walking to the fridge. Pulling the door open, I peered inside and grabbed a beer. Before closing the door, I grabbed another, handed it to my grandfather, and took the seat my father had recently occupied.

Pop opened his beer. He took a swig and made a face. "Beer and soap don't mix. Your father's going to be sorry he messed with my teeth."

"It could have been an accident," I said, trying my best to be optimistic.

"Accident my foot." Pop stomped to the table and took a seat. "The minute your father got his luggage through my door, he started hitting me up for money. He called it 'a short-term loan.' I called it 'a scam.' Next thing I know, my dentures are going for a swim in Cascade."

Pop took another swig, swished the beer in his mouth, and swallowed. "That's better," he said, looking at the bottle. Shifting his eyes to me, he added, "If I'm lucky, your father won't come back from wherever he went."

"He can't go very far, Pop," I said. "Stan doesn't have a car. Remember?"

"Oh, yeah." The glee in my grandfather's voice made me smile. "I almost forgot about that."

"I wish I could." I took a sip from my bottle. "I've been asking questions about the theft all day and haven't gotten very far."

Pop shrugged. "You will. You're the best detective in Indian Falls."

Reminding him that I wasn't a detective seemed pointless. "I'm not having much luck at the moment."

"You already found Jimmy's car. I'd call that progress." Pop upended his bottle and stood up. "I should get going. Scrabble night at the center. I don't want to miss any of the action. Last week, Eleanor caught Maryann cheating and started winging tiles."

Was it wrong to think that the Scrabble tournament kind of sounded like fun?

A cloud of depression hung over me as my Honda Civic chugged back to the rink. Lack of progress on the case. My father's abrupt departure from the first one-on-one conversation we'd had since I wore pigtails. Lionel's annoyance with me and my plan to sell the rink. Any one or all of them could have been the reason for the nagging unhappiness.

Not liking the feeling, I did what any person would do: I went skating.

Several hours later, I was tired, covered with sweat, and a whole lot happier. Handing out stinky skates and cleaning up after kids who had eaten frozen pizza and skated in circles for too long usually had the opposite effect. But, to my surprise, I found myself whistling while locking up the rink for the night. With a little skip, I headed around the side of the building to the entrance to my apartment.

I opened the door, and my heart dropped into my toes.

In the dimly lit stairway stood a man. A very large man who was currently cracking his knuckles.

And looking very unhappy with me.

Eight

The menacing guy took a step toward me.

My palms began to sweat as I took three steps backward onto the sidewalk and into the dim streetlight. I looked up and down the sidewalk. Not a creature was stirring. I was completely on my own.

The big guy took another step forward. Now at least I could see him a little better. All six feet and a whole lot more of him. The man was built like a freight train. He was wearing dark jeans, a green short-sleeved bowling shirt, and a cowboy hat. Not a guy I wanted to get into an arm-wrestling contest with.

I shuffled my feet backward, preparing for a running start.

Then the train spoke. "Rebecca Robbins?"

I barely recognized the name through the guy's heavy accent. The fact that this scary dude was specifically looking for me sent shivery waves of fear down my arms. Slowly, I nodded. I was too freaked to speak.

The guy rattled off a bunch of other words, none of which I

understood. Partly because of the accent and partly because the guy sounded upset. Really upset. Not to mention that some of the words were clearly in Spanish.

"*No comprendo,*" I squeaked out. That was all the Spanish I knew. Now, with any luck, the guy would go away.

No such luck. Another loud, angry bout of incomprehensible words came out of his mouth as he took another step toward me. Finally, there was one syllable I understood: "Car!"

"You know something about the stolen cars?" I asked.

The guy blinked at me; then his eyes narrowed. He shoved his hand into his pocket and came out with—*gulp*—a long wire. That's when the world went into slow motion.

Slowly, Mr. Freight Train wrapped the wire around his left hand. He then pulled the rest of it taut with his right. He barked out a couple of words and extended the wire toward me.

Without waiting for my brain, my feet began to move. I was around the corner, in my car, and down the street before my mind began to function. Three thoughts flashed through my head.

My life has just been threatened.

Someone doesn't want me looking into the car case. That means I'm making progress.

I didn't look at the scary guy's butt.

I pressed my foot to the gas pedal and steered the car toward the Indian Falls city limits and Lionel's house. I figured a threat on my life took precedence over any fight currently in progress.

The porch light at Lionel's house/veterinary office was on, but the rest of the building was dark when I pulled into the drive. I decided to be optimistic and knocked anyway.

No answer.

However, this wasn't the first time I'd knocked on Lionel's

door. No answer meant no one was in the house. The barn was another story.

Fingers crossed, I peered around the house. The barn was ablaze with light.

Eureka!

Legs trembling, I hurried down the path to the large white structure while shooting nervous looks over my shoulder. I was pretty sure the big scary dude hadn't followed me. Still, the crunch of the gravel beneath my gym shoes jangled my nerves.

After one last "I hope nobody is there" look back toward the house, I walked through the barn doors. The smell of hay and animals filled the air. A horse nickered from a stall.

No Lionel.

The sound of hay crunching under foot made my neck prickle. Slowly, I turned toward the sound to my right and squinted into the darkened corner of the barn, waiting for something scary to jump out at me. The minute the source of the sound came into the light, I began to laugh.

Trotting toward me, wearing a faded Chicago Cubs baseball cap, was Elwood, an ex-circus camel and current resident of Château Lionel. Elwood moseyed up to me and blew warm air in my face. All feelings of fear were pushed to the side for a moment. No one could remain terror-struck in the presence of a hat-wearing camel begging for attention. Besides, not long ago this camel had saved my life. If I wasn't safe here, I wasn't safe anywhere.

My hands patted Elwood's neck, making him grunt with happiness. He butted his head against my shoulder, and I scratched his face, careful not to dislodge his hat. Elwood needed a hat or he wasn't happy. Unhappy camels spit. I had enough problems without adding camel saliva to the mix.

I straightened Elwood's baseball cap and smiled. During his life with the circus, Elwood was the animal half of a clown/camel Blues Brothers act. When the clown died, Elwood became depressed and stopped eating. While passing through town, one of the animal keepers brought Elwood to Lionel for medical attention. Elwood liked Lionel and never left.

Since coming back to town, I'd been trying to figure out a way to adopt Elwood. However, something told me neither Elwood nor any Chicago landlord would be happy with the situation. My loss.

A muffled noise from far back in the barn made me jump a little. I looked at Elwood, who was rolling his eyes in delight. If he wasn't concerned, that could only mean one thing.

Lionel.

Escorted by the camel, I made my way to the other end of the barn. I walked through the back hallway into Lionel's favorite hangout—the poker room. The wood-paneled room had beige carpeting, in the center of which were a large round poker table and chairs. There was also a television and a large leather sofa. To make the place self-sufficient, Lionel had added a microwave and a refrigerator.

It was in the refrigerator that I found my favorite veterinarian. His head and upper body were obstructed by the fridge door. His butt was in plain sight, and I leaned against the doorjamb to admire it. Eleanor might be onto something, I thought.

Elwood nuzzled my shoulder. I gave him a small pat. When I didn't offer him food or any more scratches, the camel trotted back down the hallway in search of something more interesting.

The man attached to the butt emerged from the fridge wielding a beer. He ran a hand through his wavy brown hair, popped the top, and turned. The minute he noticed me, my throat began to ache. Tears welled in my eyes. I sniffled, trying to hold back the flood that had been threatening since I left the rink.

I failed.

Lionel put down his beer and crossed the room. The tears streaking down my face came faster. Lionel reached me, and I wrapped my arms around him and held on tight as my body shook with fear, relief, and unhappiness. My eyes and throat burned. I tried to take a deep breath and almost choked. Lionel's strong arms tightened their hold, and I sank into his chest.

I don't know how long we stood that way. It had to have been a while, because when I finally pulled away, the right shoulder of Lionel's green shirt was soaked. Worse yet, I was feeling more than a little embarrassed about my outburst. Redheads don't cry well, and I'm the worst of the bunch. My eyes get puffy, my cheeks break out in red blotches, and the rest of my face turns pink and shiny. None of which is a good thing when faced with a guy who looks like he jumped off the pages of a *Playgirl*, Veterinarian Edition calendar.

"Sorry," I said, bowing my head. To my horror, I began to sniffle again.

Lionel didn't seem to notice my embarrassment or the sniffling. He just guided me to the sofa, grabbed his open beer, and handed it to me.

"I think you could use this."

I nodded and took a sip. Alcohol was never a solution, but in this case a beer seemed like a good stopgap until I could come up with a better one.

Lionel waited in silence for me to finish half the beer before asking, "Now that you're feeling better, tell me what your father did."

The beer bottle stopped halfway to my mouth. "What do you mean, 'what your father did'?"

"You were crying," Lionel said in the same voice he used to calm nervous horses. I could tell by the flash of his eyes that he was upset. "Your father must have done something to make you cry."

I shook my head and handed back the beer bottle. Something told me that in a minute Lionel was going to need an alcohol infusion more than I did.

"My father didn't make me cry." He'd made me angry. That was entirely different. "A big man lunging at me with a wire did."

It was Lionel's turn to look confused.

I took a deep breath. "I don't know who the man was. I was going to my apartment and found him standing in the stairway, waiting for me."

A muscle in Lionel's throat twitched.

"The guy yelled at me for a while in Spanish, but I could only make out one word."

Another twitch. "What was the word?"

I took another deep breath and braced myself for impact. "*Car.*"

Lionel stood up and paced the floor. His hands raked through his hair three times. I counted. One meant he was thinking. Two meant he was stalling for time. Three meant he was trying not to yell. Four told me to dive for cover.

"I don't believe this," Lionel said in a strangled voice as he strode back and forth across the floor. Stopping in front of me, he asked, "The car thief came to your apartment to yell at you?"

"Maybe. I don't know." I was as confused as he was. "Maybe he's the thief's brother and is worried about my being on the case." Yeah, right. Shrugging, I explained, "All I know is the guy said something about a car. He could have been asking about buying a car, for all I know."

Lionel turned his green eyes on me. "And what about the wire?"

"Okay," I admitted, "the wire was scary. One minute the guy sounded like a skater who was mad at me for losing his shoes and the next he was stretching a wire between his hands and extending it toward my throat."

I tried to sound nonchalant, but my voice shook anyway. The wire and the guy holding it had knocked me off balance.

And Lionel knew it.

In a flash, his cell phone was in his hand. "We're calling Sean."

"No, not Sean," I yelled, springing from the sofa. I grabbed Lionel's hand and wrestled for the phone. Lionel was bigger, but I was scrappy. Too bad scrappy lost.

Panting, I watched him put the phone to his ear and say, "We have to let the cops know this guy is around. You don't want him to scare anyone else, do you? What if Agnes ran into this guy? Or your grandfather?"

The idea of my grandfather running into the wire thug made me weak. Pop wouldn't run. Pop thought he was Arnold Schwarzenegger and Zorro rolled into one. Pop wouldn't stand a chance.

"All right," I said. "You have a point." He also had the phone held high enough to keep me from snagging it. The combination was unbeatable.

Lionel handed me the receiver. "It's ringing."

Great. Sean would make me feel as if it were all my fault. I ignored the niggle at the back of my brain that said it might be. I was looking into the car theft after Sean had told me point-blank not to.

"Hello, you've reached the Indian Falls Sheriff's Department." Roxy's overly chipper voice boomed into the receiver. "We are busy on the other line, assisting a fellow citizen. Please leave a message and we will get back to you."

I smiled at Lionel. He had dialed the nonemergency line. Now I could do my civic duty without talking to Sean. I left a detailed message about the wire run-in and promised to check in the next morning.

I closed the phone and handed it back to Lionel. "Satisfied?"

Shoving the phone in his pocket, Lionel picked up the opened beer and chugged. When he finished, he closed his eyes for a moment and sighed. "A message is fine for now, but tomorrow morning you are going down to the Sheriff's Department to file a report. Until then, you're staying here."

"Here? As in here in the barn?" The couch was pretty comfortable, and Elwood was in the next room. All in all, things could be worse.

Lionel arched an eyebrow and crooked a finger in the neckline of my T-shirt. He gave a little tug, and I took a step toward him. "Here," he said in a low voice, "as in my house, with me."

"Oh." My heart gave a funny little skip as Lionel's mouth touched mine. I sank into his arms as his lips teased and tasted, until all scary thoughts of the man with the wire disappeared.

I didn't have to open my eyes to know that something was different. Behind my shut lids I could feel the sunlight streaming into the room. It was morning. And last night . . .

My eyes flew open, and I sat up in bed.

Last night, my life had been threatened. Last night, I'd stayed the whole night with Lionel in his house.

And nothing had happened.

I looked down at my clothing. Yep, I wasn't imagining it. I was dressed in a T-shirt and a pair of Lionel's boxer shorts. I'd slept in the house of the sexiest man alive, and I'd done it alone. I groaned, remembering the worst part. The sleeping arrangements had been my choice.

Lionel had kissed me all the way up to the house. His hands touched my shoulders, back, and arms. I unbuttoned his shirt and ran my fingers across his hard, tanned chest. He unlocked the door to the house without our lips breaking contact. Heat and desire coursed through me. My whole body tingled with excitement as we traveled up the stairs to his room. Nothing had ever felt better. I was alive and safe and ready to celebrate both.

And then my mind turned on. Maybe it was the sight of Lionel's bed, all massive mahogany, with a deep green comforter. Bachelor decor. Or maybe it was the uncertain status of our relationship and my future in Indian Falls that made my brain hold up the stop sign. One minute I was kissing Lionel as if my life depended on it, the next I was saying, "I think I should sleep on the sofa."

Lucky for me, Lionel had self-control and a guest room. He even lent me his toothbrush and tucked me in for the night.

What other guy would do that? I thought with pride. A second later, my pride turned to confusion.

What guy would do that? One who cared too much to push a girl into something she wasn't ready for, or one who didn't care enough to get upset when the girl changed her mind?

And which one did I really want it to be? My head throbbed. Thinking about my life did that.

My nose twitched as the aroma of coffee floated through the air. Coffee was somewhere downstairs. So was Lionel. I burrowed between the sheets, warring between the need for caffeine and dealing with the fallout from last night's abstinence.

Caffeine won.

I hopped out of bed. In record time, I did the teeth-brushing thing in the bathroom and padded downstairs, pretending to be more in control of the situation than I felt. My nose led me to Lionel's kitchen, which was in the back of the house. I braced myself for confrontation and walked through the doorway.

The kitchen was empty.

Huh. All that worrying for nothing.

Lionel was nowhere in sight. Instead, I found white cabinets against blue walls, butcher-block countertops, spotless white appliances, and a scarred wooden table with six matching chairs. All in all, the epitome of the cozy farmhouse kitchen.

Taking advantage of Lionel's absence, I peeked in the cabinets, then in the fridge. Lots of fruits and veggies, milk that hadn't passed the expiration date, cheese, and a couple of packages of lunch meat and other butcher delicacies. His cabinets were filled with pots, pans, and a full set of dishes. This was not the kitchen of any happily single man I'd ever dated. This was the kitchen of a man who should be married.

Eeek!

I made a beeline for the door, stopping first to set my coffee cup in the sink. My mother had taught me manners, which apparently took over when everything else flew out of control. A piece of paper on the counter caught my attention, probably because it had my name on the top. It read:

Becky, I had to go check on Bucky Davis's mare. Hope you slept well. I'll stop by the rink later. Love, Lionel
  PS. Go to the sheriff's office and file a report.

After making the bed and straightening up the bathroom, I was in my car and traveling back to town, doing my best not to dwell on the *L* word in Lionel's note. I was pretty sure Lionel wasn't making a romantic declaration with a Sharpie and a ripped-out page of a spiral notebook. Lionel had more class. Still, the word unnerved me.

To distract myself, I decided to follow Lionel's instructions and tooled over to the sheriff's office to file a report. The fact that the station was next door to the DiBelka Bakery probably added an extra incentive to do my civic duty.

Indian Falls Sheriff's Department dispatcher and all-around nuisance Roxy Moore was seated behind the reception counter when I stepped through the glass front doors. The pink-lacquered tips of her fingers flipped though a magazine as her platinum blond head bopped to the oldies playing over the speakers. At the sound of my footsteps, she glanced up. Her onyx-lined eyes widened. Then she smiled.

"Inspector Robbins. I figured you'd wander in here. Can't keep your nose out of police business, can you?"

"Morning, Roxy," I said, trying to be polite. "I need to file an official report. I left a message last night about the man threatening me outside the rink."

"Oh God, that's right." Roxy's face turned the same color as her nail polish. "Sean mentioned you had called. I had to leave work early. I must have just missed your call. I don't think I would ever have forgiven myself if something had happened to you and I hadn't been here to get the call."

Quickly, I walked Roxy through last night's encounter with the psycho Spanish guy. My stomach churned as I described the moment when the man had pulled the wire out of his pocket and wrapped part of it around his hand. By the time I'd finished my story, Roxy's face was decidedly pale under her liberally applied makeup. I wasn't sure, but I thought I preferred the snide comments and withering looks.

Roxy lent me her magazine as she typed the report. I feigned interest in Mel Gibson's life while she plucked keys on the computer. Sadly, Mel wasn't interesting enough to distract my mind from exploding cars and angry thugs. So when the printer started whirring, I asked, "How's the investigation on my dad's car coming? Does Sean have any leads?"

One perfectly penciled eyebrow raised in my direction. "Deputy Holmes is working very hard to find the person responsible. I'm sure he'll catch the thief any day, especially now that you've come in and given a description. This guy will be easy to spot in Indian Falls."

I couldn't deny that. But somewhere in my brain I wasn't sure the big guy was the thief.

Roxy handed me the report. I signed it and took my copy, all the while wondering if maybe the guy had just been a witness to the crimes and was trying to share information. He struck me as the type that would avoid cops. Then again, maybe his own car had been stolen and he wanted my help. There were too many maybes for me to swallow. Until there was some kind of evidence linking my Spanish-speaking visitor to the cars and the fire, I wasn't about to call the case closed.

As I walked toward the front doors, a question popped into my head. "Hey," I said with my hand on the door frame. "Do they know what type of accelerant the thief used to torch Jimmy's car?"

I waited for Roxy to shoot me down with a snide remark. Instead, she took her seat behind the counter and said, "Gasoline. Jimmy's car was soaked in it. So was the mannequin. Then they were both set on fire. Make sure you take care of yourself."

Stunned, I walked into the bright sunshine. Roxy had been nice. She was never nice, especially when I poked my nose into police business. And she never gave me useful information. Either Roxy had started taking Precious's medication or she thought my life was about to come to an end. Something told me I wasn't lucky enough for it to be medication. My day was going downhill fast.

I walked next door to the bakery and purchased a banana nut muffin and two chocolate croissants. By the time I pulled into the rink parking lot, I had polished off one croissant and was working on the other. The flaky combination of chocolate and butter restored my sense of optimism. Besides, if someone was waiting to kill me, I could bribe them with the muffin. No one would choose blood and death over one of Mrs. DiBelka's banana nut creations.

I drove around the parking lot, clutching the bakery bag and looking for mysterious figures lurking in the shadows. Thank goodness there weren't any. I would live another day and get to eat the muffin. Things were looking up.

I took a peek into the stairway leading to my apartment and let out a sigh of relief. No freaky guys in sight. With the coast clear, I ran upstairs to shower and change.

I flipped on the lights and crossed through the expansive living room to the bathroom, feeling safer with every step. Sensing my mother's presence always had that effect. After Dad left us, she and I had moved into the rink apartment and created a safe space for the two of us. Before that, we'd lived in a rambling old farmhouse with four big bedrooms and a big backyard. Come to think of it, the house was kind of like Lionel's.

Weird.

At the edge of my parent's farmhouse yard had stood a large oak tree. There I practiced for my dream job—an aerialist with the Barnum & Bailey Circus. My dream died the day Dad left and Mom and I had to move. Huh. Now that I thought about it, my father's desertion had probably helped me live through puberty.

I showered and changed into a pair of jeans and a copper tank top. Then, standing in Mom's gourmet kitchen, I tried to talk myself into going downstairs. This apartment felt safe. Anything outside of it didn't. But hiding felt like a wimpy, girl thing to do, and I hated feeling wimpy more than I liked feeling safe.

Well adjusted I wasn't.

Grabbing my purse, I went downstairs to work in the rink. While George skated around the wooden floor, I paid some bills and returned phone calls. Scheduling three birthday parties and enrolling six kids in the upcoming group skating lessons helped the rink's bottom line, but it did nothing for my deductive abilities. So I strapped on a pair of skates and joined George on the floor.

I pumped my legs from side to side, gaining momentum as I traveled the dimly lit length of the rink. Unless there was a class or a private lesson in progress, George and I kept the lights low and the music off. Without the fluorescent lights and pumping bass, the rink took on a relaxing, almost soothing atmosphere. The combination also helped keep the electricity bill down.

George executed a perfect triple-loop jump in the middle of the floor while I whizzed around the boards, taking mental inventory of what I knew about the car thefts. Both Jimmy and my father had parked their old cars in well-used parking lots. The thief either had liked the added risk of being caught or hadn't thought anyone would notice him. I liked to think that meant the guy was a local. That would narrow it down, since the guy who'd accosted me last night would stick out like a sore thumb in this town. However, Indian Falls's citizens were a trusting group as a whole. If a thief waved at them while hot-wiring a car, the citizen would probably wave back, whether they knew him or not.

Starting to sweat, I spun around and traveled the floor backward. The thief might have called Jimmy's insurance agent, he might have been in the diner two nights ago, and he might have attacked me last night. But might haves weren't helping me right now. I needed to study what I knew for certain. I knew for sure that the thief had stolen two cars and torched one of them with gasoline. A mannequin had also been set ablaze. And despite the fact the hay field had been dry, it hadn't gone up with the car or the doll. I had no idea why the thief had set a recently stolen car on fire or how he'd managed to save the field from going up in smoke, but I wanted to find out.

For that, I needed a fireman.

Nine

The Indian Falls Fire Department was located five blocks from the rink, right next to Dr. Truman's office. Given this proximity, I guessed that Dr. Truman wasn't just the local doctor and coroner; he was also one of the paramedics.

The heat index was climbing as I parked across from the station. Music was pumping from a small but powerful CD player while the faded red fire engine sat parked on the long and currently wet driveway. Big Red was getting a bath.

A half-naked man with a garden hose danced around the engine, spraying water. The guy didn't see me, which was probably a good thing, since my mouth was hanging open in horror. Not that I was a prude or anything. Most of the time, twenty- or thirty-something shirtless men in shorts were the best part of summer.

This wasn't one of those times.

The fireman did a stripper impersonation with his hips while his ample gut undulated in time to the music. The man gave new meaning to the words *belly dance*. Add to that the dark curly hair crawling up his chest and down his legs like moss, and suddenly you had a picture that would never appear in any of the sexiest-firemen calendars.

When the song ended, the guy turned off his hose, scratched his hairy stomach, and yawned. Then he turned. I could tell he'd spotted me when his uncovered mouth turned from a stretched yawn into a come-hither smile.

Oh joy!

I gave him a little wave and strolled up the drive. "Hi. I hope I'm not interrupting your work."

The guy winked. "I don't mind being interrupted by a hot chick."

I mentally rolled my eyes and stopped next to the truck. Now that I was closer, I realized the guy was barely out of high school. I tried to decide if I'd ever seen him before. Nope. He might have been at Pop's two months ago when the scarecrow went up in flames or at Jimmy's car fire. Either event would have warranted wearing a shirt and pants. Without those, I was too distracted to say for certain.

"Hi, I'm Rebecca Robbins. Are you the only one manning the station today?" I was hoping to find a more experienced firefighter to answer my questions.

My new friend nodded. "Robbie Bellson. The other guys went to get coffee. I'm the new guy around here, which means I get to wash the truck and baby-sit the station."

His disgruntled frown made me smile. "Not exactly the exciting job you signed on for, is it?"

"It has its moments," he said, leaning down to tie his shoe and giving me a great view of his ample butt crack.

"Like someone setting fire to Jimmy Bakersfield's car?" I

asked while feigning interest in the fire truck. Butt cracks weren't my thing.

"Yeah, that was cool. I never knew a car could light up so fast." I braved a look at Robbie. He was standing upright, with his hands jammed in his pockets. A glee-filled smile spread across his face as he reminisced, "You should have seen those flames. They were truly excellent."

"I saw them. I was the one who reported the fire."

"Then you know what I'm talking about." Robbie shifted from foot to foot, almost dancing with excitement. "The guy who started it used a lot of gasoline. I guess he didn't want to risk the fire going out."

"If that much gasoline was used, why didn't the hay field go up in flames?" I asked. "I mean, I don't know much about setting fires, but I was wondering how the car burned so fast and the dry field was barely singed. Isn't that unusual?"

Robbie stopped dancing. "I don't know," he said, walking over to the CD player. With a whack, he turned it off. He grabbed the red T-shirt sitting next to it and shimmied into it. Rolls of hairy fat shook from side to side, then disappeared underneath yards of material.

"Look," he said, turning back to me with a frown. "There are lots of reasons why the field wouldn't catch fire. Only, I can't talk to you about them."

"But I only—"

"Sorry. The guys are already giving me a hard time, my being new and all. The last thing I need is them finding out I talked to you about the fire. Besides, Deputy Stick-up-His-Ass read us the riot act about talking to anyone but him. You're hot, but you're not hot enough for me to risk pissing him off."

Robbie trudged into the firehouse, leaving me trying to decide whether I had just been insulted.

I contemplated hanging around until the other firemen came back, then decided against it. Deputy Sean had beaten me here. None of these guys would be talking to little old me. There was only one person associated with the firehouse who would risk crossing Sean Holmes to give me information, and right now he probably had his hand up a cow's behind. I was going to have to wait for Lionel to shower before grilling him.

That in mind, I went back to the rink. I walked through the front door and stopped in my tracks. There was my father, standing on the rink's sidelines, watching a class of seven- and eight-year-olds learn how to skate on one foot.

Every muscle in my body tightened as I recalled how my father had stood in that same spot and watched my mother teach me how to skate. He'd always yelled encouragement when I fell. I fell a lot back then. I still did, only now I didn't rely on Stan's voice to help me get up. I got up all on my own.

My father turned and spotted me in the doorway. His white shorts were pressed to perfection, as was his black polo shirt. A frown creased his face as he crossed to me. "Rebecca, honey, I heard what happened to you last night. Why didn't you call us? We were worried."

For a moment, I thought he was using the royal *we*. Then I spotted my grandfather making a beeline for me. Pop was wearing black shorts and a white shirt. Together, they looked like Yin and Yang. It was kind of creepy.

"I'm fine," I assured the two of them.

"That's not what Roxy said." Pop wagged his finger at me.

"She said you were threatened last night right outside the rink. You should have called me."

"You couldn't have done anything, Pop."

Pop straightened his bony shoulders. "I could have stayed here. I still can. That man won't come back and bother you with me around."

"Right." My father laughed. "You have as much chance of scaring off an intruder as a teacup terrier does."

Pop scowled. "I'll have you know I'm the Senior Center's arm-wrestling champ." He flexed a nonexistent muscle in his bicep. "I can protect my granddaughter."

My father's eyes narrowed as he looked down at Pop. "I'm back in town now, which means if Rebecca needs protecting, I'll be the one to do it."

"You'd run off at the first sign of trouble," Pop yelled, puffing out his chest. "And, yes, I might not be young anymore, but Rebecca knows I'll be around when she needs me. You can't say that."

My father's face turned three shades of red. He took a step forward, so only inches separated him and Pop. "Are you calling me a coward?"

"It's the truth." Pop adjusted his teeth and shot an evil grin at his adversary. Pop was having way too much fun. Stan wasn't. A vein in his neck throbbed as he cracked his knuckles. Yep, Stan looked ready to explode. It was time to step in, before someone got hurt.

"Hey," I hollered. Two pairs of testosterone-filled eyes swung in my direction. "Look, I appreciate your concern, but I don't need either one of you to stay with me."

Pop wasn't going down without a fight. He plopped his hands on his hips and said, "Rebecca Robbins, you need me."

I smiled. "Of course I need you, Pop. I just don't need you to be my roommate. If I am in danger, I don't want to drag you into it. I couldn't live with myself if anything happened to you." I also couldn't live with Pop's social calendar. I'd tried that once before, with great discomfort. Walking in on my grandfather while he was having sex guaranteed therapy into the afterlife. "Please understand, Pop."

Pop's shoulders fell. "Okay. But you have to promise to come get me if you're doing any dangerous investigation work. I make a good lookout."

Pop made a terrible lookout, but I said, "Sure."

"Good." Pop slapped a hand on one of his scrawny legs. "Now, I got to get over to the center. They're showing *Body Heat* in the game room. Do you want to come? I can get you in."

"No thanks," I said quickly. Thinking about watching sexy movies with my grandfather made me want to hurl. "I have to track down someone to be rink manager."

My grandfather shot me a bright smile. The dishwasher had done a good job polishing his teeth. "Already done. I hired a manager just after Stan and I got here."

I looked from my grandfather to Stan. "You took the job?"

"Me?" my father stammered. "Well, you know I'd love to work with you, honey, but I already have a job. That's why I helped Arthur hire someone for you." His eyes darted from side to side while his hands fidgeted with the buttons at the top of his shirt. "I mean, I'm in the middle of a business deal; otherwise, I'd—"

"You don't have to make excuses," I said, finally letting him off the hook. Although watching him dangle had been kind of fun. "I wouldn't have let you take the job."

My father stiffened. "Why not? I can do the job. Stan Robbins can run any business anywhere."

The blood in my temples pulsated. "Sure. Fine. Now, would someone please tell me who you hired to be the manager of my business?"

"Me."

I turned toward the sound of the sort-of-familiar voice and almost fell over. Standing there in black sandals and socks was Max Smith, the angry son of Sinbad.

"You?"

Max's curly hair bobbed as he nodded. "Your grandfather wasn't sure what paperwork you'd need me to fill out. So he said I'd have to wait to do that with you."

"But you didn't want the job."

"I changed my mind."

"A boy's entitled to change his mind," my father said. "You should give this boy a break. I like him."

"So do I." My grandfather clapped Max on the back. Max tilted dangerously forward, then righted himself.

"Good," I said, feeling cornered and not liking it. "Then the two of you can hire him."

Turning on my heel, I stalked toward my office, not sure what had me more annoyed: the fact my father thought he had a say in my business or that my grandfather agreed with him.

I flipped on the light switch and flopped into my wheeled computer chair. I rubbed my temples and leaned back, trying to decide how to go about finding a real rink manager. All normal avenues had been tapped long ago. Newspaper ads hadn't done the trick.

Neither had flyers or Now Hiring signs. Everyone in town loved coming to the rink to skate. No one wanted to run the place, including me.

"Ms. Robbins, could I talk to you for a minute?"

Max hovered in the doorway. His glasses slipped down his long nose, making him look studious. He ran a hand through his curly hair and gave me a nervous smile.

I gestured to the seat on the opposite side of the desk, and Max sank into it.

Leaning my elbows on the desk, I asked, "Why are you here, Max? We both know you don't want this job."

"But I do." Max scooted forward in his chair. "I need a job, and this is better than working for my father. The two of us don't do well under the same roof. You might have noticed."

"What about your film career?"

Max's eyes brightened behind his thick glasses. "Making movies is very expensive. That's why I need a job. I have this great script. We've been filming it for the past couple of weeks, but I can't finish it without more cash."

"What's the movie about?" I couldn't help asking.

Max raised his hands. "Imagine *Die Hard* meets *Steel Magnolias*. A southern groom walks into the church on the day of his wedding, only to discover terrorists have kidnapped half the wedding party, his bride, and the minister. Now the groom has to save the bride, rescue the minister, and do it all before the guests get tired of waiting for the wedding to start. There'll be fight scenes and chases, and a big Hollywood happy ending where the bloody groom marries his almost-raped wife. Isn't it great?"

Great? No. Flop, yes. Bruce Willis and Chantilly Lace weren't going to put butts in the seats for that film. "Sounds interesting."

I pushed my forefingers against the throbbing in my temple and rubbed.

Max bounced on the edge of his chair. "When the movie is finished, I'm going to send it to some agents and producers in L.A. Once I'm offered representation, I'll move to California."

"Really?"

He nodded. "Serious directors have to live out west to get work. At least I will until people find out how skilled I am. Then I'll be able to live wherever I want."

"What's your dad think about that?"

He stiffened. "My father refuses to believe I have any talent and says he'll only watch a movie that I made when hell freezes over."

The pain in the kid's eyes had me softening. I understood dad issues all too well. "I don't understand. How will working here help you become a serious director?"

Max smiled. "I need a job. At least until the movie is done and I get an agent. You need a rink manager who understands a creative business like skating. The way I see it, we're a perfect fit."

The logic made a warped kind of sense. And I had to find a manager for the sale of the rink to go through. Against my better judgment, I found myself liking Max. He had passion. Besides, no one else wanted the job.

"Okay," I agreed. "You're hired on a trial basis. Let's see how the next week goes. If things run smoothly, the job is officially yours."

I was desperate, not stupid.

The condition didn't deter Max's enthusiasm. He shot out of his chair with a huge grin. "You won't regret it. I learn fast."

And he did. After he finished filling out the requisite paperwork, I took him on a tour of the rink. Max jotted down notes as he trailed behind me through the ticket booth, the rental counter, the kitchen, the snack area, and the sound booth.

And then it was time to introduce Max to George.

George had just finished his class when I waved him over. He skidded to a stop in front of us. His blond hair was plastered to his forehead with sweat as he asked, "What's up?"

"George, this is Max Smith. He's going to be our new rink manager."

Max gave George a friendly smile.

George studied Max from the tips of his sock- and sandal-clad feet to the small coffee stain on his oversized powder blue golf shirt. Kids from George's last class sped around us, getting ready to go home, but George didn't move. My throat tensed. Normally, George watched over his students like they were his own children. Right now, he didn't appear to see or hear them.

This was a bad sign.

Without a word, George launched himself toward the middle of the rink and executed a perfect double-axel jump. Then as quickly as he'd left, he zoomed back toward us. Coming to a flawless stop, he asked Max, "Can you do that?"

"No."

"Can you do a sit spin?"

Max's dark eyebrows rose slightly as he turned to me. "That sounds personal. Do I have to answer him?"

George's eyes narrowed into tiny slits. Max raised his chin, as if daring George to take a punch. For the second time today, I found myself in the middle of warring male hormones. Yippee.

"You don't have to be a great skater to run a roller rink," I explained to George in my best "be reasonable" voice. "Max will

95

run the office, and George, you will be in charge of the skating. I think the two of you will make a great team."

Clearly this wasn't the answer George was waiting for. He shot me an injured look, let out an exaggerated sigh, and rolled toward the rental counter, where a bunch of kids from his class were waiting to exchange skates for shoes. Not exactly the most auspicious of beginnings. I hoped my would-be buyers would sign the papers before George left tread marks on Max's back.

With a sigh, I turned to Max. "George is very dedicated to this business. As soon as you show him that you can manage the place, he'll love you."

Max gave me a thumbs-up sign while I said a small prayer that my big fat lie would by some miracle come true. Then the two of us set off for the office to do some training on the computer.

The rest of the day passed as I taught Max the ins and outs of rink management. That meant I didn't have time to find Lionel to ask him about the car fire. Still, training kept me busy, inside, and away from any psychopaths waiting to strangle me with a wire. And by the time the office clock read 5:30, Max was up to speed on skating lessons, music systems, and staff scheduling. All in all, a productive day.

Standing up, I told my trainee, "It's quitting time for you. Be back here tomorrow at nine."

"No problem." Max stretched his lanky arms and stood up. Half-way to the door, he snapped his fingers and turned back. "Oh, boss, you forgot to give me a key for the front door."

I leaned back in my chair and peered up at Max's earnest face. "No, I didn't."

"Opening in the morning is my job. I need a key."

"In a week, it'll be your job," I told him. "Once you prove

you're ready, I'll get you a key for the front door. Until then, you'll have to wait for me or George."

Max's eyebrows knit together. He opened his mouth, no doubt to argue with me, so I said, "Go home, Max. I'll see you in the morning."

"Sure," Max said with a smile that didn't quite erase the frown from his eyes. "See you." He disappeared out the door.

I let out a sigh and dialed Doreen's number with a sense of dread. Talking to my father's bed partner wasn't in my comfort zone. I smiled with relief when Doreen's smoky voice instructed me to leave a message at the beep.

"Hi, Doreen," I said, trying to erase the picture of my father and her from my mind. "You can tell the buyer I have a manager for the rink. Once the inspection is done, we can sign the papers and finish the sale."

And I'd be able to go back to my life in Chicago. It was great.

So why didn't I feel like celebrating?

Ten

Confused and in need of distraction, I left the rink, ready to see Lionel, then remembered I already had plans for the evening. Plans I wasn't remotely ready for.

As Danielle had reminded me yesterday, I was hosting the Indian Falls Gourmet Club, a group I'd inadvertently started while investigating the town's one and only murder. The now-thriving club met twice a month at my place.

After a quick trip to the market, I raced up the stairs to my apartment and began chopping veggies. Tonight, I was making a mushroom and asparagus risotto. The other attendees would bring the rest of the meal. I would eat well, even if I didn't make progress on solving the car thefts. Then again, several of the club members were on my list of witnesses in the diner before my father's car got stolen. In between courses, I could grill my friends.

No grass growing under my feet.

The doorbell rang at five minutes to seven. I opened the front door, and Felix and Barbara Slaughter walked into the living room, carrying large pans covered with aluminum foil. Felix was the owner of Slaughter's Market and the person I'd fibbed to about starting the gourmet club the last time I was investigating a crime.

Felix shifted his hold on the food pans. A lock of light brown hair fell over his forehead as he gave me a gap-toothed smile. "I hope you were still planning on having dinner tonight. We weren't sure after Roxy called and told Barbara what had happened to you."

The FBI couldn't hold a candle to Roxy when it came to information gathering. She also spread it much like the local farmers spread manure—in liberal quantities and without much concern for quality.

"I wouldn't dream of canceling," I said truthfully. Having an apartment full of people would make me less jittery about spending the night here. A thug armed with a wire wouldn't try taking down all of us.

Barbara shook her head at her tall husband. "See, I told you Rebecca wouldn't let a silly little threat ruin our night." She turned toward me. "We should probably put these things in the oven."

Without waiting for my reply, Barbara swept past me toward the kitchen, with her husband trailing at her heels. I sighed as they disappeared around the corner. Curvy, blond, and petite, Barbara looked cuddly and submissive. She proved the rule that looks were deceiving. Four-star generals had less command capabilities than the grocer's wife.

And less volume. Barbara's high-pitched voice traveled from the kitchen. "Felix, you're doing it all wrong. Give me the spoon and get out of the kitchen before you ruin everything."

Not long ago, according to the local grapevine, Barbara had gone to see her lawyers. Sources in the know said she'd instructed them to bring out the big guns and aim them at Felix. So far, the guns hadn't fired. I just hoped they wouldn't start in my kitchen.

Straightening my shoulders, I turned toward the kitchen, in hopes of protecting my appliances, when the doorbell rang. I opened the door and smiled as Danielle Martinez and her boyfriend, Pastor Rich Lucas, walked in with dessert.

Danielle shoved the cake carrier into her boyfriend's hands and raced toward me. A second later, I was being squeezed so hard, I thought my eyeballs were going to pop.

"Rebecca, Rich and I heard what happened to you," Danielle squeaked, stepping back and giving me a thorough once-over with her perfectly pencil-lined eyes. "Are you okay? Did the guy hurt you?"

"I'm fine," I said, trying to sound more casual about the encounter than I felt. "The guy startled me, but no harm was done."

"Right." Danielle pursed her glossy lips together, then turned on her million-watt smile. "Rich," she cooed. "Would you take the cake into the kitchen for me? Oh, and could you get me something to drink?"

Red-faced, Pastor Rich nodded with a shy smile and wandered off in search of the kitchen.

"You really should be nicer to him," I said, perching on the arm of my pale yellow sofa.

"What do you mean?" Danielle raised a perfect eyebrow. "I'm very nice to Rich."

"You overwhelm the poor guy on purpose so he'll do anything you want. The pastor's sheltered life never prepared him for dealing with a woman like you."

Danielle shrugged and leaned against the wall with a pout. Even pouting, Danielle was stunning. No wonder she'd been so successful at her past profession. What red-blooded man wouldn't want to watch her dance in front of him? Heck, even in the crisp blue shorts, yellow shirt, and silver sandal heels she had on now, the woman would have men begging for her attention.

Then it hit me. Danielle was wearing heels, really sexy stilettos. And her shorts were well above the knee. I'd never seen my friend in anything that showed her knees. At least not in Indian Falls. Danielle had left those clothes in Chicago, along with stripping, in order to create a new image in a new place. Something was up.

"Hey, what's with the new look? Are you trying to give Rich a heart attack with those shoes?"

"Like he'd notice."

"He'd have to be dead not to notice." In my experience, any male with a pulse would have been panting over Danielle's legs, especially when she was wearing those shoes.

Danielle's shoulders slumped. "Or not interested. We've been dating for over three months and he hasn't tried to put any moves on me. I'm worried he doesn't find me attractive."

"He's a Lutheran pastor. They have rules against premarital sex."

"How about premarital kissing?"

I looked toward the kitchen to make sure Rich wasn't coming, then hissed, "He hasn't kissed you?"

Danielle's sexy heels traveled the beige Berber carpet. She flopped across from me on the pale blue love seat with a sigh. "Not really. He pecks me on the lips when he drops me off at home, but otherwise nothing. Every time I try to get more passionate, he claims he has a sermon to work on and runs off."

"Maybe he does," I offered. Danielle's skeptical look had me adding, "Rich has to give a new sermon every Sunday. That can't be easy."

"I know it's not." She leaned her head back against the couch and closed her eyes. "I just wish I knew what to do to get his attention. Another woman, I could handle. How the hell do I compete with Jesus?"

Apparently with high heels and short shorts.

Danielle's eyes snapped open. "No more talking about me. I want you to tell me everything that happened last night. Did some guy really threaten you at gunpoint?"

"He didn't have a gun," I said with a laugh. This was the reason no one should depend on gossip as a major form of communication. By the time the story made it through the entire town, it would have me shot, in the hospital, and hanging on to life by a thread.

Danielle sat there, waiting for me to continue.

My voice gave a traitorous quiver as I admitted, "He had a wire stretched between his hands."

"Oh my God!" Danielle's mouth dropped. "Do you think he was going to strangle you with it?"

"I didn't wait around long enough to find out." I was afraid to admit that if I had waited, I might not be here at all. Worse, I had no idea why. Not knowing the reason someone wanted to hurt you really added to the creep factor.

"Ladies," Rich's voice shattered the tension as he poked his head out of the kitchen and said, "Would you like some wine while we wait for Bryan and Reginald to arrive?"

"Bring the bottle," I suggested.

Rich appeared a few moments later holding two stemmed glasses filled with pinot noir. "Felix and Barbara are putting together some appetizers while we wait for the others." He gave a nervous glance toward the kitchen. "I'd recommend staying out of the kitchen until they're done. You know . . ."

Laughing, I took one of the wineglasses. I did know. Barbara was a little overwhelming when cooking. Especially for someone like the mild-mannered Pastor Rich. He was a lot like Clark Kent, with glasses, shirt buttoned to the neck, and neatly combed hair. For Danielle's sake, I hoped Superman lurked somewhere beneath the perfectly pressed clothes.

Rich took a seat next to his girlfriend. A small frown played across Danielle's lips and the tension in the room went up several notches. For the first time, I noticed the distance he kept between their bodies. Rich probably thought he was being respectful, but I hoped the guy would figure the boy/girl thing out before Danielle put on her Mrs. Claus outfit and took a turn around a pole. Danielle's goal was to marry Rich, not kill him.

"So," I said, trying to put everyone at ease, "where do we think Bryan and Reginald are? They're normally the first ones here."

"I don't know." Rich clasped and unclasped his hands. "We ran into them at the diner. Reginald said they were bringing a great salad and a few other surprises."

I sat up straight. "Was that the night of Jimmy's car fire?"

"It was," Danielle said, fingering the rim of her wineglass. "All the firefighters came into the diner and were talking about it. Why?"

"My father came into town and was in the diner that night. The next morning, his car was stolen out of the retirement home's parking lot. I think the person who took Jimmy's car might have been at the diner and watched my father come in. Can you tell me who you remember seeing there?"

Danielle's eyes were bright as she listed the same names I'd gotten from Zach. Rich filled in some of the bingo women, but neither of them mentioned anyone new. Drat.

"Wait," Danielle said as I took a sip of wine. "There was another guy there for a few minutes. I'd never seen him before."

I put my glass down. "Do you remember what he looked like?"

Danielle tilted her head. "He was tall, had wavy black hair, and was wearing jeans and a golf shirt."

"Age?"

She shrugged. "Thirty-five. Maybe forty." Her lips curled into a sexy smile as she purred, "And good-looking. He reminded me of Antonio Banderas."

Great. Danielle was trying to make her boyfriend jealous with my primary suspect. Worse yet, Pastor Rich wasn't looking green with envy. In fact, he looked pretty darn happy. Something told me that tomorrow Danielle was going to wear fishnet stockings to work. No doubt a fashion first for the Lutheran church.

"Can you remember anything else about the guy?" I asked.

Danielle shook her head, and I felt a twinge of defeat. Between Agnes's information and Danielle's, I was certain I had a real suspect, but I was never going to find him.

Just then, Rich said, "He came to the nine o'clock service on Sunday." Danielle and I gaped at him, and he gave me a little wink. "If you need to speak to him, he might be there again this week. I'd be happy to point him out."

My admiration for Pastor Rich went up several notches. Not only had he given me a lead; he had subtly locked me into attending church. Maybe he wasn't as innocent as Danielle assumed.

I finished my glass of wine and was about to get another, when the doorbell buzzed. Changing direction, I swung open the door.

"Hey, Bryan," I said with a happy smile. Then I glanced behind him and my smile faded. "Where's Reginald? Is he sick?"

Bryan shook his perfectly styled blond head and wrapped his arms around his body. "Reginald isn't si—si—sick," he stammered. "He's . . ."

A tear streaked down Bryan's boyishly elfin face. My heart leaped into my throat as I put a hand on Bryan's arm. "What happened? Is he hurt?"

A shudder racked Bryan's body. "He's . . ."

I braced myself for terrible news. Flashes of Reginald's happy face went through my mind.

"Oh God, Rebecca," Bryan sobbed. "They think he stole that car and set it on fire. Can you believe it? The police put Reginald in jail!"

Long dreadlocks hid Reginald's face as I walked into the small Indian Falls jail cell. Huh. The room hadn't improved any since the last time I was here.

The walls were painted white but looked almost gray under the fluorescent lights. Stainless-steel bars divided the room into the visitors' area and two separate cells. Reginald was sitting on a cot in the cell nearest the window. His tall, beefy body made the cot look like it belonged in a child's room. I would have laughed at the absurdity of his sleeping on the tiny bed had Reginald not looked up at me. The defeat in his brown eyes sucked all the amusement out of me.

I pulled an orange plastic chair up to the cell and took a seat. "Reginald," I said in a soft voice. "Are you okay?"

His broad shoulders lifted. "Bryan and I moved here to get

away from my past. Things were supposed to be different. In the city, the cops used to lock me up all the time because I was big and black. Nothing's changed."

My heart ached as Reginald slumped his shoulders in defeat. "I know you didn't do this. So does Bryan and everyone else in the club. They're back at my place, calling around for a lawyer. We're going to get you out of here. Now tell me why they arrested you."

Reginald shifted, and the cot shuddered under his massive body. He was built like a Chicago Bears linebacker. Two hundred and forty pounds of dense muscle. Personally, I was surprised Deputy Sean'd had the gumption to arrest a guy as immense as Reginald. Normally, Sean wasn't into taking risks.

The man behind bars looked down at his large hands. "When I was a kid, I used to boost cars. The older guys on the block taught me. Turned out I had a knack for it."

"And Deputy Sean found out about your gift."

My choice of words made Reginald smile. "Yeah. He found out about my gift and arrested me. Turns out I'm the only person in this town with an arrest record for grand theft auto. It doesn't seem to matter that the whole thing happened when I was twelve. Or that I've been straight ever since. It didn't matter to the cops in Chicago, either."

As Reginald's smile faded, a surge of anger whipped through me. "Reg, what kinds of cars did you steal when you were twelve?"

"Why?"

I put a hand on one of the metal bars. "Did you steal Jimmy's car?"

"No."

"Did you set the car on fire?"

"No." A spark flared in Reginald's eyes, and I felt a moment of triumph. Anger was good. It meant he would help me spring him from this joint.

I gave him my best cheesy smile. "Trust me. Now tell me what kind of cars."

Ten minutes later, I barreled down the hallway, looking for my archnemesis. But he wasn't in his office or in reception. In fact, Deputy Holmes was nowhere to be found, and according to Roxy, he wasn't on call for the night.

"Then who is?" As far as I knew, Sean Holmes was on call 24/7 and made sure everyone knew it.

Roxy applied a coat of ruby red polish to her thumbnail. Without looking up, she said, "Why, Sheriff Jackson, of course."

Of course.

The green numbers on my car's dash read 8:45 when I pulled into Sheriff Jackson's long driveway on the outskirts of town. The farmhouse was ablaze with lights, telling me Sheriff Jackson hadn't turned in yet. There was still time to get Reginald sprung before he had to sleep on the kiddie bed.

Old-fashioned lampposts illuminated the beds of colorful flowers blooming along the sidewalk leading to the front door. Sheriff Jackson had taken up gardening when his wife died. Over the years, he'd developed a real talent for it. I wish I could say the same for his investigating skills.

Shifting from foot to foot, I knocked on the door and waited. When Sheriff Jackson opened the door, he was wearing a ratty blue terry-cloth bathrobe, fuzzy white ankle socks, and an absentminded smile. "Kay, what a pleasure to see you."

The name tugged at my soul. Gently, I said, "Kay was my mother, Sheriff. I'm her daughter, Rebecca."

The sheriff closed his eyes for a moment, scratched his gray temple, and nodded. "Sorry, Rebecca. I know who you are. I was looking at some old pictures today and must have gotten stuck in the past."

"No need to apologize," I said, continuing the polite fiction that his slip was unusual. The Indian Falls populace continued to elect him sheriff out of affection, not because of his ability. For that, they relied on Sean Holmes. Strange, but true.

Sheriff Jackson grinned, pushed the screen door open, and stepped out onto the porch. "So, what brings you out here at this time of night?"

"Reginald Washington."

The sheriff squinted in confusion.

"Deputy Holmes arrested him earlier today," I prompted, "for stealing Jimmy Bakersfield's car and setting it on fire."

The sheriff's eyes brightened. "Sure. Now I remember. Young Sean said that he had a history of stealing cars in the city before moving here. And according to Sean, your friend was in the diner the night your father blew back into town. That sounds like a good suspect to me."

I couldn't fault Sean's logic when it came to Reginald's being in the diner. I just faulted his suspect.

"Is there any physical evidence?" I asked. Before the sheriff could answer, I said, "No, because Reginald didn't do it."

I went on to explain how Reginald had given up a life of crime before entering high school. I paced the porch as if making an argument in front of a jury. "And if you look at his arrest record, you'll see he stole only new cars, then turned them over to older kids, who resold them. I'm sure the district attorney will have a hard time proving that over a decade and a half later Reginald changed his pattern and is now stealing and setting fire to rusted-out cars."

On a roll, I pivoted on my heel and pointed at Sheriff Jackson. "The way I see it, Sheriff, you don't have a case."

The sheriff shoved his hands into his tattered blue pockets and gave me a stern look. "Haven't we done this before?"

I blinked and dropped my defense attorney pose. "What do you mean?"

"This." The sheriff took one hand out of his pocket and waved it in the air. "We've done this kind of thing before. I have someone in the slammer and you want me to set them free."

For a second, I worried that my diatribe had knocked Sheriff Jackson off the edge of sanity. But then I remembered. "Two months ago, when Agnes Piraino was locked up."

He nodded. "Sean arrested her, and you came out here to plead her case." A cricket chirped as Sheriff Jackson scratched his chin. Straightening his shoulders, he added, "You were right then, and something tells me you're probably right again. Don't worry. I'll take a look at the evidence myself. If it's as flimsy as you say, I'll let your friend go."

Sheriff Jackson's voice boomed in the night. The authority in it made me smile. For the first time, I appreciated why the town continued to vote him into office. Sheriff Jackson might not have had the sharpest memory around, but when he wanted to be, he was still a force to be reckoned with.

"Do you think you could look into it tonight?" I asked. "I know neither one of us wants an innocent man spending a night behind bars." Or dangling off a cot, I thought.

The sheriff puffed up his chest and hooked his thumbs under the collar of his robe. "I guess I could get dressed and go down to the station. There isn't anything on TV worth watching anyway. You have a good night and don't worry. I'll make sure justice is served."

Back straight, chin high, Sheriff Jackson marched into the house, ready to do battle for truth, justice, and the American way. Look out, world.

Smiling, I hopped back in my car and steered it into town, certain I'd upped the odds that Reginald would be sleeping in his own bed tonight. Springing Reginald was good. The downside was that Sean Holmes would have a fit when he found out, and that anger would have one target: me.

Unless I wanted to end up arrested for jaywalking and then be forced to sleep on a minimattress, I needed to find the real thief—fast.

Eleven

Unfortunately, since I had a real job in addition to my family problem, solving the car case was going to take longer than I wanted. Bright and early Friday morning, I trekked downstairs to the rink, all the while scoping out the parking lot for Sean Holmes and a pair of handcuffs. If only the handcuff thing could have been chalked up to sexual fantasy, my life wouldn't have seemed so depressing.

On the upside, Reginald and Bryan had called around midnight to tell me Reginald had been sprung. The two of them had cried and laughed so much, it had been hard to make out what they'd been saying. Still, their happiness made me feel all warm and tingly. Good deeds did that to me.

Max was talking on the phone while juggling two large cups of coffee as I approached the rink's entrance.

"Sure. We need to make sure we have enough lighting for the scene. We can't afford to do stunts twice. And make sure all the actors are ready to go on time. Have Len call me after he looks at the warehouse. I'm hoping it'll be perfect for the shoot. We have only a few more days of filming, and we have to make every minute count." Max hung up and smiled.

"Sounds like your movie is almost done," I said, fumbling for my keys.

Max bobbed his head up and down while dancing from foot to foot. "We have a couple of big scenes to film and three or four small ones. Then we start editing, and that's where a movie really comes together."

"It must be hard to hold down a day job while working on a movie." I found my key and slid it into the lock.

Max's face took on a solemn expression. "Most artists have to suffer through day jobs to make ends meet. It's part of the process."

Inside, George was rolling around the polished floor. He saw me, skidded to a stop, and began to smile. Then he saw Max and his face darkened. He shoved a blond lock of hair out of his face, then pushed off on his skates, sending himself zooming in the opposite direction.

I led Max into the office while shaking my head and praying George would get over his snit by the time the next owners signed on the dotted line. The territorial thing wouldn't play well with the new audience. It wasn't playing well with me, and I liked the guy.

Flipping on the office light, I walked to my desk and fired up the computer. Max trailed behind me, a disgruntled pout pulling at his lips.

"Why doesn't George like me?" Max asked as his eyebrows knit together.

The petulant whine in Max's voice made me arch an eyebrow. George was necessary to the running of the rink. I had to put up with his antics. But Max hadn't proved he could even do the job, which meant all bets were off. "George doesn't like change, but he'll come around. If you strapped on a pair of skates and asked him for a few pointers, he might come around faster."

Max cocked his head to the side, thinking about that for a moment. Then his face broke into a cheerful smile. All traces of six-year-old behavior vanished. Either he had heard the warning in my words or he was bipolar. I was voting for the former. Training a Ted Bundy wannabe wasn't on my agenda.

"Got it," he said with gusto. "Hey, I brought you something." He sat one of the cups he'd been holding on the desk. "A nonfat cinnamon latte with whipped cream. I wasn't sure about the nonfat, and Dad wasn't around to ask. You don't look like you need to watch your calories, but the girls I know all order nonfat. So I took a chance. I hope you like it. If not, I can run back to the shop and have my dad make another. He was really excited when I told him about the job."

Wow. Max was a brownnoser. Who would have thought it? I'd assumed filmmakers were more like me. I hated sucking up. Too many girls I'd known in high school and college got passing grades because of their brown-smudged noses, whereas I'd actually had to study.

I know. Stupid me.

I told myself I should turn it down on principle. My morals came before my chemical addiction to caffeine. My moral fiber would not be compromised. I opened my mouth to say "No thanks" but stopped as the smell of cinnamon tickled my nose. My taste buds twitched with the promise of whipped cream and smooth coffee.

I couldn't say no.

I was a schmuck.

"Thank you, Max," I said, grabbing the cup and taking a large sip. Ah! Normally, I wasn't the nonfat kind of girl, but this wasn't bad. The whipped cream compensated for the watered-down milk. "This is good."

I hit the on switch on the computer and took another hit of coffee as it booted up.

Max straightened the collar of his deep blue polo shirt while watching me enjoy my legal drug. "You know," he said in a low, purring tone, which got my attention, "I could get you a latte every day on my way to work if maybe . . ."

"If maybe what?"

He gave me a boyish smile. "If you'd talk to my dad. Tell him that you think I'm doing a great job here at the rink."

"That's all?" Free coffee in exchange for a two-minute conversation seemed too good to be true.

Max tugged at his shirt collar. "Maybe you could also watch a couple of the movies I made in college and tell my dad how talented you think I am. Things are a little tense at home. Hearing someone he respects say I have talent might help."

My brain flashed back to the scene in the coffee shop, and I felt a twinge of pity for Max. Max had a passion for making films, and his father was trying to force him to give it up. That sucked. Funny, while I was growing up, I'd always wanted a dad around to help me make decisions, but I was starting to consider the possibility that I'd gotten lucky.

"I'd be happy to watch some of your movies," I said with a smile. "And have your dad drop by. He can watch you work, and I'll tell him what a great job you're doing."

Max's thousand-watt smile told me it was definitely okay.

"Now," I said, swallowing a lump lodged in my throat, "let's get to work."

After returning messages, I took Max to the rental counter to show him how to change wheels and fix toe stops. Did I know how to have fun or what? By noon, the high school help had arrived and I left them in charge of Max's training while I went in search of food. Dairy Queen, here I come.

I considered driving, in case the psycho with the wire was around, but that felt wimpy. Besides, no one had spotted the guy since. In Indian Falls, I would have heard about it if they had.

I started to walk, smiling and enjoying the sun—for about a block. Then I got hot and sticky and stopped being happy. When the big red sign came into view, I broke into a speed walk. I needed ice cream, and I needed it now.

My hand was pushing the door to air-conditioned paradise when I heard "Rebecca!"

I jumped and looked around. No one in sight. Maybe the near-Sahara temperature was making me hallucinate.

I pushed the door again, in a hurry to be inside.

"Rebecca, I've been looking for you."

I knew that voice.

Turning, I shaded my eyes and squinted into the sunlit street. Pop's pimplike maroon Lincoln Town Car with its white soft top cruised into the restaurant's parking lot. My grandfather stuck his head out of the window and smiled. The combination of Pop's blowing gray hair and the chrome-covered car looked like a trailer for Disney's *Shaggy Dog Turns Pimp*.

Pop gave a frantic wave and yelled, "Get in."

All thoughts of ice-cream confections left my brain. "Did they find my father's car?" I asked, trotting toward Pop.

"No, but Eleanor reported her car stolen today."

I slid into the Town Car and pulled the door shut. "Someone stole Eleanor's car?"

"No. She just forgot where she parked it. Senior moment. But things were real exciting around the center before she figured that out. Sean Holmes even paid us a visit. He's not too happy with you right now."

My need for ice cream increased tenfold. "I figured he'd be upset."

Pop grinned. "*Upset* doesn't cover it. *Ballistic* is a better description. Jimmy was telling everyone in the game room how lucky the police were to have you helping, seeing as how they locked up the wrong man."

I groaned. "Don't tell me—"

"Yep." Pop slapped his scrawny Bermuda shorts–clad thigh. "Right then, Sean Holmes walked through the door. Must've heard every word, because he looked as though he'd bitten into a green tomato."

"Great."

"He told everyone that he had some questions to ask you." Pop's smile disappeared. The wrinkles in his forehead looked more pronounced as worry filled his eyes. "I snuck out of there the minute Eleanor found her car. Thought I should let you know Sean was on the warpath."

"Thanks, Pop." I gave his hand a squeeze.

"I don't want my granddaughter locked up because Sean has a burr up his butt," Pop said with a scowl. Then his eyes began to twinkle. "Now, your father is a different story. I think I might tell the cops Stan took some doodads off my dresser. A few days behind bars might do him some good. Don't you think?"

A week ago, I might have answered yes. Now that Stan was back in town and doing an impression of a father, I was conflicted.

Thank goodness Pop didn't require an answer. He just laughed and told me, "Sean is probably going to head over to the rink as soon as he's done at the center. You should steer clear until he's had a chance to cool off."

Knowing Sean, cooling off could take until Christmas. I didn't have that long. Max was back at the rink, waiting for me to return. No telling what would happen if he and George were left without a referee for too long.

"I'd love to, but I have my new manager to train." I'd just have to do it while hiding in the girls bathroom. Sean would never set foot in there.

Pop shook his head. "I'll train him while you go underground. Once Sean gives up and goes home, I'll give you the all clear."

"I thought you weren't interested in running the rink." Pop's desire to resume his retirement was what had brought me to Indian Falls in the first place.

"I'm not," Pop said. "But I wouldn't want to miss my chance at sandbagging the fuzz. It'll be like something out of *The Sopranos*."

Only if Tony Soprano lost two hundred pounds and started wearing plaid Bermuda shorts. Still, the idea made Pop happy. I wasn't about to say no.

After a quick turn through the drive-thru for ice cream, we swung by the rink. Sean's cruiser sat in the parking lot. The man himself was nowhere to be seen, but something told me he was just waiting for me to make a break for my car.

Pop must have had the same thought, because he said, "I think we should get you out of town for a while. Why don't we pay a visit to Lionel. I want to talk to him about putting Elwood in my Elvis act. I could get him a wig and a scarf. Women would go nuts for an Elvis-impersonator camel."

Nuts was a good word for it.

I was still trying to picture Elwood in sideburns when Pop pulled into Lionel's driveway and parked next to his testosterone-filled pickup. The thing looked like it should be in a monster truck rally. Black, with enormous tires and oodles of shiny chrome, the thing reeked of overcompensation. Since our relationship hadn't progressed to the mattress mambo, I couldn't wager a guess about what Lionel was compensating for.

I know. Someone should kick me.

Pop unfolded himself from the car and headed for the barn. Scrambling to collect my purse and phone, I raced after him. Elwood greeted us with a wet nuzzle and happy camel noises as we walked into the air-conditioned structure. Coming out of a horse stall was a sweaty and sexy Lionel.

"Hey, Lionel," Pop called in a chipper voice. "I hope you don't mind if I stash my granddaughter here for a while."

The corner of Lionel's mouth twitched. "This wouldn't have something to do with getting Reginald sprung last night?"

"Doesn't anyone in this town have better things to do than talk about me?" I mumbled.

Pop gave an exaggerated shrug, and Lionel's mouth twitch stretched into a Cheshire grin. "Becky," Lionel drawled, "you're the most interesting thing to hit this town since indoor plumbing."

"Great. Should I be flattered?" Being compared to a toilet wasn't exactly my idea of a compliment.

"Our family has always attracted attention. I'm happy that everyone at the center likes talking about me. Shows I'm not getting boring in my old age."

It was hard to be boring in sequins.

Pop looked at his watch. "I should get going. Don't want the new manager running the rink into the ground."

Hiking up his plaid shorts, Pop gave a jaunty wave and shuffled out of the barn into the sunlight.

Now that Pop was gone, the temperature in the barn went up twenty degrees. I gave Lionel a nervous smile. Part of me was embarrassed about the other night. My behavior wasn't what I'd call mature. The other part was annoyed. Lionel hadn't bothered to call since then. I'd have thought that some big guy threatening me outside the rink deserved at least a smidge of follow-up concern.

Lionel hooked his thumbs through his belt loop and leaned back on his heels. "You've been busy since yesterday morning. Hiring new managers and freeing innocent citizens. What's next? Leaping tall buildings in a single bound?"

Laughter and irritation colored Lionel's voice in equal measure. I did my best to fan the internal flames of female indignation for the lack of concern. Nope. No raging flames of anger. I guess I wasn't female enough. My college roommate, Jasmine, could have done it. Her emotional responses to relationships should have garnered Academy Award nominations. You would have thought some of her dramatics would have rubbed off.

I pulled my cell phone out of my purse and flipped it open. "I should call the rink and let George know my grandfather is taking charge for the day."

Lionel nodded and watched me let my fingers do the walking. His posture looked lazy, but his eyes were bright, clear, and glittering with an emotion I couldn't identify. The gaze made my stomach flutter and my nerves jangle.

Turning around, I straightened my shoulders and did an impersonation of a businesswoman, all the while feeling Lionel's eyes caressing my back. It was kind of a turn-on. Suddenly, I was trying to remember my reasons for not sleeping in Lionel's bed.

Thank goodness Max answered the phone, putting an end to my moment of sexual crisis.

"Toe Stop Roller Rink. This is Max. What can I help you with?"

"Hey, Max. It's Rebecca."

"Rebecca." Max's voice rose an octave with what I decided was a combination of excitement over the new job and relief. "Where are you? You said you were going to be back in a few minutes. Hey!" Max's voice shouted.

Then George came on the line. "Rebecca, we need you here. Now. This boy is ruining your mother's rink."

A strangled yelp came over the line. Then a loud clatter. Then all I could hear were voices that sounded as if they were underwater.

"Hello?"

No answer.

I raised my voice. "Hello. Would someone talk to me?"

Panting, George came back on the line. "Rebecca, I can't work like this. Max just assaulted me. I should report this to Deputy Holmes. I just saw him here a few minutes ago."

"Don't do that," I begged. "Look, something came up, so Pop is coming in. He'll get everything straightened out, and tomorrow I'll have a talk with Max about his behavior. All right?"

George didn't answer.

My heart skipped a beat. The rink couldn't lose George.

"George? Are you still there?" I asked.

"Yes."

George sounded petulant, but that was okay. At least he was talking. When George was really angry, he gave everyone the silent treatment. "Look, if things don't get better with Max in the next couple of days, I promise to let him go. Does that help?"

George sighed. "I suppose. And I'll try to get along with him for your sake, but I can't promise anything."

I closed my phone, shoved it deep in my purse, and said a small prayer to the roller-skating gods that peace would reign between Max and George. I didn't think it would help, but it couldn't hurt. Besides, Pop was going to need all the divine assistance he could get.

Warm hands settled on my shoulders. "Can I do something?" Lionel asked as his hands began to knead the tense muscles in my neck.

I leaned into his touch and felt the strain of the day disappear. Lionel had magic hands. "I wish. George hates Max, my new rink manager."

"I can't imagine George hating anyone."

"Neither could I, but he took a serious dislike to Max on sight. It's weird." Lionel's thumb dug into my shoulder. I closed my eyes and leaned into the pressure. "Imagine Hermie the misfit elf on too much caffeine and too little sleep. That's George. I just don't know what to do about it. The rink needs a manager, and at the moment Max is the only one interested in the job. I don't want to think about what I'm going to do if I have to fire him."

"Then don't." Lionel turned me around so I was facing him. His fingers gently brushed my cheek and my breath came faster. Then his lips touched mine and I forgot to breathe.

My hands clutched at his broad shoulders. His fingers found their way under my shirt. Yowzah. My purse slipped from my shoulder and fell with a thunk in the hay. Which is where I wanted to be right now. In the hay with Lionel. My blood churned. Electric shocks fluttered through my stomach as Lionel's hand brushed against my breast.

Without a doubt, I wanted this. I really wanted this.

My fingers itched to pull off Lionel's clothes and run over every inch of his body. Lionel's mouth trailed up and down my neck. The wet path of his kisses tingled in the air conditioning, making my breasts tighten. My knees trembled as his fingers dipped below my waistband. All the muscles in my legs turned molten as I lost myself in a haze of desire.

Then the haze disappeared.

"Do you hear that?" I asked as Lionel kissed my ear.

"Hear what?"

His voice had that sexy "I want you" quality, which almost made me feign deafness. But I couldn't. I had identified the sound, and it was coming from my purse.

"My phone," I gasped as Lionel's fingers unbuttoned the top of my jeans. "Lionel, my phone is ringing."

"Don't answer it." A zipping sound accompanied the ringing phone as Lionel's hands moved lower. For a second, I considered taking Lionel's suggestion. I didn't want to answer the phone.

Then it rang again. Visions of Pop playing WrestleMania with my two semiadult employees danced through my head. Pop was so small. And he was old. He'd get squashed for sure.

Summoning willpower I didn't know I possessed, I struggled out of Lionel's grasp and dived for my purse. "Hello?" I said in a low, breathless voice. Yikes. I sounded like a porn star.

"Rebecca, you need to come back to town." George's high-pitched voice reached over the phone line. "The guy who threatened you the other night came back to the rink. And this time, he wasn't alone."

Twelve

Lionel's truck broke all speeding records on the way back to the rink, while I clutched my seat in terror. And not because of Lionel's NASCAR driving. Pop hadn't been able to talk to me on the phone because he was being checked out by Dr. Truman. The man who threatened me had gone after Pop at the rink.

And I was the reason Pop was even there.

The terror slid up my spine and lodged in my throat. Pop was the only family I had left. My father didn't count. He'd never applauded after a high school play or bought me ice cream when my boyfriend broke up with me. Pop had. Now he was hurt, and I had no idea how badly. My phone had remained painfully silent since George had hung up.

I said a prayer that my grandfather would be okay. When that didn't make me feel better, I began making bargains with God. If Pop lived, I would attend church. I would donate my spleen to charity. I would enter a nunnery and become celibate for the rest of my life. It was the least I could do. After all, I had been preparing to fornicate while my grandfather's life was in danger. Perpetual sexual frustration was too good for me.

Sean Holmes's cop car and an ambulance were parked in front of the rink's entrance. A bunch of people were milling around near the front door. None of them was Pop. My fingers unclipped the seat belt. Before the truck came to a stop, I leaped down from my seat. My feet hit the pavement, and I started running.

Breathing hard, I skidded to a halt next to the emergency vehicles. When I spotted George hovering near the front door, I yelled, "Where's Pop?"

George pointed a long finger toward the ambulance, and I sucked in air. Trembling and trying not to hyperventilate, I walked around the side of the ambulance toward the open back doors. Sean Holmes, complete with open notepad and pen, nodded at me as I came around the vehicle's back. He wasn't yelling at me—not a good sign. I gave Sean a weak smile and held my breath as I peered into the back of the ambulance.

"Hey, Rebecca," Pop called with a delighted smile. "You missed all the excitement. You should have seen me with those guys. I gave them the old one-two."

I sagged against one of the open doors. Pop was okay. In fact, he looked like he was having the time of his life as Doc Truman looked in his ears and asked him to take deep breaths.

"Pop, what happened?" I asked weakly.

"That's what I've been trying to find out." Deputy Sean moseyed up to stand next to me, a scowl plastered on his face, a half-eaten doughnut in his hand. For a minute, our eyes locked. Then he gave a slight nod. I nodded back. We understood each other. Sean wasn't happy with me, but neither was he going to arrest me. At least not right now.

"Sean, I've already told you what happened," Pop said from his seat on the edge of the ambulance, his scrawny, steel-wool hair-covered legs swinging back and forth. "I came to the rink to help train the new manager. While I was walking up to the rink, two big guys in yellow-and-black bowling shirts approached me."

My heart lurched.

I touched Pop's arm to reassure myself he was really okay. "Did they hurt you?"

"Not exactly. They kept yelling at me, but I had no idea what they were talking about. My Spanish isn't that good yet. But I think one guy said something about a tan, which made sense, because he was. They both had really nice tans." Pop looked down at his pale, wrinkled skin and sighed.

"Then what, Pop?"

Pop's legs stopped swinging. "Then they yelled about a car, or maybe it was tar. I couldn't tell. So I shook my head to let them know I couldn't help. That's when the really big guy pulled a metal ratchet thingy out of his pocket and started swinging at me." Pop's eyes flashed with excitement. "Well, I wasn't about to take that. Just because I'm old doesn't mean people can push me around. I'm stronger than I look, you know."

Pop flexed a minuscule bicep muscle. "The guy thought he was going to get the drop on me, but I dodged him."

"And tripped on the rink's front step," Sean said matter-of-factly while glancing at his notebook. "One of the kids saw you go down and yelled, and the two men ran around the side of the building and disappeared. That's when George called the Sheriff's Department." The notebook snapped authoritatively shut. "Did I miss any details?"

Pop scratched his chin. "Not that I can think of. It's a shame

125

those guys got away. If I hadn't tripped on that step, I would have taken them into custody for sure. I've been waiting to use some moves I saw on that bounty-hunter cable show. He always gets his man."

The guy Pop was referring to weighed 250 pounds and could bench-press an elephant. Pop couldn't bench-press a Chihuahua.

"Well, I think I'm done taking your statement. You can go about your business when Doc Truman here gives you the okay," Sean said to Pop with a tight smile. Over Pop's head, Sean gave me a small shake of his head, walked to his squad car, and, without a backward glance, drove away. I think Pop's bounty hunter dreams were too much, even for ex-football tough guy Deputy Holmes.

Doc Truman looked in Pop's eyes one last time, gave me a smile, and said, "He's going to have a couple bruises, but otherwise he's just fine. Arthur, you call me if you have any soreness or dizzy spells. I'm going fishing, but I'll keep my cell on vibrate just in case you need me."

I let out a sigh of happiness and gave Doc Truman a big hug. Doc Truman had known me since I was little. He patched up my scraps and cured my sore throats. Even though years had passed, his wavy hair had turned gray, and the size of his pants was larger, I still trusted him. If he said Pop was okay, then Pop really was okay.

Doc packed up his stuff, gave a wave, and went off to catch fish.

"So now what?" Pop hopped off the back of the ambulance and propped one hand on a bony hip.

"What do you mean, 'now what'?"

"Well, we're going to look for the bad guys, right?" Pop danced from foot to foot. "I mean, they're probably the ones who took Jimmy's and Stan's cars. I say we start canvassing the town. Maybe we'll find a witness."

And maybe Elwood would grow another hump. There was no way I was going canvassing for thugs with Pop riding shotgun.

"We can't, Pop. We don't have a picture of the guys. You need one to show witnesses." I crossed two fingers behind my back in an attempt to ease my guilt. Lying to my recently injured grandfather made me feel really icky.

"Huh," Pop said, a bead of sweat running down his dejected face. "I didn't think of that."

The guilt meter went up another notch, but I wasn't about to give in. Pop's life was more important than taking him looking for scary guys. I was about to suggest we go into the air-conditioned rink, when Max came bounding up to me with an excited smile.

"Wow! That was cool. I never would've guessed that working at a roller rink would be so interesting." Turning to Pop, he asked, "Do you think they'll catch the guys who attacked you?"

"The cops?" Pop scoffed. "Nah. Sean tries really hard and he's pretty smart when he wants to be, but you have to have a knack for investigation. Rebecca here has it. I was just telling her we should go looking for witnesses, but we don't have a picture to show anyone. People need a picture to look at in order to identify the perps."

Max nodded. "Too bad the cops don't have a sketch artist. I bet you remember every detail about those guys. I know I would remember everything if someone threatened me."

"That's it." Pop snapped his fingers. "A sketch artist."

"The Indian Falls Sheriff's Department doesn't have a sketch artist, Pop." I hated bursting his bubble, but this time it was the truth.

Pop shook his head. "Ethel Jacabowski at the center takes all those art classes. I bet I could describe the guys to her and she'd be able draw a picture of them."

"You think she could do that?" Max looked hopeful.

"She's the best artist at the center. Everyone always wants to be on her team when we play Pictionary. People can actually tell what she's drawing, so her team wins every time."

"I always wanted to use a sketch artist in one of my movies," Max said wistfully. "But I've never seen one in action. That makes all the difference in putting together a realistic scene. Life experience is very important."

"You're right." Pop nodded. "The only way to really understand something is to experience it. Maybe you should come along and watch Ethel in action. I'm heading over there right now. I want to have her draw them before my memory starts to fade."

Max's eyes flashed with anticipation. Then he looked at me and hung his head. "I'm scheduled to work until five. If you could wait until then, I'd love to go with you."

Pop's shoulders slumped. Max sighed. They both looked at me with big puppy-dog eyes. Suddenly, I was the Grinch who had stolen my grandfather's crime-scene fun.

I figured Max should stay and work, but I didn't have the heart to say no again. Besides, without the two of them underfoot, I might be able to do a little snooping of my own. Being threatened had both scared and annoyed me. Someone going after my grandfather really pissed me off.

"All right, Max," I said. "You can have the rest of the day off to work with Pop. Just make up the time on another day."

Pop and Max gave me identical smiles, then turned to each other to high-five. As they took off for the center, I could hear Pop saying, "I think Sean Connery should play me in the movie. Lots of women tell me we look alike."

"Where's your grandfather going?"

I turned. Lionel was leaning against the redbrick wall of the rink, watching me. "To the Senior Center. He wants to get a sketch of the bad guys."

Lionel's left eyebrow arched. "Is he going to make it out of macaroni?"

Laughter bubbled up and out. The fear and tension I'd been holding inside since George's phone call eased. "Someone named Ethel is going to play sketch artist."

"Sounds kinky. Who's the guy going with him?"

"My new manager, Max. He wanted to see a *real* sketch artist in action."

Lionel's eyebrow arched higher. "Ethel?"

I giggled. "I guess that's as close to the actual thing as our budding film director can get."

Lionel pushed off the wall and slowly walked over to me. The sensual gleam in his green eyes stopped my laughter. He hooked a hand around the back of my neck and leaned down. His warm lips pressed gently against mine.

Pulling back, he asked, "How about going back to my place? We could pick up where we left off." His fingers caressed the back of my neck.

My mouth went dry. I was tempted to say yes. Then I remembered my bargain with God. Not that I believed God would hold it against me. After all, God was the one who said, "Be fruitful and multiply." Still, as much as I wanted to be fruitful with Lionel, I wasn't sure this was the time.

"I can't," I said, stepping away from Lionel's touch. The loss of contact left me feeling adrift. *Scary.* "I need to make sure every-thing is in order here."

"I know you do," Lionel responded in a tone of voice that said he didn't believe my explanation for a minute. "You realize that sometime or another we're going to have to talk about what we've been doing."

Or not doing.

"That would be the mature thing to do." Which was probably why I wasn't in favor of it.

The corners of Lionel's mouth twitched. "It would," he agreed. "Why don't I pick you up around seven? I'll buy you dinner, and the two of us can think about our maturity level."

Being cornered into talking about our relationship didn't in-terest me, but I did want to discuss Jimmy's car fire with Lionel. A restaurant would be the perfect place to test Lionel's firefighting knowledge, and promising to see him later would get him out of my way for the next couple of hours. That would give me plenty of time to start tracking Pop's attackers.

"Dinner sounds nice. I'll see you at seven."

Lionel nodded, planted a quick kiss on my lips, and turned to leave. I admired the way his backside filled out his jeans as he strode to his truck. Then, the minute he drove away, I sprinted into the rink to make sure George had everything under control. He did, which meant I could start looking for the bad guys who'd attacked Pop. Once I found them, I'd call Sean and he'd arrest them. Problem solved.

Of course, saying I was going to find the bad guys was much easier than actually doing it. Pop hadn't provided much in the way of details. Add to that my encounter with the big dude and I still came up with nothing. Yellow-and-black shirts, dark skin, and a penchant for wires and metal ratchets weren't details that were going to solve this case.

There was only one clue from the two incidents that jumped out at me. Pop hadn't recognized the guys.

That wouldn't have mattered if this were Chicago. There, you could be mugged by someone who lived in the same building without ever having known he lived there. But this was Indian Falls, and Pop had lived here almost all his life. He knew everyone in Indian Falls and the three surrounding counties. The fact that he didn't know his attackers or hadn't heard about their existence from the local gossips pointed to one thing: Those two men weren't from around here.

Based on that flimsy deduction, I got in my car and steered it toward the edge of town. If these two weren't locals and they were here for more than a day, they had to be bunking somewhere. Indian Falls had only two motels that were actually in town. One was located just north of the diner. Any pertinent details about strangers staying there were humming through the local grapevine within hours. No one was talking about mysterious strangers, which left me pulling my Honda Civic into the Presidential Motel's parking lot on the southernmost edge of the city limits.

Faded pictures of Abraham Lincoln and Ronald Reagan greeted me as I walked into the motel. I guess the owners thought people would flock to a place Ronald Reagan might have stayed in. Reagan had been born in a nearby town, which gave businesses a license to scam. In this case, the scammers hadn't cashed in. In fact, from the condition of this motel, I would have said there was a better chance that Abe and Mary had given one of the rooms a whirl.

The gray linoleum-tile floor was peeling, giving the cement underneath a chance to see the light of day. Cobwebs hung from the ceiling fan. A love seat meant for waiting guests had two large tears in the dusty black fabric, and the counter was missing large chunks of Formica. The only thing that looked new was the computer. With a nineteen-inch flat-screen monitor, a spotless keyboard, a printer, a scanner, and a shiny processor, the thing looked like it belonged in a NASA lab instead of this run-down lobby.

And no one was there to operate it.

I took a step toward a door at the back of the room.

"Hello?" I called. "Is anyone here?"

A scrawny, short, pasty kid with large glasses and a T-shirt that read BYTE ME appeared in the doorway.

"Sorry. I didn't hear you come in." He hurried behind the counter and smiled. "My name's Alan. Would you like a room?"

Yikes. The kid looked all of twelve years old. I wondered if maybe dad was around somewhere.

"Hi, Alan. I'm actually here to ask about some of your guests. Is there any chance I could talk to the manager?"

The kid pushed back an oily lock of black hair. "You are."

"You're the manager?" I couldn't keep the surprise out of my voice. "No offense, but aren't you a little young?"

"I'm seventeen." The kid shrugged. "My parents own the motel. Last year, they decided to take the RV around the country and left me in charge. Last I heard, they were in Seattle. Now, what can I help you with?"

I blinked at the businesslike tone in the Harry Potter look-alike's voice. He tapped his sneaker, waiting for me to answer. So I did. "I'm looking for a couple of guys who might be staying here. They're tall, dark-skinned, and speak Spanish."

The description sounded lame even to me, but it was all I had.

"That could describe a lot of people. You got anything else?" The kid crossed his arms over his geeky shirt.

I gave myself a mental thwack on the head. "They could have been wearing matching bowling shirts."

"Oh, them."

My heart skipped. "They're here?" Was I brilliant or what?

"Nah." The kid shook his head, obliterating my elation. "They came by a couple of days ago, looking for a place to stay. After seeing the rooms, they decided to go elsewhere." Alan shrugged. "My parents ran this place into the ground. Now that they're gone, I figure I can start fixing it up. Make it into a real business."

I hated to ruin the kid's entrepreneurial speech, but I had to ask if he remembered anything else. "By any chance did those guys say where they were going?"

"No." My face must have shown big-time disappointment, because the kid's face turned bright red. "But," he added, "I did give them a list of other hotels in the area. I mean, Mom and Dad would yell at me for helping the competition, but I couldn't blame them for not wanting to stay. And it was late. They needed a place to sleep. You know? They weren't like the group of college kids that came by a few days ago. The college guys had camping gear."

"Do you remember where you sent them?"

The kid scratched his greasy head, sending another lock of hair careening over his eyes. "I told them about the Indian Falls Motel downtown and about the three near the highway. Why? Did these guys rob a bank or something?"

For a second, I was tempted to say yes. Alan's eyes were wide behind his dorky glasses. This was probably the most excitement he'd had since hooking up that new computer. I hated to disappoint the kid.

"No, but they might have stolen two cars."

"Cool." Alan grabbed the computer's mouse and started clicking. "This is going to make a great entry for my blog."

Backing out of the office, I gave the blogging Alan a quick wave and, smiling, went back to my car. I had another lead. It was time to scope out the motels near the highway.

A half hour later, I pulled into the Holiday Inn Express. The very efficient clerk at the desk listened to my description of the men. He then told me not only that he didn't remember the guys but that he couldn't tell me if he did. Hotel policy.

Country Inn and Suites and the Red Roof Inn had the same party line. Guest information was confidential, and each motel had at least five different clerks who might have waited on the guys, depending on when they'd come in. I was out of luck. Worse yet, I was out of ideas.

Dejected, I steered my car back to Indian Falls. Returning to the rink was pointless. George had everything under control, and watching kids skate in circles wasn't going to help me keep my grandfather safe. I needed a plan.

I stopped at the sheriff's office, hoping Roxy would have some information. She did, but it was about a new stylist who had just opened a shop one town over. I left the station knowing where to get my hair highlighted but with no new leads. At least Roxy had promised to give Sean the message to call me. I wanted to pass along my motel lead. Maybe law enforcement would succeed where I had failed. Sean would love that.

Funny. I would, too.

Since I was in the neighborhood, I went next door to the bakery for a fresh-baked cookie. Brain food. Only my brain wasn't cooperating.

Now what?

I was about to head back to my car, when a pair of flailing arms caught my attention.

"Rebecca!" Danielle stood on the sidewalk in front of St. Mark's, looking like she was trying to land an airplane. "I have something to tell you."

A Jeep Cherokee passed between the two of us. Once the street was cleared, I trotted over to the Lutheran side. I was Catholic, which meant Mom and I had attended St. Charles, directly across the street from St. Mark's.

While growing up, I'd been intensely curious about the church across the street, mainly because our catechism instructor told us not to go in it. Two months ago, I had finally walked through the forbidden double doors and was vastly disappointed. St. Charles and St. Mark's might teach different doctrines, but the same architect must have designed both buildings. Now I was a frequent visitor to the Lutheran side. Danielle worked there, and at the moment she was bursting with excitement.

"Rebecca!" Danielle ran toward me in four-inch zebra-striped heels. "You'll never believe what I learned."

"There's an Internet sale on animal-print shoes?" And maybe another on leather skirts. The combination of the two was going to send the gossips into overdrive.

Danielle looked down at her footwear with a small frown. "Rich still hasn't made a move. I'm getting desperate. If the shoes and skirt don't work, I'm going to have to break out the big guns."

"Don't do anything drastic," I warned. "You don't want to give the man a stroke."

"True." Danielle bit her lip. "Too bad there isn't a sexy parishioner around to hit on me. That might do the trick."

"I'm sure my father would hit on you given half the chance, but he's not your type."

Danielle's eyes narrowed with concern. "How are things going with your father? I haven't had a chance to ask."

I shrugged. "Could be worse. We haven't had a chance to talk."

"Don't you think that's strange? I mean, the guy disappears from your life for a decade. You'd think he'd want to make up for lost time. Why else would he have come to town?"

"Good question. I really don't know why he's in town," I admitted.

"Have you asked?"

I clasped my hands and shrugged. Danielle gave my arm a sympathetic squeeze, causing my throat to burn and tears to well up behind my eyes. Sympathy did strange things to me.

Blinking back the flood of unhappy emotions, I asked, "So, what did you need to tell me? Is it about Rich?"

The worry in Danielle's face vanished, replaced by an anticipatory smile. "Are you still looking for the mystery guy from the diner?" I nodded, and Danielle's smile broadened. "Good, because I know who he is."

Thirteen

Clayton Zimmerman. Not only did it sound impressive, it was my mystery man's name. It turned out that Danielle had been admiring his backside while standing in line at the drugstore checkout an hour earlier. It wasn't until he hit the sidewalk that her gaze shifted to his face. Good luck for me. Better yet, my man Clayton used a credit card to purchase his bottle of aspirin, a can of shaving cream, a disposable razor, and a pack of ribbed condoms.

Ick.

Danielle had only to ask the clerk, who, conveniently, attended St. Mark's, and the name of the mystery guy was hers. And now mine. The question was what to do with it.

I thanked Danielle for her help, jumped in my car, and debated my next move. Who was Clayton Zimmerman? I needed to know, and for that I needed a computer.

Cranking my yellow Honda to life, I cruised down the street and into the rink's parking lot. As inconspicuously as possible, I dodged two kids on Rollerblades, sneaked into my office, and closed the door behind me.

Sitting at my mother's desk, I turned on the computer and logged on to the Internet. I cracked my knuckles and smiled.

I Googled sexy butt's name and waited for the search engine to spit out an answer. All 367 of them, as it turned out. Hmm. The first six entries documented the athletic prowess of a minor-league baseball player. The next entries brought up a kid's Web page from somewhere near Los Angeles, two sites for German restaurants, and a collection of impressionist art by an artist who painted with his toes. Interesting, but none of them was my guy.

I clicked to the next page of entries. That's when I saw it.

Clayton Miguel Zimmerman, Chicago lawyer. My "Spidey sense" started tingling. I clicked on the Google entry and waited for the page to load. A picture of a way-too-tan-to-be-real Clayton Zimmerman appeared on the Web site of Phillips, Parra and Powell, LLP. According to his bio, Clayton was a tax and contracts man, an associate who specialized in wills and prenups. Just reading about the job made me want to yawn. Well, while the guy's work didn't seem all that interesting, the fact that his picture matched Danielle's description was. A phone call seemed in order.

After punching in the law firm's number, I gnawed on the side of my thumbnail and waited. A perky female voice came on the line and asked how I wanted my call directed.

"I'd like to speak to Clayton Zimmerman," I said, feeling a bubble of anticipation rise in my chest.

"Sorry, Mr. Zimmerman no longer works here." The perky voice had popped my bubble. I rested my head against my hand in defeat. "But I would be happy to direct you to the associate who has taken over his cases."

"That would be great," I said, and a synthesized orchestra come on the line, playing a normally enjoyable Billy Joel tune. I drummed my fingers on the desk, waiting for the musical torture to end.

"Good afternoon. My name's Patrick Grimes. I hope that I can be of service."

"Can you sue the company that makes hold music? I think I've been emotionally scarred."

A fake laugh boomed through the receiver. "Right. Now, the receptionist said you were looking for Clayton. Unfortunately, Clayton is no longer with the firm."

"I'm so sorry to hear that," I gushed in a voice that sounded like it came right out of one of Pop's daytime dramas. I should know. Pop DVR'd shows on three different channels and watched them religiously. He said it helped give him and his dates something in common. "When did Clayton leave the firm?"

"Two weeks ago. All of his current cases have been assigned to me."

I smiled, glad the lawyer couldn't see me. Patrick sounded so proud about inheriting Clayton's boring cases. How sad was that?

"Do you know where he went? I really need to get hold of him." Especially if he was the suspect I was looking for.

"He moved out of the city to start his own practice in some little town." I sat up straight. "Said he wanted to try his hand at small-town life. But I would be more than happy to do any legal work you might need."

"Thanks. I'll think about it," I said. I dropped the receiver back in its cradle. Clayton was definitely my guy.

Armed with a printout of Clayton's law-firm photo, I locked the office and headed for the door. If Clayton Zimmerman was living in or around town, he must have talked to a Realtor. Indian Falls didn't do a brisk real estate business. There were only so many Realtors around. Being the competitive sort, Doreen would know each and every one.

"Rebecca, honey," a voice boomed over the loud eighties music, "I've been looking all over town for you."

I turned toward the voice. A lead brick dropped into my stomach as I forced a smile. "Hi, Stan."

My father's wide grin shrank. "Call me 'Dad.' You used to, you know."

I also used to eat dirt. Goes to show some people can learn from their mistakes.

"Why were you looking for me?" I yelled over the rink noise, choosing to ignore the parental-title discussion.

The narrowing of my father's eyes told me my omission hadn't been as subtle as I thought. "I wanted to have a heart-to-heart. You know, get to know my grown-up daughter. Is there somewhere we could go to talk, or are you too busy for your old man?"

Guilt was a powerful motivator even when it wasn't warranted. I looked down at my shoes, wishing the ground would suck me under. When that didn't happen, I looked up and nodded. "We can talk in the office."

Once again, I found myself seated behind Mom's old desk, but now I was less happy than I had been only minutes ago. I was going to have to talk—really talk—to my father. My stomach churned. I was sure I was going to throw up.

My father sat on the wooden chair on the opposite side of the desk. Crossing his right leg, he asked, "So, pumpkin, how are things going?"

"Fine," I replied cautiously.

"I hear you've been dating the local vet." His eyebrows danced. "Does that mean I'll be walking you down the aisle soon?"

"Nope. No ring. No aisle walking. We're not that serious." And even if we had been, Pop would be the one bopping with me to "Here Comes the Bride."

My father nodded. "I hope you'll let me know when you get serious. Weddings are wonderful things." Stan cased the office with his eyes. I could see him taking in the pictures, the computer, and the large events calendar hanging on the wall. The rink was booked solid. "Besides running this place, what else have you been doing with your time?"

"I've been trying to track down the person who stole your car." Duh.

Stan gave me a sage nod. "I appreciate your looking into it, but it's probably too late. The car is long gone by now. Even if the cops find it, it'll be stripped, or worse."

I rolled a pencil through my fingertips, not sure what to say. Failure left a metallic taste in my mouth.

"Anyway"—Stan leaned back in his chair with a smile—"the car situation is what I wanted to talk to you about." He cleared his throat. "My work depends on having reliable transportation. Can't meet clients if I can't get to them, you know?"

You also can't skip town without saying good-bye, I thought.

Stan uncrossed his legs, and his eyes met mine with great sincerity. "Honey, your father needs a loan. I have a couple of big deals ready to come through, but I don't have a car or the cash to see them to fruition. All I need is a couple of thousand and I'll be flush."

My heart did a free fall all the way to my toes.

Money.

Stan's father/daughter bonding moment was about money. I

should have seen it coming, but something inside me had dared to hope he was going to explain his absence. That he was going to tell me why he'd abandoned me in the first place. That he was going to say he was sorry.

How stupid could I get?

"Honey," my father crooned, "I know this is a lot to ask. I wouldn't if I had any other choice, but Doreen hinted at how much the rink is going to sell for. You'll have a lot of extra cash floating around. Surely you could float some my way, seeing as how I'm family."

Family? I considered Elwood the camel a more immediate family member than my father. Elwood had taken a bullet for me, and he'd never hit me up for money.

I looked at my father's warm smile. A white-hot rage traveled through my bloodstream, making me tremble with emotion. Tears built behind my eyes while an invisible fist closed around my heart and started to squeeze. Suddenly, I couldn't breathe.

"Honey? Are you okay?"

My fingernails dug into my palms. "No."

"What's wrong?" My father's face filled with such concern, I almost believed him. "Do you need a doctor?"

"No, I'm okay," I said as my throat tightened. "I meant no, I won't lend you any money."

Good old dad's concern dropped like a two-ton Acme anvil. "You don't mean that."

"Yes, I do." I stood up slowly, doing my best to hide the wobble in my legs. "You left Mom to run a business and raise your daughter all by herself. Never once did you call. Not on Christmas or my birthday. And now you want me to lend you money that my mother, the woman you abandoned, earned with this rink?"

My father tried to smile as he shifted in his chair. "I don't think you understand how hard things were back then. I didn't really want to leave you and your mother, but I had to."

"Funny," I said, yanking open the office door. "I didn't think I was going to want to throw you out of the rink without giving you a red cent. But trust me when I say I absolutely have to."

Stan considered my words for a moment, gave me one of his boyishly winsome smiles, and waited. Something told me most women caved when faced with his charming bull. Not this chick, I thought as I met his stare with a condemning one of my own.

Our staring contest stretched out as "Don't Go Breaking My Heart" pulsated through the building. Appropriate, if not helpful.

My eyes itched with unshed tears, but I still didn't blink. I summoned every scrap of anger and stood there, waiting.

Finally, my father hung his head. Heaving a large sigh, he pushed himself out of the rickety chair. Then, with one last wounded glance, he walked out of my mother's office.

I closed the door behind him, sat at my desk, and stared at the walls as time passed.

When the shock of throwing my dad out had worn off, I wiped my runny nose. Then I gathered up my wounded heart and made a break for the door, determined to track down the car thief. Stan was a complete jerk and deserved his bad car karma, but that didn't mean I was going to give up. Pop's well-being hung in the balance, not to mention my pride. I'd be damned if I'd give those up because of my father.

Cell phone in hand, I hopped in my car and hit Doreen's speed-dial number.

No answer.

I left a message, asking her to give me a ring, then steered my way over to the diner, hoping that maybe someone there could confirm that my suspect, Clayton Zimmerman, had been the guy ordering takeout.

Sammy was at the counter, pouring coffee for the diner's sole customer, when I strolled through the door. I gave him a smile and took a seat at a booth with a window view of the parking lot. If Doreen passed by, I'd spot her.

Sammy came over to my booth, coffeepot still in hand. I gestured to the empty bench, and he sat down with a grateful sigh. "Been on my feet all day. The new kid we hired didn't bother to come in today, which left me and Mabel on our own. My corns are killing me."

More information than I wanted to know.

"Do you want some coffee?" Sammy held his coffeepot at the ready.

I shook my head and unfolded my laser-printed picture. "I just came by to ask if you've seen this guy in here. He might have moved to town recently."

Sammy set the coffeepot on the white Formica table and took the picture from me. Squinting, he stared at it for several seconds. Then he smiled. "Meat-loaf sandwich with extra fries."

I blinked.

Sammy slapped the table and let out a sandpaper-sounding laugh. "He's been a regular take-out customer for the past couple days. At least I think it's him. His hair is longer than it is in the picture, and he's never worn that suit. Mostly slacks, jeans, and polo shirts."

Made sense. Only funeral directors wore suits every day in Indian Falls.

"You wouldn't happen to know where he's living, would you?" I asked.

Sadly, Sammy shook his head. "Never came up. He's been here a couple of times, but only during our busy hours, so I didn't have time to welcome him to Indian Falls like I should've."

"Sammy!" Mabel poked her head out of the kitchen, a scowl on her face. "Are you going to get this food while it's still hot, or are you going to keep talking?"

Pink spots brightened Sammy's age-lined face. He scooted out of the booth and gave me a sheepish smile. "Gotta run. Mabel can get ornery if an order gets cold."

I gave him a fond smile as he picked up the coffeepot with a wrinkled hand and shuffled back toward the kitchen. Once he was gone, I pulled out my cell phone and called Doreen.

No answer. Again.

Suddenly, I had an idea. I flipped open my cell phone and punched in Pop's number. After one ring, Pop's voice came on the line.

"Hello."

"Hey, Pop," I said with a grin. After today's scare, it was nice to know Pop was still safe. "How did the sketch-artist thing go?"

"We're still working on it. Ethel was having a hard time concentrating at the center. Too much activity with the bridge tournament going on. So we brought all of Ethel's gear to the house and ordered a pizza."

"Is it any good?"

"Sausage and pepperoni from Dom's. Doesn't get any better than that."

I rested my forehead against the heel of my hand and sighed. "Not the pizza, Pop. The sketch. Does it look like the guy who attacked you?"

Silence. I could almost see Pop cocking his head to one side to consider my question.

"Well, Ethel's first try didn't look much like him, but that was because she was using watercolors. Tell you the truth, it looked a lot like Bozo the Clown. So she decided to switch to charcoal and try again after we eat the pizza. She thinks we'll get it right this time. Hey, I gotta get going. Ethel needs me to describe the guy's eyebrows. I thought they looked like two caterpillars, but I learned not to say that. Ethel is a literal kind of artist. The watercolor she did showed the guy with two fuzzy bugs on his face."

I choked back a laugh and said, "Wait, Pop" before he could hang up. "Do you have any idea where Doreen is today? She isn't picking up her phone."

"Hey, Arthur, we need you in here." Max's voice traveled through Pop's house to my phone.

"Be right there," Pop called to the crack investigating team of Max and Ethel. To me, he said, "I bet you'll find Doreen at the center. She never misses a bridge tournament. Oh, and come by here later. Ethel should be done in another hour or two. She'd draw faster, but her arthritis is acting up."

Pop disconnected before I had a chance to respond. I shook my head, shoved my phone in my purse, and headed for my car. Two minutes later, I was on my way to the Senior Center to crash a bridge tournament.

The last time I'd been at the Senior Center to play cards with Pop, the place had buzzed with loud conversation and a couple of snores—even card night wasn't enough to keep some of the seniors awake. I figured a bridge tournament would be much the same, so no one would notice me crashing the party.

Wrong.

As I walked down to the main common room, the only sound in the place was the echo of my footsteps on the linoleum floor. It was kind of creepy. Where were all the old people?

I turned the corner and found them. They were seated in groups of four around small tables. The rustle of cards being shuffled and an occasional cough were the only disruptions to the eerie silence. If it hadn't been for the slapping down of cards on the table and the occasional superior look, I would have thought they were all in comas.

It took me several moments to spot Doreen at a table in the back. I did a double take and let out a gasp. The last time I'd seen her, Doreen's hair had been champagne blond. Today it was fire-engine red. If Pop thought Ethel's picture looked like Bozo the Clown, I couldn't wait to hear his take on Doreen's new do.

Doreen glanced up from her cards, and I waved. I could have sworn she noticed me as her narrowed eyes panned around the table to study the other three players. Then, with a frown, she looked back down at her cards.

Huh. I figured I was too far away for her to see me. Well, that was easy to fix.

Weaving around chairs, tables, and mute cardplayers, I crossed the room to Doreen's table and stood behind the player sitting kitty-corner to her.

"Doreen, can I talk to you?" I asked.

Several dozen heads snapped toward me, all eyes wide with a combination of surprise and outrage. Something hard thwacked my leg.

I jumped, but not quick enough. Something whacked my calf again.

"Ow!" I yelled, turning around and looking for the source of the pain.

An old man with wrinkles that strongly resembled uncooked pie dough was tapping a wooden cane menacingly on the floor.

"Did you hit me?" I demanded, feeling slightly foolish for raising my voice at a basset hound look-alike.

An angry frown appeared under the wrinkles. "Only a bidding player can talk during a tournament. You broke the rules."

Several voices murmured agreement, sending my indignation to new levels. "You could have said something. You didn't have to hit me."

"Talking breaks the rules," he said. "Didn't want my team disqualified. We're winning."

I really wanted to stick out my tongue and give the guy the raspberry. Juvenile? Absolutely. But he'd started it.

Before I had a chance to revert to childhood behavior, Doreen held up a single perfectly manicured nail and mouthed the works *one minute*. And then the game continued, with all the players in the room dead silent.

The clock on the wall ticked. Another card was played. A player said something, which I assumed must be bidding. Another card. I was both clueless and restless.

Finally, after what felt like hours but what my watch had the nerve to claim was only twenty minutes, the tournament was over. Doreen and her cane-happy friend came in first. Yippee. Now we could get down to business.

"Sorry about that," said Doreen, walking over to me. She was clutching a gaudy gold-framed certificate declaring her bridge-playing prowess. "Bridge tournaments are a serious thing around here."

A shuffling man with two wisps of gray hair and nearly tooth-less smile said, "Nice play, Doreen."

This was followed by the approach of two frail-looking ladies. "If you ever need a new partner, let me know," one of them said before turning to me. "Tell your grandfather that Nan says hello. He threw me a scarf at his last performance."

Something told me Nan thought Pop's Elvis gesture had a deep hidden meaning. She didn't know Pop got a deal on the Internet if he bought twelve cases of multicolored scarves. The boxes were currently sitting in his living room, obstructing the view from the couch to the TV. The sacrifices he made for art.

Still, between Doreen's cardsharp abilities and my grandfather's conquests, I was never going to get the information I needed.

"Is there somewhere else we can talk?" I asked.

Doreen tilted her bright red coif and nodded. "Come with me."

I followed Doreen as she headed out the side door, down the long hallway, and into the ladies' room. Doreen tossed her award onto the bathroom counter and sighed. "Thanks for waiting. I worked hard to finally snag Myron as my partner, and I didn't want him throwing a fit and getting disqualified."

"Myron was the one hitting me with his cane?"

She nodded and adjusted her glasses. "Best bridge player at the center. Normally, he plays with Marjorie, but a month ago I asked him out and convinced him to jump ship."

"If you're dating Myron, what was the thing with my dad?" I couldn't help feeling a twinge of indignation. My dad might be a jerk, but that didn't mean I wanted Doreen to break his heart. Even if the jerk deserved it.

Doreen gave me one of her tsks. "Don't worry about Myron. He agreed to be my partner and broke it off. Said he didn't want to taint the game of bridge by mixing it with romance. He's dating Marjorie now. So I'm free to see whoever I want." Her chin jutted out, as if she were challenging me to warn her off my father.

Yeah, right.

"Look," I said, changing the subject. "I was wondering if you have a client named Clayton Zimmerman. He just moved to the area, and I figured you might have showed him some properties."

Doreen pursed her pink-tinted lips. "Nope, I can't say I did." I could tell Doreen was annoyed to have missed a potential sale.

"Do you know of any properties in town that were recently purchased? The guy is a lawyer," I said. Doreen wasn't much of a Watson, but she was all I had. "I'm betting he was looking for a house that could also function as an office."

Doreen's eyes brightened behind the rhinestones. I'd hit pay dirt. "The old Miller place went off the market about three weeks ago. It's at the edge of downtown, on Main Street. You probably know it. Donna Miller used to run a taxidermy shop out of the place until her husband up and died. He wasn't around to bring in inventory, so she folded and moved to Miami."

I wasn't sure I remembered Mrs. Miller and her stuffed menagerie, but I had a good idea which house she'd lived in. I left Doreen to polish her tacky gold frame and made a beeline for my Civic. Soon I was cruising down Main Street, with one eye out for Spanish-speaking thugs and the other for the old Miller place.

The minute I drove up to a faded green Colonial with yellow trim, I knew I was at the right house. Six very large boxes with animal heads peeping out their tops sat on the front porch. I approached the house in a warped haze of fascination. Raccoons with beady little eyes, possums with perfectly curled tails, and molting squirrels watched my approach. It was like walking into the Hundred Acre Wood gone zombie.

The front door flew open. I looked up and froze. One of Winnie-the-Pooh's really angry cousins was coming through the door—fangs, claws, and all. The thing launched down the porch steps. Right at me.

Oof.

I hit the ground with a thud. Right on top of me, giving me a big hug, was the icky bear. I sneezed. The thing wasn't only dead and creepy; it was incredibly dusty, too. Yuck.

I tried to push the bear off me, but he wouldn't budge. I was trapped.

"Help!" I yelped, hoping the person doing the bear shoving hadn't gone back inside.

Nothing.

I opened my mouth to holler again and stopped as the bear rolled off me. Squinting into the sunlight, I looked up at a tan, dark-haired man with a big smile.

I had found Clayton Zimmerman.

Fourteen

Clayton offered his hand while grinning like the Joker. "Can I help you up?"

"It's the least you can do, since you knocked me over." I took his hand. Clayton yanked me upright and almost dislocated my arm in the process. Ow. The man packed a wallop. So did his bear.

I sneezed.

"Are you okay?" Clayton's smile dimmed.

"Dust," I said between two more sneezes. I was coated in it. The bear must have been collecting the stuff for years. He had just been waiting to transfer it to some unsuspecting stranger.

My eyes narrowed as I took in Clayton's perfectly pressed khaki pants and powder blue polo shirt. Not a speck of dust in sight.

"You're clean," I said, a decided edge to my voice.

He gave me a crooked, slightly baffled smile. "Thank you."

"Why are you clean?" I demanded. "I look like Pig Pen, and you are—" A girly sneeze ruined my diatribe.

Still, Clayton got the point. "I kept my distance while moving the thing," he explained. "Once I got it to the stairs, I decided to let it find its own way down."

And smack into me.

Clayton tucked one hand in his pocket and held out the other. "My name is Clayton Zimmerman."

I took his hand and grimaced at the gray cast to my skin. Sweat and grime weren't a good look for me. "Rebecca Robbins. I run the Toe Stop Roller Rink in town."

Clayton didn't seem to mind my grimy hand, since he continued to hold it. In fact, his thumb did this little caressing thing on my palm. Either I didn't look as bad as I thought or Clayton was hard up.

The guy gave me another crooked smile and lowered the pitch of his voice. "So, what are you doing here, Rebecca?" The guy sounded a lot like the announcers on smooth jazz radio.

I reclaimed my hand and took a step back, trying not to trip over the mangy bear. "I heard a new lawyer had moved to town. I figured I'd see if you were open for business yet."

Okay, my excuse sounded lame even to me. Being tackled by Smokey the Bear had thrown me off my game.

Thank goodness Clayton bought it. He straightened his shoulders and puffed out his chest. "Not yet. I'm working on getting the place cleaned up. I didn't think potential clients would be interested in sharing the living room with stuffed woodpeckers. So, what kind of business do you need a lawyer for?"

Good question. I racked my brain for a legal problem. "The rink. I'm selling it. There are a couple of conditions in the contract of sale that I want a lawyer to look over. My Realtor is local. I don't want it getting back to her that I had someone double-check her work."

Clayton scratched the back of his head. "I hadn't realized that people in small towns were really that nosy about everyone else's business."

"Gossip beats baseball here as the American pastime." I tried not to look too interested in Clayton's obvious concern. "I guess you're new to small-town life?"

He gave a distracted nod. "I moved here from Chicago. After working for a large firm in the city, I thought I'd try something different."

If different was what he was looking for, Indian Falls had plenty of it. "So, how long have you been in town?"

"A week. That's why this place is such a mess. I bought the house after seeing pictures on the Internet. It looked like the perfect size. The inspector I hired told me about a chimney problem and some plumbing issues. I guess he just assumed I knew about the furry tenants."

He launched into a description of how the living room looked when he arrived. Meanwhile, I was mentally doing the math. If Clayton had gotten to town a week ago, he could have stolen both cars. But I doubted it. The guy was up to his elbows in moving hell. While I questioned his sanity for coming to Indian Falls by choice, the guy didn't strike me as completely nuts. No one would go around stealing cars and blowing them up in the middle of moving.

With a sigh, I mentally crossed Clayton Zimmerman off my suspect list.

"Well," I said, interrupting Clayton's monologue. "I should let you get back to work. It sounds like you have a lot of it to do."

A flicker of irritation marched across Clayton's Latin good looks. The lawyer wasn't used to being interrupted. "Sure. When you have the contract for the rink's sale, let me know. I'll be happy to go over it for you. And maybe when I'm done getting the house in shape for company, you'll join me for dinner? I'd love to get to know you better."

I knew I should just say I had a boyfriend. Using the *B* word didn't necessarily imply long-term commitment. Only, my mouth wouldn't do it. Instead, I found myself saying, "I'm not all that interesting. Besides, I'm moving back to the city." Turning away from the disappointment that darkened his eyes, I took a step toward my car, then stopped. "Three nights ago, you were in the diner getting takeout, right?"

Clayton blinked. "Wow. You weren't kidding about the grapevine. Do you know what I ate that night?"

"The meat-loaf sandwich with extra fries. A really good choice."

"Wow," he said again. His face went pasty white under his tanned skin. Even his curly dark hair looked like it went a shade lighter. My Spidey sense told me the guy had a hell of a secret in his closet, along with a lot of stuffed critters. But it wasn't the secret I was looking for. Whatever the guy's reasons were for ditching the city lights, it wasn't because he yearned for small-town life. The guy was hiding. People who were hiding didn't blow up cars. Period. But they might be watching everyone around them more carefully.

Before Clayton fainted, I asked, "Did you notice anyone suspicious in the diner that night?"

"I don't think so. The place was kind of crazy, especially when the firefighters showed up. Do you have many car explosions out here?"

"Cow tipping, yes. Explosions, no. Are you sure you don't remember anyone acting strange?"

155

Clayton rubbed the back of his neck. "Everything was strange. Some guy was talking like a used-car salesman about needing a new car, the firefighters were bragging about how much better they were at using the hose since the last fire, and two old women were talking about my ass. I almost left before getting my order, like the guy standing next to me. If my oven didn't have stuffed ferrets stashed in it, I would have."

Guy? What guy? "The guy who left," I asked, trying to sound casual. "What did he look like?"

"I don't know." Clayton shrugged while continuing to rub hard at the back of his neck. If he wasn't careful, it was going to chafe. "Shorter than me. Tan. Dark hair. Accent."

My brain immediately conjured up the scary dude with the wire. "Would you know him again if you saw him?"

Clayton stopped rubbing his neck and studied me. "Why?"

I considered my options. I could lie. In fact, during my tenure in Indian Falls, I'd become moderately skilled at it. Still, Clayton had helped me. I decided that telling the truth was the neighborly thing to do. The guy should have the option of getting out of Indian Falls while he had the chance.

"There have been two cars stolen in the past couple of days, and I think the man you saw might have done it."

Casting a nervous look at his garage, Clayton nodded. "I think I might remember the guy if I saw him again." Then crossing his arms, he gave me a stern look. "You didn't come here for legal advice, did you?"

Busted.

Shrugging, I gave him what I hoped was a winsome smile. "No, but I would like a lawyer to look at the contract. Let me know when you clear out the ferrets, and I'll swing by with the paperwork."

Heading for my Civic, I caught a glimpse of his car sitting in the open garage. A very shiny Corvette.

"Don't worry," I said. "The guy stealing cars is taking the old and rusted ones. Yours should be safe."

Leaving a stunned Clayton behind me, I steered my yellow Honda toward Pop's house. With any luck, Ethel had created a usable sketch of the guys who'd attacked Pop. If Clayton could identify the one who was in the diner, I'd solve the case by dinnertime.

I stared at the drawings laid out on the Formica kitchen table, trying to keep my jaw off the floor. Behind me, Pop, Ethel, and Max waited for my opinion of their efforts. Only I didn't have one. I was speechless.

Okay, I wasn't expecting Ethel to be the greatest artist ever. In fact, when my initial enthusiasm after talking to Clayton disappeared, I remembered that this sketch artist thing was a long shot at best. Then Pop and Ethel's proud expressions made me think I'd been wrong in my underestimation.

I wasn't.

While I wasn't sure what the guys who'd threatened Pop looked like, I was certain they weren't Bert and Ernie on a bad hair day.

"What do you think?" Pop asked from behind me. I was sure if he could see my face, he'd already know what I thought. Academy Award–winning actress I wasn't.

Forcing a smile, I turned away from the Muppet-like drawings and looked at the expectant trio. "These aren't bad." They weren't good, either, but I didn't think that needed to be said.

Ethel gave a tinkly little laugh. Her pale skin puckered as she grinned. "I'm so glad you like them. Arthur made me do them over three times to get the faces just right."

"That's the way police sketching works," Pop said, puffing out his chest. "It's all in the details. Well, I should drop Max off at the rink and take Ethel back to the center. Tonight is board-game night."

I thanked Ethel for her hard work, told Max I'd see him tomorrow morning, and watched the two of them parade out the door. Pop followed for a couple steps, then said, "You two get in the car. I have something I need to talk to Rebecca about."

Once the door closed, Pop turned back to me with a sigh. "Sorry about the pictures."

"What do you mean?" I asked. "The pictures might be a real help." If Big Bird and gang come to town.

Pop raised a shaggy gray eyebrow and plopped one hand on his leather-clad hip. "Don't kid me. Those things are awful. Ethel kept saying she was a true artist and that she needed to add her own creativity to her work. When I tried to explain how we needed her drawing ability, not her creativity, she started crying. By the time she emptied the tissue box and got around to drawing again, she had me so confused, I barely remembered what the guys looked like. I used to think it might be fun to date an artist, but I've changed my mind. Two artistic temperaments in the same house might not be a good idea."

"Probably not," I agreed. Pop and Stan were an interesting mix all on their own. Thinking about my father prompted me to ask, "Have you seen Stan?"

Pop snorted. "Upstairs. He came in grumbling about needing a loan and how he couldn't get one. After stomping around the kitchen, he asked what we were doing. I told him about getting attacked by the Spanish dudes. Stan actually looked concerned. I didn't know he had it in him. He looked at Ethel's pictures, asked if the cops were looking for the guys, and went upstairs. Didn't even mooch a slice of pizza. Guess hearing about how I fought off those two attackers made him think twice about snitching my food."

"I bet that was it, Pop." Pop was allowed to dream. Reminded about the presence of pizza, my stomach growled. I grabbed a slice, knowing I still had time before my dinner with Lionel.

While I appreciated the flavor of cold cheese and pepperoni, Pop stared at the drawings and snapped his fingers. "You know what I need? One of them cell phones with a camera. Next time those big guys come after me, I can just snap their picture and— *bam*—we got 'em."

Personally, I thought the cell phone was a pretty good idea. Not for the camera. By the time Pop figured out how to take a picture, he'd be trussed up like a Thanksgiving turkey. Still, having 911 at the ready seemed like a smart plan.

"Gotta run." Pop gave my arm a pat and sauntered toward the back door. "I don't want to leave Max and Ethel alone for too long. Ethel has a thing for younger men."

Yikes.

Ignoring that visual, I considered going upstairs to talk to my father. I hadn't changed my mind about loaning him money, but he had shown concern for my grandfather. That rated pretty high in my book. And I wasn't all that keen about having him angry at me. Our relationship was historically one of mutual indifference. I was uncomfortable knowing that delicate balance had shifted to hostility.

Walking toward the stairs, I caught a glimpse of my reflection in the hallway mirror and stifled a shriek. I was a mess. Streaks of sweat and bear dust meandered down my arms. A black smudge was perched on the edge of my nose, and a host of dust bunnies had taken up residence in my hair. Pop, Ethel, and Max must have noticed my strange appearance, but none of them had commented. For a minute, I wondered why, before realizing it was me. Ethel and Pop expected me to do strange things. Everyone in Indian Falls did. They probably thought I had a good reason for looking like I'd just rolled around in dirt. I did, but that wasn't the point. I was supposed to go on a date with Lionel in less than an hour, and no one had bothered to tell me I looked like something Agnes's cat had dragged in.

Turning away from an inevitably unhappy confrontation, I slipped out the back door and tooled over to the rink in search of a shower. Stan and our father/daughter problems could keep for another day. Heck, they'd been on ice since before I'd hit puberty. Waiting twenty-four hours wouldn't kill either one of us.

I'm a coward. Sue me.

I steered into the rink's parking lot and noted it was starting to fill up for the night's free skate. Growing up, I never understood how anyone wanted to exert physical energy when the weather was hot and sticky. The community pool was just a couple blocks away. Why pay to go inside and sweat when you could be in the water, laughing at the heat? Funny, but now that I was older and in charge, I almost understood the lure of the rink. There was something hypnotic about the music, the disco ball, and the round-and-round-the-floor pattern.

Smiling at the muted sounds of laughter and bass coming from inside, I climbed the stairs to my apartment and then stopped, my hand on the doorknob. A folded sheet of ripped spiral notepaper was taped to the door.

Huh. I pulled the paper off and went inside my apartment. Flipping on the light, I opened the note and felt the hair on my neck stand on end. I had no idea what the note said, but I had gotten heartburn from enough Mexican food to know it was in Spanish.

Not even I was naïve enough to believe this note wasn't connected to the guys in Ethel's *Sesame Street* sketches. Calling the cops was a must, but there was no way I would face Sean Holmes wearing a layer of taxidermy dust. Flipping the dead bolt, I headed for the kitchen.

Tacking the note under a smiley-face refrigerator magnet, I grabbed a large knife, just in case, and headed for the shower. Once the dust was washed from my body, I felt more equipped to deal with the current crisis. Under the hot water, I'd decided I needed to know what the note said before picking up the phone. Once Sean got his sticky little fingers on it, I'd never see it again. And he sure as hell wasn't interested in sharing information. The fact that the note involved me wouldn't make any difference. That meant I had to do a little Internet magic before dialing for the cavalry.

The computer booted as I blow-dried my hair and got dressed, taking extra care to look sexy and vulnerable. The combination might help when talking to Sean. If not, the flirty green sundress with a hint of cleavage might distract Lionel from the relationship talk. I wasn't ready to nail down what we had going on.

I sat down at the computer and surfed for an Internet translator, then started typing out the words on the note. Or what I thought the words were. Whoever had written this had gotten an A in intimidation but had flunked penmanship. I hit Enter and waited. A few seconds later, the English version came back.

"Running is no good. We will find you. Then . . ."

Then what? The translator didn't know. My best guess hadn't been good enough.

Gulp. The sense of dread that I'd been keeping at bay settled into my stomach. Not knowing what I was being threatened with was worse than knowing what was coming. At least in the latter case, I could prepare myself.

I tried a couple other guesses. None of them worked. I was stuck. So I did what I hated doing: I called the Sheriff's Department. An excited Roxy told me to wait in my apartment for a deputy to arrive. So I took a seat on my living room couch and waited, knife in hand.

Mom's crystal clock on the end table ticked off the seconds. After two whole minutes of waiting, I got up and went to the kitchen. Nothing in the fridge looked good. Possibly being threatened had killed my appetite. Grabbing a diet soda, I went back to the living room and stared at the clock some more. I had never been one to wait around for something to happen. I wasn't sure how to do it. My feet crossed and uncrossed while my hands did the nervous wringing thing. Waiting was something I needed to practice. I sucked at it.

A knock broke the agonizing silence, sending me to the door in record speed. Knife in hand, I asked, "Who is it?"

Lionel's disgruntled voice came from the other side of the door. "Your date. Are you expecting someone else?"

I tossed the knife onto the end table behind me, flipped the lock, and opened the door. Standing in the doorway with a sexy gleam in his eye was Lionel. And wow, was he decked out. Gray fitted pants showed off his legs and a button-down green shirt matched his eyes perfectly. He even wore shoes that weren't boots or sneakers. Impressive.

So were the flowers he pulled from behind his back. Roses. Lots and lots of red roses. I was stunned. Lionel wasn't a roses kind of guy. Or maybe I wasn't a flowers kind of girl. Up till now, flowers and other romantic gifts hadn't been in our dating paradigm. I didn't know what to do.

Lionel didn't have the same problem. He leaned down, gave me a peck on the lips, and headed into the kitchen. A few moments later, he returned with the roses, which were now resting comfortably in one of Mom's vases.

"Thanks," I said, feeling slightly light-headed. Sitting down on the arm of the couch, I added, "You didn't have to."

"My mother taught me manners." He gave me a lazy grin, which made my heart flutter. "Besides, I realized it's hard to take a relationship seriously if you haven't done any of the normal dating rituals. I thought some flowers and a romantic dinner might get us on the more traditional path."

"I like nontraditional." At least I thought I did. I wasn't sure. My success rate with relationships wasn't exactly off the charts. Still, the disappointment in Lionel's face at my lack of enthusiasm had me saying, "But dinner and flowers are a nice change of pace."

Stepping toward me, Lionel took my hand and pulled me upright. My throat went dry. The two of us were standing so close, I could feel the perfectly pressed creases in his pants. Tilting my face upward, I succumbed to temptation and leaned in for a kiss.

Only I met air instead of lips. I opened my eyes, baffled. Lionel was leaning his head back while grinning like a fool.

"What gives?" I asked, taking a step back.

"Becky, I'd love nothing more than to kiss you, but I don't want to start something I can't finish. We have dinner reservations in a half hour. We have to leave now if we're going to get to Dixon in time."

"I don't think you're going to make your reservation."

Lionel and I turned toward the voice. Standing in the doorway, a scowl on his face and a gun strapped to his belt, was Deputy Sean Holmes. "Roxy said you called. Where's the note?"

Lionel looked at me with one eyebrow raised. "What note?"

Oops. "When I got home today, I found a note taped to my door. It was written in Spanish. Considering everything that has happened lately, I decided to let the cops handle it."

Personally, I was proud of my explanation. I sounded calm and completely rational. By the red cast to his face and the clenching of his jaw, I could see Lionel was neither of these things. Fairly certain there wasn't anything I could say at this moment to change that scenario, I grabbed the note off the kitchen fridge and handed it to Sean.

His eyes narrowed. "When did you find this?"

"About forty-five minutes ago."

Sean's eyes panned up from the note to mine. Oops again. Only fifteen minutes had passed since I'd called the station.

And Sean knew it.

I was batting a thousand with the men in the room.

Much to my surprise, Sean decided to focus on the problem instead of giving me a hard time. He went back to studying the note while asking, "When was the last time you left the apartment?"

I filled him in on my morning while watching Lionel out of the corner of my eye. He was leaning against the far wall, arms crossed, doing his best to look unconcerned.

"Can you read Spanish?" Sean asked.

"No. Can you?"

Sean smirked. "As a matter of fact, I can. I won the Spanish award in high school."

Color me surprised. Back in our high school days, Sean had been known for having big biceps and a great throwing arm. No one had ever accused him of having a brain. Go figure.

"So what does it say?" I asked.

Sean's face turned serious. "It's a threat."

Even I knew that much without being God's gift to high school Spanish. "What kind of threat?"

Deputy Sean took a step closer and put his hand on my arm. "They say you can't run from them. That they will find you and that something will happen when they do."

"Something? What kind of something?"

Sean's skin took on a pale green cast. "Look, I wouldn't worry about it, Rebecca. The words in the last sentence are pretty hard to read. Who knows what they say."

"But you think you know. Right?" I was trying not to freak. It had to be bad. Sean's idea of fun was tormenting me. If Sean was being nice, bad things were about to happen.

Lionel must have had the same thought. He lost his angry stance and walked over to stand next to me. "What do you think they say, Sean?" His hand rested protectively on my shoulder.

"Well," Sean said, clutching the paper, "the words are smudged and hard to make out. But I think this word here is . . ." He swallowed hard. "*Muerte.*"

Good thing Lionel was holding me upright, because even I knew that word. *Muerte* means "death."

Fifteen

Dead was bad. I didn't want to be dead. In fact, while my life had some downsides, I was pretty happy to be living it and I wanted to stay that way. While Sean and I had our differences, putting them aside in order to keep me breathing seemed like a good idea.

I took a deep breath. "I think the guys who wrote this are staying at one of the motels off the highway. The desk clerks there wouldn't give me any information, but they'll probably talk to you."

Mr. Nice Guy disappeared, leaving typical Sean in his place. "How the hell do you know that? I told you to let the real authorities handle this."

"As far as I can see, the real authorities haven't been able to handle anything," I shot back. "Since I reported the guy with the wire, my grandfather has been attacked and I've been threatened with death. The only person you've managed to arrest for a crime lately was innocent. I'd say the real authorities are doing a bang-up job."

"Maybe if a certain redhead wasn't poking her nose into places it didn't belong, the sheriff wouldn't have to worry about her getting death threats."

"This is my fault?" I marched up to Sean and poked him in the chest. "Jimmy asked me to look into finding his car because he didn't trust you to take his case seriously. If anyone in this town trusted you to do your job, I wouldn't need to be doing it for you."

Sean's ears turned crimson. He looked like he was ready to have a heart attack. Much to my surprise, he didn't make a move for his gun. In fact, he didn't do anything for several long seconds. Then he straightened his shoulders, snapped his cop book shut, and gave a stiff nod. "I'll follow up on the hotels off the highway. Until then, try not to get into any more trouble."

A second later, he was out the door.

Stunned, I rocked back on my heels and waited for him to reappear and start yelling again. He didn't.

"Do you think pushing a cop like that is a good idea?" Lionel asked, sounding a little shocked.

I sighed. Lionel was right. I had probably taken things a little too far. But I'm a redhead. Redheads are known for their nasty tempers. For the most part, I kept that genetic predisposition under control. Unless provoked. Sean's words had definitely provoked me. Still, I couldn't help feeling a twinge of regret at what might have been unhappiness in his eyes. Sean annoyed me, but I didn't want to hurt him.

"I know, but he pushes my buttons," I admitted. "I couldn't help myself."

"Like you couldn't help forgetting to tell me about the note?"

Lionel's tone sounded reasonable, but I wasn't stupid. This conversation was a potential land mine. I'd already stepped on one with Sean. I needed carbohydrates before I hopped onto another.

"I meant to tell you." Maybe. Stranger things have happened. "The flowers took me by surprise. By the time I thought about it, Sean was already here."

Lionel looked like he was going to argue the point. Then he shook his head and sighed. "It's too late to drive to Dixon. How about we go to Dom's and get a bottle of wine. Both of us could use a drink."

Ten minutes later, we were seated in a back booth at Papa Dom's, Indian Falls's answer to Italian cuisine. The restaurant was located at the far end of town but never had trouble drawing a crowd. The food was great. The decor erred on the side of checkered tablecloths and melted-down candles in Chianti bottles. What else could you want?

Dom himself came over to take our drink order. He was a short man with almost Transylvanian black hair and a weathered face. Still, the expressive Italian in him made Dom appear larger than life.

"The two of you do no come in here enough," he said, rubbing his tan, wrinkled hands together. "Young people in love are good for my business and for my heart. I will bring you wine, yes? A nice white to go with your pasta."

He shuffled off toward the bar without waiting for us to agree with him. Dom was allowed to serve you whatever he wanted. House rule. If you didn't like it, he wouldn't charge you. That almost never happened. What the guy lacked in hairstyling taste, he made up for with his palate.

He came back with two glasses. Our waitress, a tiny blond

woman I'd seen rolling along my rink floor with her kids, trailed behind him, holding a bottle of pinot grigio. After putting the glasses down and popping the cork, Dom poured the wine. "Rebecca, your mother would be happy to see you with such a nice young man. It is time to be settled and have a family." Giving me a pat on the hand, Dom shuffled off to chat up another table.

The waitress took Dom's place tableside. She ran down the specials and asked if we were ready to order.

"Yes," I said quickly. Food was a safe subject. "I'll have the special pasta." I wasn't even sure what the special pasta was, but it sounded like there was a lot of it. If I had food jammed in my mouth, I couldn't be expected to hold a conversation. When it came to discussions about relationships and scary notes on my door, saying as little as possible was a good thing.

Lionel ordered the eggplant, my favorite, and then we were left alone. Before he could launch into his agenda, I started on my own. "I have some questions about Jimmy's car fire. I was hoping since you're a volunteer fire guy, you could fill in some blanks."

I dropped the gauntlet and sucked down half a glass of wine while waiting to see if Lionel picked it up. He eyed me over the Chianti candle while fingering the stem of his glass. I could tell his naturally curious nature was warring with his need to keep to his desired conversation topic.

After several long moments, curiosity won out. "What about Jimmy's car fire?"

"The fire burned really hot," I explained. "I could feel the heat singeing my eyebrows from a hundred feet away."

Lionel arched an eyebrow. "So? Fire is hot. What's so strange about that?"

"The field didn't burn." I emptied my glass and put it down with a clatter. The perfect punctuation to my Sherlock Holmes moment.

Only my Watson didn't get it. "You're upset that Alan Schmitt's field *didn't* go up in smoke?"

"No," I said, leaning forward. "But I do think it's strange. Look, it hadn't rained for days. The field was dry. That means either God decided to keep Alan out of trouble or our arsonist did something that kept the field from catching on fire. I'm betting God doesn't have a personal stake in Alan's life."

Lionel put his elbows on the table and leaned forward. "Okay, you're right. The fact that the field didn't catch on fire is strange."

I poured myself another glass of wine. Being told I was right was something to celebrate.

Our waitress arrived at that moment with our food, and I stared in amazement at the plate in front of me. Looking at me from atop a large helping of rigatoni were several little fish heads, eyes and all. I poked at one of the fish with my fork. It wasn't moving, which was good. But I was expected to eat it, which was bad. Sampling unusual food at the gourmet club was one thing. Beady-eyed fish were something else.

Lionel smiled at me over his plate of steaming eggplant. "Problem?"

Yes. Only I wasn't going to admit it. Trying to look pleased, I pushed the fish to one side, stabbed a pasta tube, and shoveled it into my mouth—except that I couldn't chew. The fish were still looking at me.

So I did what any self-respecting person would do: I scooped up the fish with my unused spoon and put them on my bread plate.

As a final gesture of respect, I covered them up with my cocktail napkin. Now they could rest and I could eat in peace.

Without my aquatic friends, I was able to taste what was in my mouth. I didn't hate it. In fact, it was pretty good. There were raisins, tomatoes, and pine nuts swimming in a zingy sauce. I took another bite and smiled for real. Dom might want to rethink the garnish, but the pasta itself was outstanding.

Now that my meal wasn't wigging me out, I could get back to business. "I'm guessing someone put something on the field to keep it from catching on fire. That baffles me. I mean, what arsonist would do something like that? I don't think an arsonist would be worried about adding a couple of extra Hail Marys to his penance."

Lionel nodded. "It sounds weird, but I can't think of a better reason the field didn't catch fire."

"I know you do the firefighter thing on a strictly volunteer basis, but I thought you might know what kind of fire retardant could be used in this situation." And if he didn't, I was hoping his interest would be piqued enough for him to stop by the firehouse and find out. The guys would talk to him. Getting him to share the information after he got it might be problematic. I'd just have to hurl myself off that bridge when I got to it.

He ate several forkfuls of his meal while deep in thought. This gave me time to scarf down some more pasta, a slice of bread slathered with seasoned olive oil, and another glass of wine. If the bad guys made good on their threat tonight, I'd die with a happy stomach.

I grabbed another slice of bread while eyeing Lionel's half-eaten meal. "Are you going to eat all of that?"

Lionel cut off a piece of the eggplant and put it onto my plate.

Then he said, "Every Fourth, the fireworks guys spray some kind of retardant on the grass to prevent sparks from flaring up. I don't think that kind of thing is strong enough to work on a car fire, but I can find out. If the guy who did this stopped the fire from spreading, then the thief might be one of—"

He cut himself off and slugged back the rest of his wine, then refilled the glass and drained it again.

I knew where his thought had been heading. Right to the front door of the Indian Falls firehouse. I couldn't believe one of the firefighters could be our pyromaniac car bandit. But only a person looking out for the safety of the town or maybe the welfare of the firefighters themselves would care enough to prevent the fire from spreading. Plus, all the firefighters had been in the diner the night my father blew into town.

Damn. Suddenly everyone associated with the big red truck was on my suspect list.

I pushed my almost-empty dish away. The pasta sat like a big ball of wax in my stomach. I knew all of those guys. Lately, poker night at the barn had included at least one or two members of the IFFD. I really didn't want one of them to be the car thief. From the look on Lionel's face, he didn't want that, either.

Our waitress cleared our plates and offered us dessert. Dom's tiramisu had taken first place in the Fall Festival Cook-Off three years running. It said so on the menu. Normally, I'd have considered it my duty to make sure he wasn't slipping, but not tonight.

Lionel drove me back to the rink. I hopped out of his megatruck and walked with him upstairs to my front door.

No notes. No scary guys lurking in shadows. Both good signs.

"You're going to question the guys at the firehouse, aren't you?" Lionel asked as I put my key in the lock.

I stepped into my apartment and waited for him to follow. He didn't. I sighed. "Would you rather Sean talk to them?"

"I'd rather you'd forget the whole thing." His face was partially in shadows, but I could hear the frustration in his voice. "None of those guys would do anything to hurt people in this town."

"Don't you think I know that?" I said, getting annoyed. "I like those guys. I liked Annette, too. She was my mother's best friend, and still I questioned her when it looked like she might have committed murder. Liking someone doesn't make the person innocent."

I was pretty sure I was right. Expert I wasn't, but every *CSI* episode I'd watched backed me up.

Lionel tilted his head to one side, considering my logic. Finally, he leaned down and planted a kiss on me. The tension that had been building in my neck dissolved as a tingle of anticipatory pleasure built. Reaching up, I started to wind my hands around Lionel's neck. But he pulled back, taking his lips with him.

"I don't want to leave you alone tonight," he said in a satisfyingly reluctant tone. "But I've got to go. I promised Doc I'd look in on his horse. She's ready to foal."

I searched his face to make sure he was telling the truth. Being ditched for a pregnant horse wasn't all that flattering, but it was better than having your boyfriend leave angry. "So you're not mad at me?"

He gave me one of his sexy grins. "Becky, there's someone setting fire to cars and guys with death threats running around town. Somehow you're messed up in both. I can't even begin to describe what I'm feeling."

He leaned down and kissed me again with a lot of emotion. None of it was angry. All of it was exciting. And then he was gone, leaving me staring at an open doorway and feeling a little wistful. Then a little scared. I was here alone. Yikes.

I closed the door and threw the dead bolt. For a moment, I contemplated scooting the end table in front of the door. It would keep the bad guys out. But it would keep me from making a quick escape if they decided to set fire to the place. I decided against re-decorating and went to bed instead.

Not that I slept much. Without the security of having Lionel nearby, I tossed and turned most of the night and woke without my alarm at seven. There was sand in my eyes and a dull throb in the back of my head. On the upside, I had a plan. Hours of not sleeping had given me lots of time to think out my next move.

I got dressed in a pair of jean shorts, a stretchy blue Chicago Cubs shirt, and my best sneakers. I figured I might end up running for my life. I wasn't about to risk doing myself in over a pair of sexy heels, no matter what they might do for my legs.

Grabbing a bagel from the kitchen, I munched as I headed down the stairs to the rink. No bad guys were lurking around the front door. I grabbed the handle and froze. The rink was already open.

Huh. Maybe George was here.

I walked inside the dimly lit rink. "Hello?"

My voice echoed in the large, completely empty space.

"George?" A strange tingly sensation a lot like fear tickled the back of my neck. "Hello? Is anyone here?"

"You're up early."

I spun around as a spandex-clad George waltzed through the front door. He smiled at me and hefted his green army backpack up on his shoulder. "Is Max coming in early, too?" The sneer in his normally perky voice spoke volumes.

I wasn't interested in his power play for king of the rink.

George hadn't opened the rink this morning. So who had? Had it been open all night?

"Who locked up last night?" I asked, walking over to the sound booth and hitting the light switch. The large fluorescent lights hummed and sputtered to life. Nothing looked out of place. The CDs in the booth looked a little less than tidy, but that was to be expected.

George cocked his head to one side. "Brittany closed. Why?"

"I didn't use my key to get in. The door was already open." I hurried back to my office, leaving a stunned George in my wake. The door was locked. I inserted my key and hit the light switch. Fine. Everything was fine. The computer was on the desk, all my knickknacks were accounted for, and the money from last night was locked in the box in the desk. Unless someone had raided the stash of Tombstone pizzas in the kitchen, everything was as it should be.

George poked his blond head into the office, frowning. "Are you sure the door wasn't locked?"

I nodded. "Brittany must have forgotten."

"She couldn't have." The creases on George's forehead deepened. "I came back to the rink last night to make sure things were running okay. New management—" George took one look at my face and swallowed the rest of that sentence. "Anyway, I helped Brittany close up. She locked the door, and I walked her to her car. I didn't want her to be alone in the parking lot with those Spanish guys on the loose. I even tested the knob to make sure the place was closed up tight."

Crap. Crap. Crap. Someone had broken into the rink.

"Okay," I said, taking several deep breaths. "Let's split up and make sure the rink is okay."

Twenty minutes later, we reconvened on the floor of the rink.

If someone had broken in, I had no idea why. Money, sound system, and pizzas were all in their places. Strange.

I debated calling the cops. The shouting match with Sean last night made me less enthusiastic than usual at the prospect. Besides, what would I tell them? The door had been unlocked, but there were no signs of forced entry—no crowbar marks, no scratches, nothing. Sure, George said he'd checked it and it was locked, but more than one person had a key to the joint. The cops weren't going to be impressed. I figured the best thing to do was make sure the keys were all accounted for. It might not solve the problem, but it would make me feel better.

There were six keys floating around in people's pockets. I had one. George showed me his. That made two. Brittany, Doreen, Pop, and a pimply yet responsible high school senior named Mike had the others.

I grabbed my cell and texted Mike and Brittany. No one under twenty ever answered the phone. They were too busy texting or instant-messaging on the computer to do anything as ordinary as talking. Moments after I'd hit Send, both kids confirmed they had keys in hand.

As did Doreen. She seemed incensed that I had the nerve to ask if she had her copy of the rink key, but after I soothed her hurt feelings, she answered the question. The key was in her desk at her office. I asked her to call me back when she verified that it was still there, and she asked, "How is your new manager working out?"

I was going to give her a lengthy answer, but I heard a man chuckle in the background. It was one of those low, husky laughs guys use when they're interested in sex. Oh God! The guy was probably my father. Yuck!

"Max is doing just fine. In fact, he'll be here any minute. Gotta go."

I snapped the phone shut, wishing the visions in my head would disconnect, too.

Four keys were accounted for. Once Doreen called me back, the number would be up to five. That just left Pop's. No answer at the house or on his cell. He was probably sleeping, showering, or, like my father, otherwise occupied. I turned to give George an update. He was pale as a ghost. His bottom lip trembled like that of a four-year-old ready to have a tantrum. I should know. I'd seen a lot of kids with just that look on this very floor.

"Are you okay, George?" When I was dealing with a toddler, this question was always followed by tears or throwing up. I was hoping George would do neither. My nerves couldn't handle it.

George sucked in some air and gave a brave little nod.

"You sure?"

Another stoic movement of the head. George was scrappy.

"It just hit me that someone actually broke into your mother's rink," George said with a sniffle. "This is a place for happiness. It is hard to believe someone would think of ruining that."

Happiness wasn't the first word I'd use to describe the rink.

"Hey, guys. I brought coffee." Max sauntered into the rink. He was sporting a three-piece suit and juggling a tray of Styrofoam cups. "And I even got here thirty minutes early just to impress you, George."

George didn't look impressed. He just looked stunned. I was, too, but that only heightened my need for coffee. "Thanks, Max." I took a swig and hoped the caffeine would jump-start my brain. Maybe then the break-in would make sense.

"What's wrong?" Max asked, looking from me to George and back again.

"The rink wasn't locked when I got here," I said. "George swears he doubled-checked to make sure the place was closed up last night. We think someone broke in."

Max's raised eyebrows, dropped jaw, and wide eyes reminded me of the pictures taken at amusement parks of the people strapped into the ride that drops two hundred feet before swooping to safety. Max was in drop mode.

"A break-in. Wow! Although, if there were no signs of forced entry, then George could be wrong about the place being locked." Max shifted from foot to foot, looking almost giddy to be in the middle of such intrigue. He also looked happy to be getting back at George for his bad behavior. "I mean, who would break into a roller rink?"

George's pale face turned bright pink. "I didn't get it wrong, you idiot. For all we know, you broke in here to make me look bad." He took the medium latte off Max's tray and drew back his arm as if ready to launch.

"Stop." My voice bounced around the rink like a pinball. "Max, I'd trust George with my life. If he says the rink was locked, then it was locked. There's no reason to throw accusations around." That also applied to coffee.

"Now, I need to go find my grandfather. George is going to be in charge of the rink for the day. Max, I need you to stop by the sheriff's office and fill out a report about the break-in. I want to cover all the bases just in case something turns up missing."

And there was no way I could leave the two of them here un-supervised. It would be coffee at thirty paces.

George glowered at Max.

Max ignored him and buttoned his jacket. He then straightened his padded pinstriped shoulders. "I'll call you when I finish at the station, in case you have other important details you need taken care of."

Chin in the air, Max strutted past us. I grabbed George's arm just before it had a chance to fly. He stumbled at the change of momentum, shot me a wounded glare, and stomped to the side of the rink to get ready for his first lesson.

Ignoring the huffing sounds coming from George's general direction, I headed out into the already stifling heat on a mission to find Pop. I steered my Civic toward his house, hoping to find his Toe Stop key safe and sound.

The minute I turned onto Pop's street, the sound of an amped-up bass hit me square in the chest. Tooling into his driveway, I stopped the car and gaped. Pop was in the middle of the garage, strutting around with a mike. He was wearing brown leather shorts and a black T-shirt that was at least a size too small. To his right, performing a loud, ear-piercing guitar riff was Mr. O'Rourke, former high school science teacher. Behind him, a rhythm-impaired Doc Truman pounded away on the drums. Pop's next-door neighbor, Ed, did his best impression of a bass player.

No wonder Pop hadn't answered his phone. There was no way he could have heard it. In fact, the lack of musical talent in the group was so shocking, I was amazed anyone on the block could even think.

The only person present with any melodic skill was Mary Margaret on keys. Not that I could hear her playing above the din, but she'd played for my mother's funeral and done a nice job. Currently, the elderly organist was seated demurely in the back at her keyboard. Her eyes were glued to my grandfather's butt, which was swaying to the inconsistent beat.

Plugging my ears, I walked up to the garage and shouted, "Pop!"

He didn't see me. My grandfather was busy pretending to riff along with the out-of-tune guitar.

I walked through the mess of cords and amps. Then, braving deafness, I took a finger out of my ear and tapped Pop on the shoulder. He swung around and held up a fist. One by one, the band members stopped playing.

Thank God.

Pop put down his microphone and said, "Take five, everyone. We'll try that song again after a break."

The musicians all said hello as they exited the garage. Mary Margaret did a little finger wave at Pop and giggled as she walked by. Oy.

"What song were you rehearsing?" I asked before I could stop myself.

Pop hitched up his shorts. " 'Love Me Tender.' "

I blinked.

"I know. They haven't gotten the hang of it yet, but they want to learn, and they come cheap." Pop gave me a bony shoulder shrug. "Most headliners have their own band. I thought with my career taking off, I should put one together. Mary Margaret has some talent, don't you think?"

I looked toward the front lawn, where Mary Margaret sat with her hand on Mr. O'Rourke's leg. Mary Margaret had all the makings of the next Yoko Ono.

"Don't the neighbors mind that you're rehearsing here?"

"Nope." Pop gave me a toothy grin. "Most of them are at work, and I let Ron O'Rourke be in the band. He's the first one calling the cops if an ant farts on this street. So what's up? If you came by to see your father, he's not here. I don't think he came in last night."

"No, I wanted to see if you had your rink key."

Pop's eyebrows scrunched together. "Did something happen to the rink?"

"I don't know. The door was unlocked when I got there this morning. The door hadn't been forced open. Either both Brittany and George forgot to lock up last night or someone took one of our keys. I've accounted for the others."

"George must have gotten it wrong because I have my key. It's right here in my—" Pop's expression went from amused to shocked horror in a second flat as he reached into his pocket. He raised his eyes to meet mine. "My key. It's gone."

Sixteen

Damn!

"Are you sure?" I asked, though I could see a key was missing from Pop's rabbit's foot ring. Pop had three keys: home, car, and rink. Today there were only two. Subtraction sucks.

Pop looked stunned. "I don't know what could have happened. The key was here yesterday afternoon. It's not like I leave them lying around all over the place. I keep them in my pocket."

These days, Pop's pockets were so tight, lint had trouble getting in. Stealing keys out of his pocket would take serious elbow grease.

"Could you have left them on a table at the center last night? It would've taken only a few seconds for someone to slip the key off and put the ring back."

Pop shook his head back and forth. "Didn't happen at the center. I know better than that. Too many fans hanging around. If you leave your keys out, you never know who might end up naked in your trunk. I learned my lesson the first time."

I opened my mouth to ask and decided I was happier not knowing.

"I guess it could have been at the diner. Mary Ellen asked me to serenade her mother, and I left my keys on the counter for a few minutes. Wait. I know!" Pop snapped his fingers. "Your father was moping around after you turned him away empty-handed. I bet he took the key when I wasn't looking. No wonder he didn't stay here last night. Rebecca, I hate to say this, but your father is a skunk."

Pop was right not only about my father's character but about the possibility of his being the key thief. Stan was more than capable of lifting Pop's rink key without Pop being any the wiser. Stan's need for quick cash was a strong motive for breaking into the rink. Only, the lockbox with today's bank deposit hadn't been touched. Weird.

"I'll go find Stan and ask him," I said with a sigh.

"I'm going with you." Pop shifted his weight from foot to foot like a prizefighter ready to do battle. "It was my key. I've earned the right to pummel him."

"Let me talk to him first," I said. "If he sees you clenching your fist, he might make a run for it."

Pop thought about that for a minute and nodded. "You're right. We don't want to scare him off before he confesses to the crime. Once he does, I'll come in and cuff him. I should probably get a pair of handcuffs before then."

I left Pop browsing the Yellow Pages for police supply stores. Waving good-bye to the band, I steered my Civic toward Doreen's retirement apartment to search for my father.

Doreen's door loomed in front of me. Somewhere on the other side, my father and Doreen were doing something I didn't want to imagine. I figured I could wait to talk to my dad another time, except I couldn't. I'd put off a confrontation yesterday, and look what had happened.

My first attempt at knocking was barely audible. Nerves. I raised my hand and rapped louder.

"One minute," Doreen's voice sang from behind the door. True to her word, less than a minute later, the door swung open. Doreen stood in the doorway wearing a purple lace negligee and a black-and-purple robe. She squinted at me. Doreen was not wearing her trademark glasses. Apparently, they didn't go with the ensemble. "Rebecca? Did we have an appointment?"

"No appointment." The light behind Doreen made her outfit almost see-through. Help. "I'm looking for my father. Is he here?"

Doreen's eyebrows knit together, and her voice went up an octave. "Uh, no. I haven't seen your father since yesterday afternoon. He came by the office for a chat and asked me to meet him for dinner at the diner."

"Doreen, darling," a deep male voice bellowed from inside the apartment. "Where's my Realtor? I'm waiting to close the deal."

Doreen's cheeks turned bright red. "I waited at the diner for an hour, but Stan never showed. He stood me up. And, well, I met someone else, and nature took its course. I'll call you later today about the key and the closing."

Doreen ducked behind the door and slammed it shut.

Ugh! I wished she hadn't said the word *closing*. Not after hearing her friend inside. Well, I might not have known where Stan was, but I knew Doreen wasn't holding him in escrow. That was something.

I stopped by the rink to make sure everyone was in one piece. George was busy teaching classes, the pasty look of fear replaced by the rosy tint of exercise. Max was in the office, booking a birthday party. He hung up and gave me a copy of the incident report. He had shed the suit coat but still looked like he was dressed for a funeral. I filled him in on the missing key and he patted me on the back and told me everything was going to be all right. The kid was okay.

Leaving Max looking concerned but in control, I waited on the sidelines of the rink for George to finish his class. He skated over, executed a perfect T-stop, and grabbed a towel. I gave him the same story I'd given Max. George flashed me a triumphant smile while his body quivered with the need to jump up and down and say "I told you so." To his credit, his feet never left the floor. Probably because the skates were weighing him down.

George's next class arrived, and he raced back onto the floor with a giddy smile. I didn't share his sense of glee. Some unknown person had a key to my rink. Pulling out my cell, I dialed Zack and asked for a locksmith referral. Five minutes later, I'd arranged for the guy to come by and change the locks after lunch.

Leaving George and Max in charge, I headed back out into the heat. There was nothing more I could do about the key issue until my father surfaced. Sad but true. Time to take a trip to the firehouse and see if anyone had Guilty Pyromaniac written across his face.

Cruising Main Street, I kept my eyes peeled for signs of Dad or the scary Spanish duo. Nada.

I pulled into the firehouse's parking lot and got out of the car. Middle-aged muscleman Chuck Culver was standing outside in his navy blue firefighter's uniform, having a smoke. There was something ironic about a smoker having a job that involved putting out fires. Especially around here. Aside from Jimmy's car explosion and Pop's blazing scarecrow, most of the calls to the firehouse involved someone at home smoking in bed.

Still, I was happy to see Chuck. He'd taken twenty dollars from me at Lionel's last poker game. I figured my losing cash to him would grease the information wheels.

I figured wrong. Chuck took one look at me, raked the hand not holding a cigarette through his shortly cropped dark hair, and frowned. Chuck was not happy to see me. Either rookie Robbie had told him about my last visit or Lionel had called. I was betting on the latter. Lionel and I were definitely going to have a chat.

Giving Chuck a big "I don't want anything from you" smile, I crossed the asphalt. Chuck didn't smile back. He flicked his cigarette butt and crossed his arms over his chest.

"You should put the cigarette out with water," I said. "Then again, I guess if you start a fire, you have everything you need to put it out."

Okay, this was probably more confrontational than necessary, but I couldn't help it. Throwing lit cigarette butts around was never a good idea, firefighter or not.

Chuck didn't look amused. "Lionel said you might come by."

Since Lionel had already blown my cover, I just nodded. "I thought it was strange the hay field didn't catch fire along with Jimmy Bakersfield's car. Lionel thought you guys might have some idea why."

"Or maybe you started thinking that one of my firefighters started the fire. Right?" Chuck glowered at me. Every muscle that I could see sticking out of his clothes bulged with not quite suppressed anger. On a normal day, I would have appreciated his body like a connoisseur appreciates a fine wine. Today, his muscles were no longer sighworthy. They were scary.

"Look," I said, resisting the urge to take a tiny step back. "Lionel and I find it hard to believe any of your guys would set fire to a car. But someone knew enough to keep the fire from spreading. If I put two and two together, Sean Holmes is going to." Chuck's muscles relaxed a tiny bit, so I pressed my case. "I need to figure out how the bad guy kept the fire contained, then nail him before Sean arrests your entire department. Sean tends to ask questions after he puts people behind bars."

Chuck thought about that for a minute. Finally, he unfolded his arms.

Now that Chuck was more receptive, I asked, "What kind of fire retardant did the fireworks guys use? Would it work on hay?"

Chuck looked up at the sky and put his hands behind his head—a modern version of Rodin's *The Thinker.* "They used something called Safety Zone. They had gallons of it. Used to be harder to get your hands on the stuff, but the Internet has made it easy. Stuff worked like a charm. A couple fireworks exploded on the ground and we didn't need our hoses."

If Chuck was right, anyone could get their hands on the right kind of fire retardant. Which meant anyone paying attention to the fireworks setup was a suspect. My suspect list was getting longer instead of shorter.

Chuck walked into the firehouse and returned a minute later with a jug. "After I talked to Lionel this morning, I went back to the scene and found this in the field opposite. I thought about giving it to Sean, but I figured he'd use it to point the finger at one of my guys."

He handed me the plastic jug, which had a black-and-red sticker that read SAFETY ZONE. The fact that the IFFD guys were all familiar with this specific retardant pointed the finger squarely inside the firehouse. I understood why Chuck was nervous.

"I get that you're friends with the other fighters, so you want to protect them," I said. "But how can you be so sure they didn't start the fire?"

Chuck jammed his hands into his pants pockets. "There are only six of us, so we're pretty easy to keep track of. Three of the guys were here at the firehouse eating Chinese food. I got a receipt that even says what time it was delivered. Robbie's date canceled, so he was watching *Titanic* with his parents. And Kevin and I were at my house, watching the game, when the fire was called in. Everyone has an alibi."

I was confused. "Why not tell Sean and move on?"

"Can't."

Pithy but not helpful. "Why? Tell Sean about the alibis and give him the fire retardant. You'll help save the day."

"And ruin Kevin's marriage. He told his wife he had to work, so he didn't have to visit his in-laws in Iowa. This is the fourth time he's skipped making the trip, and his wife is getting angry. If she finds out he was drinking beer instead of eating her mother's borscht, she'll kick him to the curb."

For Kevin's sake, I promised to keep quiet about the alibis and the fire retardant for as long as I could. If someone was going to make me eat borscht, I'd lie, too.

I hit the rink in time for a grateful Max to go find lunch. I guess snack-bar food wasn't his idea of a balanced meal. Some days, I would have agreed. Not today, though. I grabbed a big salt-covered pretzel and a cup of melted yellow cheese. Thus fortified, I went back to my office to check e-mail and review the stuff my trainee had been in charge of this morning. While the business wasn't the driving force in my life, I wasn't about to let Max run it into the ground.

According to the records, Max had booked a couple of parties and done some lesson scheduling. He'd misquoted the price for one of the parties, but it was in my favor, so I couldn't really complain. The customer would be thrilled when I called and gave her a lower price. I'd be a hero. Gotta love that.

A half hour later, the rink's paperwork was complete. Logging on to my e-mail account, I munched on a pretzel and smiled. My best friend and former Chicago roomie, Jasmine, had sent me a long dissertation on her life. Apparently, it sucked. I wasn't sure it really did. Jasmine knew how badly I wanted to get back to the bright lights and pollution-filled air of Chicago. She might be overstating her unhappiness so I wouldn't feel jealous. She'd been doing that kind of thing since I'd come back here and gotten stuck.

I typed a long e-mail to Jasmine, instructing her to get off the ledge. If things were bad on her end, I told her, she could come join me. Jasmine was a city girl through and through. The mere thought of joining me in the middle of farm country would act like shock treatment and force her to be happy. Was I a good friend or what?

Hitting Send, I finished off my pretzel and contemplated my next move in the car-fire investigation. Safety Zone had a Web site, and the stuff was cheap and easy to order. Anyone could do it. I picked up the phone and dialed the customer-service number listed on the screen. The woman's voice was perky and very friendly. The tone got even friendlier when she refused to tell me if someone in Indian Falls had purchased the stuff. I hung up, trying to decide if I was frustrated or impressed with Safety Zone's staff. Probably both.

The problem was, I didn't have any other leads to help me ferret out who had started the fire. Nor did I have any new ideas on the death-threat front. I figured Sean had been busy checking out hotels. If everything had gone as planned, he would have the guys in a cell by now. Maybe I should check that out, I thought. Knowing they were off the streets would do wonders for my blood pressure.

"Rebecca."

I spun around when I heard the voice coming from the doorway.

Holy crap. I sucked in some air.

Danielle was wearing a pair of short red shorts that barely covered the bottoms of her butt cheeks. The top of her was in a white lacy corset-looking shirt that displayed a lot of ample chest. The whole look was capped off by white four-inch strappy sandals. Danielle no longer looked like the girlfriend of mild-mannered Pastor Rich.

She gave me an uncertain smile. "Too much?"

Danielle sat down in the chair and let out a squeak. Her short shorts had no doubt ridden high into her butt crack.

Danielle pushed a lock of her dark hair out of her eyes. "I don't know what to do. This is the first time I've dated anyone who won't make a move on me. I'm getting desperate."

"Do you love Rich?" I asked. Pastor Rich was the epitome of respectability and moral living—everything Danielle had come to Indian Falls for. But was she in love with him? I wasn't sure.

Danielle bit her bottom lip. "I think I do, but this relationship is so different. All my other boyfriends had me on my back after the first couple dates. I loved feeling close to them, but after a while, the whole thing fizzled. With Rich, we don't make out or do anything improper. So I can't tell if we have any chemistry. Can you be in love without having sex?"

I wasn't the queen of healthy relationships. My relationship with Lionel had a lot of problems, mostly mine. Still, I was pretty sure I knew the answer to this one.

"Do you enjoy talking to him and spending time with him?"

She nodded. The sadness in her eyes made me believe that she felt a lot more than just enjoyment when she was with him. Danielle had it bad.

"Then, yes, you can love someone you haven't slept with. What you need to do is change clothes and then talk to Rich. Tell him you think he isn't attracted to you. See what he does. I bet you'll be surprised." Move over, Dr. Phil.

Danielle chewed the bottom of her lip some more. "Do I have to? I'm not like you. Talking about my feelings isn't my strong suit."

If I was better at talking about relationships than she was, we were in serious trouble.

"Well," I said with a laugh, "the guy with the great ass from the drugstore is nice. I'm not investigating him anymore. I guess you could always flirt with him and see if Rich gets jealous."

I was joking. Only Danielle's pursed lips told me she was considering the option. This was bad.

"Look, I really think talking to Rich is the best plan. Honesty will help you build a lasting relationship." Clearly, I was better at giving advice than following it.

Danielle stood up and gave me a high-wattage smile. "Thanks for the help. Do you mind if I change back into my other clothes in here? Everyone was at lunch when I arrived, but it sounds busy out there now. I wouldn't want to give anyone the wrong idea." Her tone had taken on the singsong quality of a Stepford wife. It was scary.

"Of course. But I don't think I helped."

She closed the office door and pulled a pair of tan Capri pants from her bag. "You did. These clothes aren't the answer. I think I know what is."

191

She shrugged a purple T-shirt over the bustier. In the new ensemble, she looked like a housewife ready to do battle with the grocery store. "I've got to go. Thanks for the help, Rebecca. And call me if you need someone to stay with you. Sleeping upstairs after a death threat and a break-in can't be easy." With that, she walked out the door.

Danielle's skimpy outfit had momentarily shocked me into forgetting about my current predicament. I had enjoyed the momentary break from indigestion. Now it was back.

Car thefts, fire retardants, scary men, death threats, and a missing rink key. No matter how I tried, the pieces wouldn't fit together in a way that made sense.

Restless, I checked the clock. One-thirty. The locksmith should be here. I grabbed my purse and headed into the rink.

Sure enough, my locksmith, Ollie Black, was hitching up his overalls and starting work on the door. My supervision wasn't exactly needed, but I was grateful for the excuse to get out of the office. I stayed out front with Ollie and watched the small balding spot in the middle of his ashy hair turn bright red under the heat of the sun. It's the small things.

When Ollie was done, he gave me a set of six new keys for the door. I, in turn, gave him a check. Money well spent, since otherwise I knew I wouldn't sleep. I slipped the old key off my key ring and replaced it with the shiny new one.

Ollie strolled off with his toolbox in hand, and I went inside to find George. He was guzzling water from a bottle near the entrance. I gave him three of the keys: one for him and the others for my two most responsible high school employees.

"What about my key?" Max pouted as he approached. Between the heat outside and the physical activity involved in the day-to-day running of the rink, Max's suit was looking a little less than fresh. "I can stop by at night and make sure the rink really is locked. We don't want any more mistakes."

George started to lunge. I grabbed the back of his shirt and pulled. The whole scene reminded me of something out of Looney Toons. Wile E. Coyote goes after the Road Runner, but something holds him back. He's suddenly running in place and the Road Runner gets away. Only in this case, the Road Runner was standing there taunting Wile E. with a smug smile. The cartoon version of the Road Runner was way smarter than my manager, Max.

I gave George's sweaty T-shirt a hard yank, which sent him stumbling two steps backward, and said, "You can have a key after you finish your probation period on Monday."

I could tell Max was tempted to stick his tongue out at George, but he restrained himself and said, "Makes sense to me. Oh, I left a couple of DVDs on your desk for you to look at when you have a minute. I hope you enjoy them."

And with that, he strolled off toward the rental counter. After taking three deep breaths, George gave me half a smile, blew his whistle, and skated off. The Toe Stop all-skate session had begun.

With George and Max separated and occupied, I went to perform key-delivery service. First stop: the retirement home. I found Doreen in her apartment, fully clothed and with no men in sight.

She took the key and said, "We need to be careful nothing like this happens again. The buyers don't live in town and don't understand how Indian Falls works. One more incident and I'm certain they'll pull out of the deal."

Something else to worry about.

I assured Doreen that the rink was in perfect condition and nothing else would spook the buyers. Of course, while saying this, I kept my fingers crossed behind my back. I had no idea if anything else would happen and had no control over stopping it if it did. Scary, but true.

At Pop's house, all evidence of the band had cleared away and my grandfather's car was parked in the garage. I walked into the house and almost ran smack into Pop as he headed out.

"Sorry, Rebecca. I can't talk long. I have to do my Elvis Serenade act for Eleanor's birthday party. Her friends thought I'd be more fun than watching Alex Trebek on *Jeopardy*. Eleanor has a thing for Alex, so I'm not so sure."

It wasn't until he mentioned his Elvis act that I noticed his clothes: a black-and-silver studded jumpsuit unzipped down to his navel and a black pompadour wig. When a seventy-six-year-old guy in an Elvis getup looks completely normal, you know it's time to reevaluate your life.

I pulled out one of the new keys and handed it to Pop. "That's okay. I was just dropping off your new key."

Pop took it with a frown. "Your father hasn't been back to the house today. I'll bet my false teeth he took the other key." He put the key on his rabbit's foot key chain and shoved it down deep into his pants. The bulge it created made me grimace.

I shrugged. "If he did, I can't figure out why. None of the rink's money was taken." Figuring out my father would take a team of well-trained therapists years. I'd had only a few days.

"Well, let me know if you find him. I've got a pair of cuffs with his name on it."

"Sure thing."

Pop and I walked out, got in our respective cars, and headed toward town. When I started to turn left on Main Street, Pop honked his horn and gave me a jaunty salute as he drove off to his big gig.

I cruised up and down the downtown streets, looking for signs of my father.

Nothing.

Feeling brave, or at last moderately bored, I cruised up to the highway and did drive-bys of the hotels. No big Spanish dudes in sight. And the clerks still weren't talking. In fact, one guy glared at me and told me the cops had been by. From the angry balling of the clerk's fists, I assumed Sean had made his usual good impression.

I staked out the last hotel for a while with the hope my karma would improve and the big guys would come walking through the door. Two hours later, my armpits were sweaty and my butt had fallen asleep. I decided to end my first attempt at surveillance. Next time, I'd bring a book, a large icy soda, and a big bag of popcorn.

The sky was darkening as I turned off the highway and pointed my Civic back toward Indian Falls. I was feeling a little bummed. I hadn't found the bad guys. Worse, Sean hadn't found them. That meant they were still out there, waiting to make good on their threat. I needed a lead.

A loud crash of thunder made me swerve my car slightly onto the shoulder. I looked up at the sky. No rain clouds in sight. Another thunderclap rocked the air.

I knew that sound.

My head spun around and I surveyed the surrounding fields.

There.

In the distance, a bright burst of light lit up the blackening sky.

Fire. And I was pretty sure it was my father's car I was watching burn.

Seventeen

Pedal to the metal, it still took me almost fifteen minutes to reach the blaze. Every time I thought I was on the right road, a field got in my way. And it was getting dark. I felt like a rat in a maze, looking for the cheese. While hunting for the path to the fire, I hit number five on my phone and connected to the Indian Falls PD. I had their number on speed dial. Not a good sign. Ever.

Roxy's voice got all high-pitched when I reported the fire. She instructed me to stay on the line until help arrived. I did her a favor and hung up. She'd be able to pass the gossip quicker, and I wouldn't be distracted enough to drive into any cows. A win-win proposition.

I screeched to a halt in front of a smoke- and fire-filled field. The car in the center of it looked like it might match the description of Dad's old Skyhawk, but it was hard to tell with so much smoke.

I jumped out of my Civic and took a few cautious steps toward the car. As in the previous incident, the field itself wasn't on fire, only the car.

Sweat from the heat trickled down my back as I took another step forward and squinted to see through the smoky air. The tires had already exploded. And like last time, there was a body in the driver's seat. Probably a mannequin. But *probably* didn't make me feel good about watching the flames burn, whatever was inside.

Stepping forward through the smoke, I put my hands up to ward off the heat. Leaning to my right to get a better view inside the car's window, I choked back a scream. That was no manne- quin. It was a man. And his arm had just moved.

Sirens sounded in the distance, but I knew the firefighters would never get here fast enough to save the guy. My brain made the connection between Stan's sudden absence, the threatening Spanish dudes, and the car. The guy inside might be my father.

Stripping off my shirt, I wrapped it around my hand to act as a kind of oven mitt. Then, before the rational part of my mind could question my actions, I raced forward, grabbed the door handle, and pulled.

The door was locked. I peered into the window and saw the little lock thingy was up. Not locked. Stuck.

I yanked again. The heat from the handle radiated through my shirt, but I wasn't about to let go. I yanked again, this time throw- ing all my weight away from the car.

Oof. I landed on the steaming ground with a thud. Looking up, I saw that the car door was wide open. I scrambled over trampled cornstalks to the car and, ignoring the wave of heat, turned the guy's head to face me.

Not my dad.

Relief shuddered through me. Then I noticed this guy wasn't breathing. Crap. Crap. Crap.

The flames had reached the floorboards of the car and were starting to lap at the guy's pants. Grabbing his arm, I tugged. He slid out of the car toward me. I gripped him around the chest and dragged him out of the car as the car popped and sent sparks flying. I knew we needed to get away from the car before something else blew.

Sweat poured off of my face and chest, and the guy was slick with perspiration or gasoline—I smelled both. Either way, it was like trying to keep hold of a greased pig. Wiping my hands on my shorts, I grabbed hold of him and grunted a lot while dragging him through the rows of plants to the edge of the field.

The man looked to be in his thirties and had medium-length hair, a soul patch, and glasses. And he still wasn't breathing.

CPR training from my summer as an Indian Falls Park District lifeguard took over. I opened his mouth and puffed into it. Breath. I pushed on his chest.

Nothing.

I repeated the process.

Still nothing.

The sirens came closer. Out of the corner of my eye, I could see the lights. Breath. Push. Push. Push. Breath. Push. Push. Push.

Car doors slammed. I heard feet pound against the nearby pavement.

Breath. Push. Push. Push.

"There's a man down. Rebecca, we need you to give us some room." Hands pulled me up and away from the man on the ground. Two guys swooped into the space I had just occupied and took the man's vitals.

"Rebecca?"

No signs of life. They tried the CPR trick on him, too. Except they used four pushes against his chest instead of three.

"Rebecca?"

The paramedics on the ground shook their heads. The guy I had worked so hard to save was dead.

"Rebecca."

I blinked and looked up. Sean was standing there watching me. And for a change, he wasn't angry. He looked, well, freaked.

"Are you going to arrest me?" I asked, sounding like a frog was lodged in my throat. All the smoke I'd inhaled made it difficult to talk.

"Did you set the fire?" Sean asked with a ghost of a smile. Cop humor.

I shook my head. "No, but I saw the explosion as I was driving home from the highway motels. I figure the snotty clerk ratted me out."

Sean's smile grew. "He did. But arresting you for obstruction doesn't have its usual appeal. Maybe another time." I tried to smile, but my lips felt like they were ready to crack.

"Here. You should take this." Sean unbuttoned his shirt and handed it to me.

"Why?" I asked. Then I looked down and about fainted. No shirt. I was wearing only my Pretty in Pink push-up bra.

Yikes. I snatched the shirt and shrugged it on. My fingers struggled with the buttons, but after a few moments I was dressed.

"What did you do to your hand?"

I blinked.

Sean didn't wait for a reply. He took my right hand in his and turned it over. It was red and in a couple of places the red patches were starting to swell. No wonder buttoning my shirt had hurt. The hot door handle had done a number on my fingers.

"Ow," I said. Now that he'd pointed out my burns, I realized several places on my arms and legs were feeling tingly. And not in a good way.

"Maybe we should have one of the paramedics take a look at you." He escorted me over to the ambulance before I could object.

Doc Truman examined me under the ambulance's fluorescent light. His gray hair looked a little like he'd jammed his finger in a light socket. I couldn't blame him. The trauma of trying to save a guy had almost done me in. While Doc did lifesaving stuff all the time, I doubted it involved raging fires in the middle of cornfields. We had both earned the right to looked unhinged.

My pulse was checked and my lungs listened to. Then my wounds were examined while I sat on the back of the ambulance, legs dangling over. Seen under the lights, the angry red color of the burns made me cringe.

"Does this hurt?" Doc prodded at my hand, and I almost hit the ambulance roof.

"Yow!"

"I'll take that as a yes." Doc rummaged through his bag and came out with a syringe. "Why don't we give you a painkiller to help take the edge off. Once it takes effect, I'll clean the burns and bandage them. Are you allergic to any medications?"

"Nope." I scrunched my toes together while staring at the roof of the ambulance. Needles wig me out. I hate them. I watched *Rocky IV* as a kid and almost lost it when the Russian guy got a shot in between his fingers.

"Ouch!" My upper arm stung where the shot had gone in. Doc excused himself for a moment, saying he'd be back when it took effect. I watched him walk over to the firefighters, who had finally put out the blazing Skyhawk. Chuck and Robbie were in the group. No Lionel.

That was strange.

Lionel had been at the only two fires I'd seen in Indian Falls, and he'd gotten there fast.

I leaned forward and looked around. Nope. No Lionel. What did it say about the state of our relationship and what did it say about me that I wanted to cry because I wasn't wearing his shirt?

I looked at the shirt. The polyester material didn't breathe well in the humid night. Still, I was grateful for it. I smiled up at Sean to say thank you, but the words wouldn't come out.

In the haze of smoke and the overwhelming shock of it all, I had failed to notice that Sean was now naked from the waist up. And he didn't look at all like what I'd expected. Almost every time I saw Sean, he was eating an ice-cream cone or a doughnut. I'd assumed that, like most aging high school football stars, Sean had left himself go soft.

I was wrong. Way wrong. Sean was all muscle. Instead of drinking six-packs, Sean had sculpted them on his torso.

Wow. Maybe it was all the drugs that were making me light-headed, but one thing was certain: Deputy Sean Holmes was sexy. Big-time. How creepy was that?

"Okay." Doc came back into view. "The painkillers should have taken effect by now. Let's get those wounds cleaned up."

Sean gave my shoulder a light squeeze. "The fire's out. I've got to go over the scene. Are you going to be okay?"

Was it me, or was Sean acting human? The drugs were really screwing with my perception of reality. But it was nice not to be yelled at for a change. I decided to go with it.

"I'll be fine."

Doc touched a cotton swab to my hand, and I almost took that back. Even with the drugs, treatment was going to hurt.

Sean gave me one more squeeze, nodded at Doc, and went to do his cop thing. Good thing he'd left. The cure was much worse than the injury, as far as I was concerned. I winced, yelped, and almost cried as Doc patched me up. I was a wimp. Worse, I was a wimp who had just been through a traumatic event. Not a good combination.

Thank goodness Doc worked fast. He medicated my right hand, upper right arm, and right thigh and wrapped them in gauze, then cleaned my scrapes and singe marks and patched them with Band-Aids. Something told me I wouldn't want to look in the mirror anytime soon, unless I wanted to go into shock a second time.

Doc helped me ease off my perch on the ambulance. I took a couple of wobbly steps. My legs wanted to go home. In fact, my entire body ached to curl up in bed and sleep for days. My nosy brain had other ideas.

The street and field were aglow with emergency-vehicle lights. I scanned the scene and spotted Sean leaning up against a fire truck, talking to one of the firefighters. Willing my legs forward, I gingerly crossed the fifty or so feet between us. At least that was how many steps I took.

Now that I was closer, I could see the firefighter's face under his big yellow hat. It was poker-playing Chuck. And he didn't look happy. "My guys would never set a fire. You're going to have to look somewhere else."

"Maybe. I don't want my suspect to be one of your guys, but that doesn't mean I'm not keeping all my options open. I need a list of every firefighter who's worked for the Indian Falls FD for the past five years and their whereabouts for both tonight and four nights ago. I want every minute from five o'clock to midnight accounted for. And I want it by tomorrow. Otherwise, I'll start bringing people in for questioning."

I smiled. Here was the annoyingly pompous Sean I'd come to know and expect. It made me feel better. The kind, understanding one had wigged me out.

Chuck looked about ready to commit assault. Not that I blamed him. Still, I figured the town was safer if he was free to respond to fires rather than being in jail for decking an officer.

"Sean, do you need to ask me any questions, or can I go home?" I asked, squeezing in between Chuck and Sean.

Sean frowned. "Shouldn't you go to a hospital?"

"Doc said I didn't have to." At least he did after I said no and started to cry. "I just have to stop by his office tomorrow so he can check my bandages. The burns aren't all that bad." Or they wouldn't be after I took a bottleful of Motrin and got twelve hours of sleep.

"If you can handle it, I have a few questions to ask." Sean guided me away from Chuck. "Let me know if you get too tired, and we'll finish this tomorrow."

He flipped open his cop notebook and asked, "Can you remember what happened?"

Sadly, yes. I walked Sean through hearing the blast and the time it occurred. I figured the department should have that logged in from my call, but you never knew. Then I quickly told him about seeing the man inside move and doing my best to save him. I even mentioned that I'd thought it might be my father. The drugs made me want to share.

"I'm guessing the car door wasn't locked?" I must have given

203

Sean a blank look, because he added, "The driver's side window wasn't broken."

"No, the car door wasn't locked. That's weird, don't you think?"

Sean made a noncommittal grunt and scribbled in his book.

"Do you know who the guy is?" I asked, kind of scared to hear the answer.

Sean shifted uncomfortably. "I'm not supposed to release that information until his family has been notified."

It was a good answer, but I needed to know. "Sean, I tried to save the man and I couldn't. I just—" A wayward tear streaked down my cheek, and my vocal chords knotted. "I want a name to put with the face."

I thought Sean was going to say no. The hard-ass cop version would have turned me down flat. But this version said, "Kurt Bachman. At least that's what the license in his back pocket says. He's not local. Once I confirm, I'll contact the family. He's also probably the guy who stole both cars. Boosted them both, set fire to the first successfully, but got trapped in the car this time or—"

"Or what?"

"Or he committed suicide. That would be consistent with the unlocked door." He gave me one of his stern cop looks. "I trust you'll keep this information under wraps until the official findings are released."

Under wraps, yes. But suddenly sleep didn't sound as necessary as it had mere moments before. I needed to know who Kurt Bachman was and why he'd been in that car. The idea of a guy stealing a car, setting fire to it, and then climbing inside wasn't doing it for me. Nope, my untrained gut was telling me this was more than an accident or a suicide. Kurt Bachman had been murdered.

Doc Truman followed me home, just in case. Chivalry wasn't dead. Too bad it had skipped my generation. I gave him a small wave and headed upstairs. No notes. No bad guys. No break-ins in progress. All good things.

Entering my apartment, I was scorched and sore but incredibly motivated. Time to boot up the computer and see what the Net had on Kurt Bachman.

My Internet search came back with a punk-rock singer, an auctioneer, an attorney, and a couple of accountants. I limited my search to Illinois. A Realtor, a lawyer, and a musician/Web designer.

The Realtor looked to be about a hundred years old. The lawyer didn't have a picture, but according to his site, he had graduated from Iowa State in 1970. I crossed him off my list. I clicked on the Web designer and sniffled. There was Kurt Bachman, alive and smiling. I flicked away a tear and clicked on his bio.

Huh. The guy was thirty-eight years old and had an eclectic work history. He'd drummed for a couple of wannabe cover bands, then given that up in favor of Web design. He'd also moonlighted as a stage tech for a Des Moines community theater group.

I clicked around for a while longer. I couldn't find any connections to Indian Falls or the car thefts. Kurt wasn't a known car thief. At least he'd never been caught. And I had a hard time believing Sean's theory that the guy had been suicidal. Even when Kurt had been having a bad day, his blog read like the *Idiot's Guide to Optimism.* Kurt hadn't allowed comments on his blog, so I couldn't search for responses from any online friends. I was at a loss.

In need of pain relief, I limped to the kitchen, grabbed some Motrin, and washed them down with a large glass of orange juice. The minute the liquid hit my stomach, I realized I was hungry. Hard to believe after everything I'd been through tonight. I slid a bag of popcorn into the microwave and waited for the *ding*. Dinner was served.

I had settled onto the couch when the door swung open. In my drug-induced haze, I'd forgotten to turn the lock. Popcorn flew as I scrambled off the couch, wielding the metal popcorn bowl as a weapon. Heart banging, I waited for a scary criminal to come through the door. Instead, it was Lionel, decked out in a tight-fitting pair of jeans, a black button-down shirt, and a tense expression.

"You scared me." I put the popcorn bowl on the end table. "What are you doing here?"

"*What am I doing here?*" Lionel's expression went from concerned to bewildered to annoyed in about half a second. "First, I get a message from the fire station, telling me there was another fire. Then I get one from Roxy, saying you called in the incident and were at the scene. The last message was from Doc Truman, telling me I shouldn't worry about your injuries."

"And?" I shifted my feet and heard the crunch of popcorn beneath them.

"*And?*" Lionel raised his voice. "And none of the messages were from you. I know we haven't talked about our relationship, but I would think that being in a life-threatening situation would merit a phone call."

"It wasn't my life being threatened." Hmmm. Wrong thing to say. The vein pulsating like a ready-to-strike snake on Lionel's neck was frightening.

"Look," I said, taking a percussive step forward. "You always get a call about fires, and you always show up. After the way last night went, I figured you were taking a break from the strange feature-film turn my life has taken. I wouldn't blame you. I'm not sure I want to be part of my life right now."

The vein in his neck stopped undulating. "I was at the Bloniarz Farm, delivering a breach calf, when the calls came in. I heard my phone ring, but I couldn't answer with my hands jammed up into the cow."

Personally, I could have done without the visual. And I noticed that each word Lionel said got progressively more clipped. Lionel was working on a serious case of pissed. What a coincidence—I was, too.

"I'm sorry I didn't call you. Things were a little busy on my end," I shot back in a not very friendly tone as I waved my arms in the air. "I saw the fire. I called the cops. Then I noticed that this time the body inside the car was real. So instead of calling you and crying on your shoulder, I decided my time would be better spent trying to rescue the guy. And I tried to save him. But I couldn't. He died. And I had to watch him die. And now I can't even figure out why the hell he was in that field in the first place. So if you want to be mad at me, do it somewhere else. I've had enough drama for one night."

A tear leaked out from under my eyelashes, then another. I couldn't help it. A guy had died, and my boyfriend was busy complaining that I hadn't followed dating protocol. Call me crazy, but I was pretty sure the manual didn't cover these kinds of situations.

Lionel seemed to agree with me. Instead of yelling back, he reached over and grabbed the empty bowl. Leaning down, he picked up the popcorn decorating my floor. By the time he'd finished cleaning up, my tears had stopped. Good planning on his part.

He took the bowl into the kitchen. I heard it clatter as he put it in the sink. A few moments later, he reappeared with a large glass of water and the crooked smile that always made my breath catch.

Without a word, he offered me the glass. I took a drink and stepped into his arms.

"Do you mind if I stay here tonight?" he asked, brushing his lips gently against my hair. "Between the death threats and what happened this evening, I don't like leaving you alone."

I settled against him and sighed. "I'd like that."

"Good," he said, guiding me toward my bedroom. "And once we get comfortable, you can tell me why the hell you are wearing Sean Holmes's shirt."

Eighteen

As it turned out, I didn't get around to telling Lionel about Sean's shirt. I remembered the painful process of putting on an oversized Northern Illinois University shirt and a pair of sweats. After that, I must have fallen asleep. The next thing I knew, I was waking up as sunshine crept through the blinds.

No Lionel. But he'd left a note reminding me to see Doc Truman. I was also supposed to call him later.

The Motrin from the night before had worn off, as had the nifty drug Doc had given me in the ambulance. Now that I was drug-free, one thing was absolutely clear: I hurt. Every muscle in my body ached, and the burns were worse. They screamed for attention. Ouch. Action flicks always make being the hero look cool and exciting. Now I knew the truth. Being a hero was painful and a bit of a letdown. Then again, I hadn't really done anything heroic, since the person I'd tried to save had died. Success was probably a really good painkiller.

I took some more Motrin with a glass of juice. Thus fortified, I braved a look under the gauze of my right hand. Yikes. My knees sagged. I leaned against the counter and thanked my lucky stars I hadn't chosen nursing for a profession.

The burns had left my hand looking wrinkly and splotchy. In two places, tiny white blisters looked ready to pop. I shivered and slid the gauze back into place. Doc Truman was definitely first on today's to-do list. Then I'd do my best to figure out why Kurt Bachman had died in Indian Falls.

I took a mildly warm shower, taking care to keep my wrapped hand out of the water. I washed the rest of my injuries gently and rebandaged as best I could. When it was over, I was still in pain but clean. A definite improvement. Pulling on a denim skirt, I rummaged through my wardrobe for a shirt that would cover up the majority of my burns. After shimmying into a black polo shirt, I slipped on my sneakers and headed for Doc's office.

Eleanor Schaffer was manning the front counter as I walked in. She had been Doc Truman's secretary and girl Friday since I was a kid, which was probably how Doc convinced her to work on Sunday. Eleanor had dyed black hair, brightly painted red lips, and a big personality to go with her equally large physique.

I smiled and tried not to remember the time Pop had attempted to get information out of Eleanor. He'd promised to show her a good time. That's when I'd walked in and found Eleanor lounging on this very counter, looking like the dominatrix from hell. Today she was dressed in a breezy blue top and a pair of white pants. Good thing. Dominatrix was not her color.

"Oh, Rebecca." Eleanor squeezed her ample body around the counter and gave me a careful hug. "Doc told me all about last night. I swear I almost broke down and cried when I heard how you tried to save that man. You're a genuine hero. Your mother would have been so proud."

Tears pricked the back of my eyes. "I hope so."

Eleanor beamed. "I know so, honey. And Arthur was busy bragging about your finding both stolen cars."

Great. Once Sean heard about that, the nicer, kinder version of him would be gone forever. "I would rather have found them before they were set on fire," I said with a grimace. The pain in my hand was getting worse.

"Well, you couldn't help that," Eleanor clucked. "Just like you couldn't help finding a man unconscious in that car. Doc did the preliminary part of the autopsy this morning. Poor man. Unofficially, he died of smoke inhalation, but there was a big bump on his forehead. Doc says the bump must have happened just before the guy died. He was probably unconscious during the whole thing. I've always said I want to die in my sleep, but now I'm not so sure."

I blinked. Normally, I had to employ unusual methods to get information out of Eleanor. Almost saving someone had given me a free pass. Strange.

Eleanor's excited monologue had confirmed one thing: Sean was definitely wrong about suicide. Kurt Bachman had been knocked in the head and was unconscious during the fire. That meant someone had murdered him. And that someone was still out there.

Once Doc examined my burns and gave me a prescription for some happy pills, I motored off toward the drugstore, pondering the strange turn my life had taken. I'd been so busy tracking down leads and training my new manager that I hadn't had the chance to do anything normal—like celebrating finally selling the rink. I wasn't even sure I felt like celebrating. Not that I wanted to keep the rink. I was on emotional overload. Once my dad turned up and people stopped setting fire to things, I'd be ready to celebrate my good fortune.

The store was blissfully empty, so I didn't have to recount last night's adventure to the patrons. Still, I had to tell Lenny Bemis, the pharmacist. Lenny had graduated the year before I got to high school. The minute he got his pharmaceutical degree, he moved back into his mother's basement and resumed his duties as president of the Indian Falls *Star Wars* Fan Club. Hearing about my strange evening was big excitement for Lenny.

Pills in hand, I headed out of the store and back to the parking lot. As I rounded the corner, I heard my father's voice yell, "Leave me alone." He sounded scared. Stan was never scared.

Feet flying, I raced into the parking lot. The big Spanish guy from the rink lot was back. And he'd brought friends—four of them.

The guy who'd threatened me waved his arms in the air at my father. His face was so red, it looked ready to pop. The four shorter guys next to him were nodding. The shortest of them was holding some big metal object that looked like a torture device.

Not sure what else to do, I charged.

"Hey," I yelled. "Leave him alone."

The five big men turned toward me. I stopped dead in my tracks. Okay, charging five angry guys hadn't been one of my better ideas. Now I had their attention squarely on me.

"What do you want?" I asked, trying not to sound terrified. On the inside, I really wished I were cowering under a bed.

The big dude from the other night yelled something at me in Spanish. I shrugged and turned toward the other men for a translation. They all looked at me blankly. I guessed none of them *habla*'d English.

The big dude said something again, put his hand in his pocket, and came out with a really long wire. The second guy pulled out some kind of wrench. The third and fourth pulled out other metal things and began waving them in the air at me. Then they all started yelling at once.

Stan gave me a wild-eyed look. Then he turned and ran. It took a second for the gang in front of me to realize he had gone. With a shout, the shortest guy whacked the big guy in the arm and pointed down the street. The big guy yelled something else and the four little guys pounded the pavement after Stan.

The big guy didn't move. He stared at me in a way that made my spine tingle. It was hot as hell outside, so no one was roaming the streets. And none of the businesses was crazy enough to forgo air conditioning and open their windows. I realized no one would get here fast enough if I screamed for help.

I clutched the bottle of pills and prepared to launch a surprise attack if the guy charged. But he shook his head and turned away from me, muttering something else I couldn't understand. Then he raced after his compadres, leaving me alone and wondering what had just happened.

For a second, I considered chasing after them. Then I came to my senses and called Sean. He answered after only one ring and asked how I was feeling. Sean was still in nice mode. I gave him a rundown on this morning's events. Then I described the guys who had chased after my father and the direction they had all run in. Sean told me not to worry and disconnected.

Chewing my bottom lip, I got in my car. Despite Sean's self-assured tone, I was seriously disturbed. Stan was being chased by a small but angry mob. Sure, the guy had ditched me years ago, but I didn't want him beaten like a piñata.

I revved up my car's engine, hit the gas, and followed in the direction my father had taken on foot.

Nothing.

No Stan. No bad guys. Just Sean's cruiser coming up the street toward me. It was reassuring to know Sean had moved so quickly. I waved at Sean as our cars slowly passed. He waved back and shrugged. He hadn't seen the guys, either.

After driving up and down the streets for a while longer, I steered my car toward the rink. Pulling into the parking lot, I scanned the area for the angry quintet. None of them was here. Weird. Not that I wanted them here. Personally, I would have been happy if they decided to move to Greenland. But up until today, all their intimidation had been directed at me. First the wire dude, then the two guys looking for me but running into Pop, and, finally, the threatening note. The whole thing with Stan might have made sense had they not run after him. I, the object of their escalating intimidation, had been standing right in front of them and they'd left. Why?

When I walked into the rink, all thoughts of the Spanish guys and my father's plight flew out of my head. The place was going wild. A strange synthesized version of Bizet's *Carmen* was pounding out of the speakers. A dozen kids were jumping up and down on the sidelines, screaming. Parents were trying to get their offspring under control, which only added to the chaos. And that was nothing compared to what was going on in the center of the rink.

A dozen women dressed in hot-pink spandex, silver elbow pads, and silver-pink-and-black-striped helmets were zipping around the rink on speed skates. One chick, who looked more like a linebacker than a lady, flung out her arm and clotheslined the girl trying to pass her. That girl went flying face-first into the wall. Another one skated around a couple of high school students. Then she made a beeline for the linebacker. She squatted on her skates, stuck out her leg, and tripped the linebacker, sending her skidding to a halt right on her ass. Meanwhile, in the center of the rink, George was blowing his whistle so hard, it looked like his head was going to explode from the pressure. Only no one could hear him.

I scrambled through the sideline mayhem and into the sound booth just as one of the spandex gang was shoved toward the sidelines. One moment she was on the rink, the next minute her face was smashed into the glass window. Right in front of me. She slid out of view, leaving a wet lip print behind.

Yuck.

Before another skater put her lips on my glass, I killed the power on the stereo. Then, grabbing the microphone, I hit the On switch.

"Open skate is at noon. Any skaters who are not here for private or group lessons will leave the floor immediately. Or I will call the cops." I didn't think Sean could take the insane speed skaters singlehandedly, but he had a gun. That counted for something.

My announcement worked. The pink ladies whizzed off the floor, leaving George looking dazed and confused in the middle of the rink. After exiting the booth, I reassured the parents that class would begin immediately. That handled, I turned and faced roller skating's answer to the Dirty Dozen.

"Thank you for clearing the floor."

The linebacker chick pulled off her helmet and shook out a large mane of streaky blond hair. "Are you in charge?"

I nodded.

The woman held out a callused hand. "I'm Typhoon Mary, captain of EstroGenocide."

I had no idea what to say to that. I just smiled and let her shake my hand.

Mary shook it hard, then grinned, revealing two gold caps on her bottom front teeth. "This is a great rink. Our team has been looking for a new home since our home rink asked us to relocate. Yours would be perfect."

"Perfect for what?"

"Roller derby." The women behind Mary nodded their Technicolor helmeted heads. I must have looked at her blankly, because she added, "It's a sport. Team against team. Each team needs a home rink to practice and hold meets in. We'd like it to be yours."

Okay, I knew what roller derby was. Sort of. At least I'd seen Hollywood's take on the sport. Yet full-contact sports on hardwood floors wasn't something that appealed to me. Contrary to recent events, I liked my health. Normally, I didn't do much to jeopardize it. Roller derby looked like a good way to get dumped by your health insurance provider—fast.

"This rink has always been focused on artistic and family skating." My professional translation of "No way in hell."

Mary nodded. "Roller derby is a great way to bring in new clientele. Rinks that have derby teams have seen their profits rise significantly. More people means more lessons and more concession sales. Concession items sell big during derby meets. Something about watching violence builds up an appetite."

216

Maybe it was the pain pills, but Typhoon Mary was making sense. The new owners would no doubt appreciate a profitable addition to the balance sheet. Still, I had one question. "If you are so great for business, why did your last rink dump you?"

"There was a personal conflict."

"You didn't get along with the owner?"

Mary threw back her head and laughed. It was a deep, throaty sound, one that could bring in serious cash in the phone-sex business. "Actually, Kandie Sutra got along great with the owner. His wife found out and made him choose between the team and a divorce. Guess he decided losing us wasn't as bad as losing half his stuff."

Made sense.

"Look." Mary gave me a no-nonsense look and propped one hand on her hip. "We need a rink to skate out of. We'll pay our practice fees on time and cover any damage that might happen. The big stunts we use for exhibitions are staged, so that rarely happens. But the best stunts sometimes go awry. It doesn't matter how much you practice. I tried explaining that to your manager, but the kid didn't want to listen."

"You talked to Max?"

"Young kid, about so tall?" She held up her hand slightly over her head. "Dark hair?"

"Sounds like Max. He didn't like the idea of roller derby here?" Max was a guy who liked action. From what I'd seen, roller derby had plenty to spare. Heck, he could even make a movie about it. What was the problem?

Mary shrugged. "He got into it at first. Until I explained about the stunts. Then he got all holier than thou, saying my team shouldn't be doing stunts if we couldn't control them. Then he stormed away. I thought if he saw us in action, he'd understand, but he didn't stick around for the show."

Huh. "Max will come around. He's young and a little excitable, but he's a good guy." I looked out at the class of students on the rink and sighed. "Did you have a chance to talk to George? He'd have to be on board."

"The hottie teaching the class?"

I checked twice to make sure George hadn't morphed into Brad Pitt. Nope. George was still George. "George is the rink's primary private teacher," I explained.

Mary nodded. "He told me. Said he wouldn't mind drumming up some new students and maybe being part of an exhibition match. He can't be a real part of the team, considering he's not a woman."

I'd always thought the rink was in danger of losing George to the Ice Capades or something equally as exciting. If roller derby would keep him here, I was willing to give it a go.

"Okay. The rink might be changing owners soon, but I, for one, would be happy to have your team call the Toe Stop home."

The team let out a cheer and started doing some kind of shoulder-slapping ritual. Meanwhile, I wondered if I would come to regret the decision. Derby might mean money, but with names like Typhoon Mary and Kandie Sutra, there was bound to be drama. Lots of it. At least I'd be around for only the first few weeks. Then the new owner would inherit whatever windfalls and disasters EstroGenocide would bring.

Mary agreed to stop by the office after lunch to book practice time and explain the special floor they'd use for meets. She then skated off with the team toward the women's rest room.

George was giving his class a five-minute bathroom break. All the excitement must have shaken up their bladders. So I verified that he was okay with roller derby taking up residence at the rink. He gave me a cheesy smile and a thumbs-up while his eyes took on a faraway, glassy appearance. Something told me George was dreaming of glory in pink spandex and false eyelashes.

When George regained focus, I asked, "Have you seen Max?"

George dropped the smile and scowled. "He was twenty minutes late this morning and looked like he'd just rolled out of bed. Then when the roller derby team tried to explain their sport, he stomped out in a huff. If you ask me, the kid isn't management material."

Maybe not, but I needed him. And he wasn't answering his cell phone.

I left George in charge of scheduling practice times with Estro-Genocide and headed out to look for Max. I figured that maybe in the process of searching, I'd run into my father. Not knowing where he'd run off to or if he was safe was eating at me.

My first stop was Something's Brewing. Max's father might know where he'd gone off to, and I could get a shot of caffeine. Multitasking at its finest.

Sinbad was behind the counter as I strolled in the door. He gave me a tired smile and began pouring skim milk in a stainless-steel pitcher.

"A large cinnamon latte, right, Rebecca?"

"You got it," I said as a tug of small-town belonging made my throat tighten. No one in any of the Chicago coffee shops ever remembered my drink of choice, let alone my name. I'd thought I liked the anonymity of the city. No one knowing your business was a good thing, right? Sinbad handed me an oatmeal cookie on the house while I waited for the espresso to brew. Oatmeal cookies were another one of my favorites. Munching, I decided privacy was overrated.

"My son likes working for you," Sinbad yelled over the buzz of steaming milk. "I hope he does a good job."

I polished off the last bite of cookie and brushed crumbs off my hands. "So far so good. Although, he left work this morning before I got there and didn't leave a note saying where he'd gone. Do you have any ideas?"

Sinbad frowned. "Max must have gone home to shower and change. Every day this week he has come to work with me in the morning. Then, just before he leaves for his job with you, he makes coffee to take to the rink. Today, he was still asleep when I needed to leave. So his mother brought him here this morning. He did not look presentable for his management position." He poured four shots of espresso into my large cup and reached for the steamed milk. "I tell him you must always look the part of a manager, but he does not listen."

"He wore a very nice suit yesterday," I offered with a smile.

The news didn't please Sinbad. In fact, his frown deepened. "I made him. Managers wear suits. I tell him he will only get the respect that comes with his position when he earns it."

A suit at the Toe Stop was more likely to earn you a hot dog upside the head than any kind of acknowledgment of authority. But I wasn't about to tell Sinbad that. He might not give me any more free cookies. Besides, Max was an adult. He'd fight this battle himself.

However, remembering my promise to Max, I assured Sinbad that Max was doing a fabulous job no matter what he wore to work.

Sighing, Sinbad made change for a twenty and passed over my latte. "I appreciate your kind words, Rebecca, but I know my son.

I hope you will have patience. He needs to grow up and learn life is not like the movies he dreams of."

"I could never replace Max," I said emphatically. It was true—no one else would take the job.

I headed out, with Sinbad trailing behind me, giving pointers on dealing with his kid while I pretended to listen. Suddenly, a black car with shiny hubcaps and a black cloth top went whizzing by. The driver was going way over the speed limit. The car had come and gone before I could make out how many people were in it. More than two. It could have been the men threatening me and my family.

I turned to ask Sinbad if he had gotten a better look. He looked as if he'd been socked in the gut. His mouth was slack, and his eyes were bulging.

"Are you okay?" I asked, putting my hand on his arm to steady him.

"Call the sheriff," he said with a croak.

I was more inclined to call Doc Truman. Sinbad looked like he was having a heart attack. "Why the sheriff?"

He took a step forward, pointed down the street, and yelled, "That was my car. Someone has stolen my car."

Nineteen

My fingers hit Sean's number on speed dial. Calling him multiple times a day was becoming a habit. I didn't even cringe while waiting for him to pick up.

I got Sinbad seated inside and sucking down a glass of water. Then I hightailed it to the tiny parking lot behind the store to make sure the car wasn't where Sinbad parked it every day. No car. Just a small wet mark on the ground. The perps had probably let the air conditioning rev up before peeling out. The car was black and the sun was really hot. That's what I would have done.

Back inside, I paced the hardwood floor, waiting for Sean to arrive. Five minutes later, he strolled in the door, eating a croissant.

Sinbad stood up and shook his fist in the air. "My car has been stolen, and you stopped for breakfast? Do you know what I paid for that car?"

Everyone in Indian Falls knew what Sinbad had paid for it. He'd gotten a very good deal on a special edition Impala at Jake's

Car Emporium. Jake had ordered the car for his father, but his dad racked up his third DUI charge the day the car came in. Needless to say, Jake's dad lost his license. Jake was stuck with the car for months, until Sinbad made him an offer he wanted to refuse but couldn't. Three weeks ago, Jake had been telling everyone in the county how Sinbad had cheated him. Sinbad happily told them by how much.

Sean didn't rise to Sinbad's bait. He just flipped open his cop book and asked, "When was the last time you saw your car?"

"At six-thirty, when I got to work." Sinbad's skin reddened. He began to pace the hardwood floor. "I parked my vehicle out back, like always, and some dirty thief came and stole it while I was earning an honest living."

One could have argued that charging four dollars for a cup of coffee was far from honest, but this probably wasn't the time.

"Who did you see in the shop today?" Sean asked while scribbling in his book. "Anyone who might be holding a grudge?"

The question didn't sit well with Sinbad. He huffed and pointed a callused finger at Sean. "I run a reputable business. No one has a reason to feel disserviced here."

I decided to wade into the fray. "Sean wasn't implying your customers would be unhappy with your service." I waited for Sean to agree with me. The look on his face said I'd be waiting until pigs took wing and hell had a snowstorm. Great. "Could there be someone who has a personal problem with you? Maybe someone who sold you the car?"

Sinbad shook his head with a proud smile. "No. Jake was angry about the price, but he did not get cheated. I paid exactly five hundred dollars above what the dealer pays for the car. I did not want to be swindled, but Jake is in business to make money. He said a lot of angry things, but he came here to thank me yesterday. Jake sold seven cars this month to people who believed he was not a good negotiator, and he made a lot of money on each one."

So much for that theory. Not that I actually thought Jake had repossessed the car. I was hoping that Sinbad would get the idea and offer up a few more suspects for Sean to run down.

Sean gave me a superior smile that said, Watch this. He turned to Sinbad and asked, "Do you remember who came in for coffee today?"

"Of course I do." Sinbad puffed up his chest and listed off a dozen names of people who'd picked up prework coffee. Which meant they all had alibis.

Sean asked a few more questions and assured Sinbad he would find his car. Probably up in smoke. At least, that was the trend. Then again, this car was shiny and new. Either the thief had started a new trend or this was someone different.

Sinbad went to the counter to call his insurance company. Sean and I walked out to the sidewalk. His squad car was parked behind mine, right in front of a fire hydrant. I gave the hydrant a deliberate look and glared at Sean.

He just smiled. Who was I going to report him to? Sean wasn't about to write himself a ticket just to amuse me.

I decided to switch topics. "Did you find any sign of my father or the guys chasing him?"

"No. Annette said she saw a couple of the guys running past the salon but didn't think much of it. No other sightings."

"Maybe they decided to get out of town and used Sinbad's car to make a getaway?" I floated the idea aloud, even though it didn't feel right. If the men were staying by the highway, they had to have driven here. Why would they steal a car to get back?

While I had problems with the idea, Sean didn't. His eyes brightened as he snapped his little black cop book closed. "I'll let you know if I get any information on your father. Just make sure you're careful. Someone threatened your life. You're lucky those guys didn't decide to chase you instead of your father."

No kidding.

Sean folded himself into his cruiser and drove off in search of bad guys. I got in my car and chugged toward Max's house, hoping that maybe Mrs. Smith would know where her kid had gone.

Max lived with his parents on the east side of town, right next to the high school grounds. When reading his work application, I knew exactly which house was his. It used to belong to the family of a kid named Ralph. Because of his name, his lack of fashion sense, and his scholastic aptitude, Ralph was more often than not chased home by the dumber but more physically fit members of the wrestling team. Personally, I'd liked Ralph. In kindergarten, we'd bonded over our lack of coordination. I cheered the loudest when Ralph finished his valedictory address before heading off to Harvard on a full scholarship.

Sometime after my high school experience, Sinbad had moved into Ralph's old house and painted it a very neon yellow. I pulled into the driveway and put on a pair of sunglasses to shield my eyes from the color. Astronauts on the space station could see Sinbad's house even on the cloudiest of days.

Yellow and red flowers lined the sidewalk up to the front door. I rang the bell and waited. No one answered, but there was shuffling on the other side.

"Max?" I asked in my most authoritative tone. "Are you in there?" More shuffling. "If you don't answer the door, I'm going to assume a burglar is inside and call the cops."

That did it. The yellow-and-white door swung open. Max appeared in a rumpled long-sleeved turtleneck. He had bags under his eyes, stubble on his chin, and his hair looked as if he'd spun on it while he slept. Max was a wreck.

"Are you sick?" I asked, talking a tiny step backward.

Max shook his disheveled head. "No. Maybe. I didn't sleep well last night. It all caught up with me at work, so I decided to leave before I made another mistake."

At least Max had figured out his yelling at the derby team was uncalled for. Still, I said, "You should have called me or left a note. When you didn't answer your cell, I got worried and went to see your dad."

Max winced. His olive skin went pasty white. "You saw my dad? Is he really mad?"

I shrugged. "He wasn't thrilled to hear you'd disappeared, but he's not likely to give you a hard time about it. He has other things on his mind. His car was just stolen."

"His car was stolen?" Max knees sagged, and he hung on to the door frame for dear life.

"The two of us were outside the coffee shop when the thieves sped by."

Max's skin turned a strange shade of gray. Not an improvement.

"Don't worry about the car." I used my most confident voice but prepared to catch him if he fainted. "Deputy Holmes is working the case now."

"Deputy Holmes? My dad talked to Deputy Holmes?"

I risked contamination and patted Max on the arm. He was shivering, despite wearing a high-necked shirt in the middle of a heat wave. He probably had a fever. "You really don't look well, Max. Maybe you should go back to bed."

The kid looked back into the house and nodded. "You're right. I'm sorry about work today. I promise to be there on time tomorrow, and I'll even stay late if you want. My dad will be really angry if I lose my job."

Max's issues with his dad made mine seem almost minor by comparison. Then again, he knew where his dad was at this very moment. That counted for something.

"Don't come back to work until you feel better," I said with a smile. "We'll get by without you. Have your mom give Doc Truman a call."

"Sure." Max gave me a brave grin, said good-bye, and closed the door. I started to turn, then paused. Max was talking to someone inside. I couldn't make out what he was saying, but it didn't sound happy. Maybe he was telling his mother about Sinbad's car. But if Mrs. Smith was home, why was a very sick Max answering the door?

While I was vaguely worried about Max and his illness, I had bigger problems. Like my missing father. When I got back to my office, there was still no Dad and no message from Sean. Plus, the fact I was interested in hearing from both was more disturbing than I cared to admit.

Since Max wasn't going to be around for a while, I dived into the pile of work I was planning on using to train him. Ordering pizzas and popcorn oil wasn't all that exciting, but it kept my mind occupied while eating up a bunch of time and it made me feel useful—something you definitely didn't feel when waiting around for missing relatives to turn up.

I was scribbling my name onto the last payroll check when Pop stuck his head into the office. "Doc told me you were okay, but I had to come over and see for myself. You're big news at the center."

Just what I'd always wanted.

Pop walked in and leaned on the desk. His eyes dropped to my bandaged hand. A frown puckered his already wrinkled face. "Are you really feeling okay?"

I touched his arm and smiled. Pop liked gossip as much as any Indian Falls senior citizen, but he loved me more. It was a fact of life I counted on. "I'm a little singed, but basically fine."

"Doc said almost those exact words. He was a real attraction this morning when he stopped by to give Ethel a new prescription." Pop's eyes twinkled with excitement. "Everyone wanted to know the scoop. Once they heard you were involved, they looked to me for information. I played it close to the vest and kept my mouth zipped." He made a zipper motion across his mouth and pursed his lips together.

"You hadn't talked to me, so you didn't know anything," I reminded him.

"Yeah, but the folks at the center don't know that." He flashed his very white false teeth. My grandfather bleached daily. "I have a reputation for knowing what's going on in this town. Especially when it involves my granddaughter. How would it look if I showed surprise at hearing you'd rescued a guy from a blazing vehicle last night? I don't want people to think I'm a neglectful grandfather."

"You are the best grandfather a girl could ever want," I said, feeling teary. "I should have called you this morning to let you know I was okay. I wasn't thinking clearly."

Pop held my good hand in his. "It's okay. Although I wish I could have seen the fire. Doc said your father's car went up like a torch."

I swallowed hard. "When I saw the car and the guy inside, I thought it was Dad. I thought Dad was going to die."

My grandfather's hand tightened on mine, and I squeezed my eyes shut in an effort to fight back the tears. I lost.

"This is stupid," I said, opening my eyes. Reaching for a tissue, I tried to dislodge the strange daughterly feeling taking root. "Even when Stan was here, he was never much of a father. The one time he remembered to come to my school play, he sold my principal skin-care products that turned her purple. He never cared about me. So it's stupid for me to cry over him. Right?"

I waited for Pop to agree with me. To hear him call Stan every name in the book. But he didn't. In fact, he was looking sad and more than a little conflicted.

"Rebecca." Pop perched himself on the corner of Mom's old desk. "Your father is a horse's ass. He's a cheat and a con artist. More than once I wanted to take off my belt and give his behind a lesson he'd never forget. But—"

But? What but? Pop was on a roll. I was remembering why I didn't dwell on my lack of father-daughter bonding. That was good. No buts.

"But your father loves you." Pop's clenched jaw spoke volumes about how much it cost to admit that. And he wasn't done. "When you were born, Stan hated letting you out of his sight. He had dozens of pictures in his wallet. Even stopped traveling for months at a time so he could be home with you."

Mom had always claimed my father loved me, but I figured her speeches had more to do with Oprah's show on improving teenage self-esteem than with Stan's true emotional state. Hearing my father's archenemy confirm it was a little surreal.

"Then what changed? He left us without a word and has been missing for most of my life. That doesn't sound like unconditional devotion to me."

Pop shrugged. "Just because he loves you doesn't mean he can change his nature. And it's in his nature to be a wart on my hairy ass."

Ick. Thinking about my grandfather's hairy behind was enough to scare me out of my wistful mood. Still, I had decided something. When Stan surfaced, maybe we'd talk about our past nonrelationship. Maybe we'd find a way to act like father and daughter. The combo of fear and sadness was enough to make me want to try.

I stood up and kissed my grandfather's stubbly cheek. "Thanks, Pop."

"No problem." Pop stood upright, grinning. "That's what grandfathers are here for. That reminds me. I do have one question I'd like you to answer before I go."

I raised an eyebrow, wondering what piece of my parental past he wanted to delve into. My reality had gotten really skewed when Pop wanted to talk about feelings. I clasped my hands and waited.

"Did you really have a high-speed chase with the guys who stole Sinbad's car? I have it from three different sources that you did. Bingo is going to start in another hour, and I gotta have the dirt."

After Pop got all the details, he bopped out of the rink, excited to spread gossip to friends and fans alike. Meanwhile, I was still feeling guilty for making him worry in the first place. I should have called.

That reminded me: If I didn't call Lionel, someone else would.

A lot had happened since last night's fire. Third-person news didn't set so well with him, so I punched his number into my cell and waited to get chastised.

Voice mail.

I did a little happy dance for my luck. Normally, voice mail was frustrating. I rambled and in general felt like a complete nitwit. Today, I was willing to put aside my prejudice against technology. The details of the morning were related. A slight sniffle might have been audible at the part where I talked about Stan's disappearance, but otherwise I thought I sounded okay.

That finished, I grabbed my purse, waved to George, and hit the road. I wasn't sure if the car thefts, subsequent explosions, and my father's disappearance were linked, but I needed to explore the possibility. I motored over to the scene of last night's car fire, figuring maybe there was a clue there that would help me put both cases to rest.

The field was scorched but empty when I arrived. No police. No torched car. There were a couple of guys working the field to my left and a few guys mending a fence in the distance. None of them was close enough to chat with. Just me communing with nature.

I walked to the center of the blackened field, trying to ignore the smell of burned rubber mingling with overcooked soybeans. The odor brought back memories from last night, which I pushed away. Crying wasn't going solve my problems. Shaking my head, I did my best television-cop impression and walked the crime scene in search of clues.

Like the last car fire, this one had left all but a small area of the field untouched. Green flourished all around me, minus the sections where the firefighters had stamped down the plants beyond saving. Wait. One other spot was just as trampled, and it wasn't anywhere near where the emergency crews had operated. Weird.

Wiping my sweaty brow, I crossed the field to a spot about fifty feet away from where the car explosion had taken place. A guy working in a field across the way waved. I waved back and stared down at the decimated vegetation. Six parallel lines of smashed foliage looked up at me.

If I'd had to guess, I would have said a car or three had driven here. Rewinding my memory, I confirmed none of the emergency vehicles had been in this area. Which meant someone else had. Who?

A welcome breeze rippled across the field. I turned to face the wind, letting it cool off my face, and spotted something small and gray stuck in the vegetation. Kneeling down, I snagged the thing with my fingers and gave it a squeeze. Spongy. The thing had a hole on one end and easily fit my thumb. It was either the most boring finger puppet ever or a new dishwashing device. Neither option was very helpful in finding the pyromaniac and bringing him to justice. Still, I pocketed the gray sponge and stamped down plants, looking for more clues.

There were some burned rubber bits from the exploding tires and a few pieces of blackened fabric and plastic. Sean must have done a good job of collecting evidence, I thought. Either that or there was nothing to find.

Hoping Sean was on his way to pegging the killer, I cranked the air conditioning to high and steered back toward town. While my body returned to a nonbroiling temperature, I contemplated what I'd found. The little gray thingy wasn't high on my clue me-ter, but the tire tracks were. No farmer would park his car on a crop. Kids might have done it, but the damage looked recent. The squashed vegetation was still green and flattened. The activity in nearby fields made it unlikely kids would hang out there during the day. Any farmer worth his job title would run them off or call the cops.

I turned the wheel and coasted into the Sheriff's Department's parking lot. Sean and Sheriff Jackson were nowhere to be found. However, Roxy was hard at work flipping through a *Cosmopolitan* magazine. Her bare feet were propped up on the counter. Cotton balls were wedged in between each toe as she carefully applied a sparkly pink polish. Beach Boys music poured out of the radio sitting nearby.

I squashed the urge to yell "Fire." Watching Roxy try to save both her pedicure and herself was tempting, but I needed information more.

Next time.

"Hey, Roxy. Are you busy?"

Roxy jumped. The glossy magazine careened to the floor, and her hand flew out of control. Next thing I knew, a streak of sparkly pink trailed up her leg. I smiled. Almost as good as the fire drill.

Roxy eye's narrowed as she considered her polished leg. With one perfectly manicured hand, she whacked the radio's Off switch and glared at me. "What do you want, Rebecca?"

Good question. "Do you know if Sean has any news about my father?"

Roxy's eyes softened, and I felt the kernel of hope I'd been harboring fade. When Roxy was kind, good news never followed. "Sorry, Rebecca. Deputy Sean and Sheriff Jackson have been all over town trying to find your father and the men who chased him. No luck."

Knowing it was coming didn't make it any easier to hear. I shoved the unhappy feelings to the back of my brain. I'd deal with them later. Or not.

"How are you feeling? Deputy Sean said you got burned while trying to rescue that poor man."

Somehow I'd forgotten the burns and the pain that went along with them. Now that Roxy had mentioned them, the pain was back full force. "I'm fine," I said, trying not to wince. While Roxy was still in sympathetic mode, I changed the subject. "Do you know if there have been any complaints from farmers about kids parking in fields? I know that can sometimes be a problem."

Roxy grabbed a tissue and a bottle of nail-polish remover. "Not that I know of. Last year, it was a big problem. The kids wanted to create a new make-out spot but were killing crops in the process. Sheriff Jackson didn't want to lock the kids up, so the farmers got together and started their own neighborhood watch. Now the kids just neck behind the bowling alley."

Personally, I was glad they'd chosen the bowling alley instead of the rink. A parking lot filled with steamed-up windows and panting teenagers wasn't my idea of fun.

I said good-bye to Roxy and went back to the Toe Stop for some pain pills and a spot check. "Sweet Home Chicago" blared from the speakers, and kids and parents rolled around the wooden floor. At the far end of the rink, I could see the members of Estro-Genocide lacing up and putting on their gear. The afternoon open skate session would be over in fifteen minutes. Time for roller derby practice to begin.

After returning a few calls and helping with skate returns, I watched my derby girls take the floor. The music had changed to a fast techno song with a lot of bass. George stood on the sidelines, his whistle clutched tightly in his fist. He yelled a couple of pointers to some of the weaker skaters and cheered every time a girl was elbowed into the Crayola-colored walls. Instead of the team getting pissed, they high-fived George and yelled for more advice. By the time I walked out of the rink, George had become the team's new coach. The world was getting stranger by the minute.

I considered going back to my apartment for a nap but then found myself returning to my car. Napping alone didn't sound like fun. Pulling up at Lionel's place, I smiled at the sight of his testosterone truck. Napping with someone sounded way more interesting.

The front door to the house was locked. The sign told me the doctor was in, so I headed down the gravel path to the barn. Elwood greeted me, and I gave his flank a scratch. Today, Elwood was sporting a military camouflage beret.

"Where's Lionel?" I asked.

Elwood turned and trotted down the center of the barn. I followed. The sound of spraying water made me smile. Lionel had installed a full bath in the barn so he could clean up after his messier procedures. By the sound of things, he was currently scrubbing away.

All thoughts of car explosions, scary men, and my missing father went out of my head as I imagined Lionel's well-muscled body lathered up and glistening. I heard the water being turned off, and I waited outside the bathroom so I could jump Lionel when he emerged. The handle turned. The door opened. And I let out a scream.

Twenty

"Dad, what the hell are you doing here?"

Hair dripping, my father smiled. "Hi, honey. I hated leaving you earlier, but I had to get out of there. You understand."

I didn't understand anything, especially why my father was standing outside Lionel's bathroom in a partially closed bathrobe. Black chest hair and wet skin made me avert my eyes. "I've had the cops looking everywhere for you."

Dad retied the bathrobe belt and shrugged. "Guess they didn't look everywhere; otherwise, they would have found me."

My father the comedian. "You disappeared two days ago without a word, and then I see you this morning surrounded by the same guys who threatened me. What the hell is going on?"

"Nothing." My father watched to see if I would let it go.

Nope. I crossed my arms and waited.

A cow mooed. A horse neighed.

Finally, my father said, "I needed coffee and a decent breakfast, so I went into town. Those guys must have spotted me going into the pharmacy for a few personal items. Then you showed up. By the way, you really need to have a conversation with your boyfriend about his shopping list. No bacon or hash browns in his fridge. That can't be healthy. Although I can't complain about the view. There was a blonde dropping off a pony today that was va va va voom, if you know what I mean."

I blinked. Stan had been here this morning for breakfast. That meant he'd stayed here overnight. Who the hell was the blonde? My blood pressure started to rise. "Lionel knows you're here?" I asked, balling my hand into a fist.

"I would never stay somewhere uninvited. I thought about bunking inside the rink, but I'm not much for sleeping on the floor." Stan ran a hand through his wet hair and smiled at something behind me. "Hey, here's my roommate now."

Sure enough, Lionel was standing directly behind me. He didn't look pleased. That made two of us.

"How's it going, buddy?" Stan's voice echoed in the barn's hallway. "I was just telling Rebecca here how good you were to put me up for the past two days. No telling what would have happened to me without you."

Two days?

Lionel shot a dirty look at my father and then gave me one of his smiles. Normally, I found that smile irresistible. Being lied to made me immune. "I think we should have this talk alone."

To emphasize his point, Lionel grabbed the sleeve of Stan's robe and helped propel him down the hallway.

"I can take a hint." Stan gave me a wink. "I'll be in the back room, in case anyone needs me. Lionel has a great setup in there. Could use a softer couch and some import beers in the fridge, but who am I to complain?"

We watched my father disappear into the back room. Then, turning to Lionel, I asked, "You've been letting my father stay here?"

Lionel shrugged. "I didn't know what else to do. He showed up two nights ago, looking for a place to stay. I couldn't tell him no. He's *your* father."

Somehow Lionel made it sound like this was all my fault. "You're right. He's my father. So why didn't you tell me he was staying here with you?"

"He asked me not to."

Wrong answer.

"He asked you not to? I left a message on your phone this morning, telling you how scared I was. And you let me worry even though you knew my father was shacked up in your backroom eating pork rinds and checking out your top-heavy blond clients."

"Okay." Lionel took a step toward me. "I probably should have told you your dad was safe."

" 'Probably'?"

Lionel's left eyebrow twitched. "Definitely. But he said he was worried about you and thought it was best no one knew where he was."

"Why?"

"He said something about being scared the guys who are after you would use him as a hostage. He was trying to keep you safe."

I raised an eyebrow. "Did he try to sell you some swampland, too?"

A slow flush crept up Lionel's neck. "Look, it was late and I was half-asleep when he showed up. I figured you'd thank me for taking him in. So I did. Sue me."

I looked for something to throw at him. Nothing. Unless I

chewed through a wooden beam, which I was almost angry enough to do. "I've been worried sick and you want me to thank you? A decent boyfriend would never have kept his girlfriend in the dark."

Lionel's eyes narrowed. "A decent girlfriend would've pulled the rink off the market and decided to stay here where she belongs."

The rational part of my brain told me to stop now before I said something I would regret later. Unfortunately, Lionel had waved the proverbial red flag. I couldn't help myself. I had to charge. "I was hoping you'd understand that I was selling the rink because I had to. Mom loved that place, and it deserves an owner who feels the same way. Instead of letting me deal with it in my own way, you decided your macho way was right and I was wrong. Well, since we both obviously suck at this relationship, there's only one thing left to do."

I marched down the hallway to the poker room. *The Simpsons* blared from the TV while my father sucked down an orange soda from his perch on the couch. My father's clothes were strewn all over, a pair of BVDs hanging on a lamp. Yuck.

With a flick of the remote, I faded Bart to black. "Come on, Dad," I said, grabbing his duffel bag and shoveling clothes in. "It's moving day."

Dad grunted. His mouth was too crammed with cheese puffs to talk.

I didn't wait for his conversational skills to return. I just grabbed his arm and hauled him to his feet. "Let's go."

We were halfway down the hall when Dad said, "I can't go anywhere. Those crazy Spanish guys will still be looking for me."

"They're looking for me, too. Guess they'll find us together."

My feet kept moving down the barn aisle toward the entrance. The crunching of hay told me my father was following behind. Elwood made a move toward me and then stopped as I kept trucking. I felt a twinge of sympathy for the affection-seeking camel. Then I got angry. Elwood wouldn't be lacking attention if it weren't for Lionel's keeping my father's whereabouts a secret. The man was a menace.

The menace was leaning against my car door as I approached. He gave me a tense smile. "Becky, we should talk about this problem like adults."

He might have been right, but I wasn't feeling particularly adult at the moment. Popping the trunk, I pitched Dad's duffel inside and turned toward Lionel. "Talk to Elwood. You and I have nothing to say to each other."

I got into the car and watched Dad shrug in Lionel's direction. He got into the car as I revved it to life, then asked, "Where are we going?"

Stepping on the gas, I said, "The rink. From now on, you're staying with me."

I should have learned by this point that being impulsive always got me into trouble. At a high school sleepover, I'd accepted a dare to make a snow angel while naked. That got me a trip to Doc Truman's office for a mild case of frostbite in a place I'd rather not mention. This time, my knee-jerk reaction had landed me with my father for a roommate.

"Where should I bunk?" he asked, strolling around the living room. He picked up a framed photograph of Mom and me at high school graduation. "I wish I had been in this photograph. It would have been nice."

That would have required his actually being there. I clenched a fist. "You can sleep in my room. I just have to clean up a bit."

Stan flipped on the television, and I went to relocate my stuff. Maybe it was an extension of my earlier juvenile behavior, but I wasn't about to let him sleep in my mother's bed. He'd lost that privilege a long time ago. The fact that she was no longer in it didn't matter.

Once my clothes had changed closets, I popped some Motrin, left Dad alone in the apartment, and headed back down to the rink, hoping that maybe loud music and hyperactive kids would take my mind off my problems.

For a while, it worked. "Dancing in the Streets" blared from the speakers. The Motrin helped ease the ache in my hands, and scooping popcorn into colorful bags allowed me to take my aggression out on butter-flavored kernels instead of Lionel's head. I had calmed down enough to admit ending our relationship was a bit drastic, but not enough to forgive him for keeping me out of the loop. I needed to scoop a lot more popcorn for that.

One of my teenage employees arrived to relieve me. I headed to my office for some serious investigatory thinking.

"Rebecca."

I looked up and was almost blinded. Pop was decked out in a black pompadour wig and a skintight jumpsuit. Every last inch of it was covered with sequins. Pop looked like the disco ball from hell.

"What's with the outfit?" I asked.

Pop's face fell. "Tonight is the Indian Falls Dinner Dance at the center. That agent is coming to see my act. You didn't forget, did you? You said you were going to come cheer me on."

Damn! I had forgotten. There was even a notice at the front of the rink telling everyone we were, like all other local businesses, closed tonight for the big event. Considering the week's events, it wasn't surprising I'd forgotten. Too bad that didn't alleviate the guilt.

"Don't worry, Pop," I said, forcing a tight smile. "I'll be there. What time do you go on?"

"The gig starts at eight. You and Lionel should come early and get a good spot up front. We're going to have a big turnout. There were even some college kids eating at the diner who wanted to know who could attend. I made sure they knew the whole town was going to be there." Pop shifted from foot to foot, sending his already-sparkly sequins into high gear. I hoped the center had good insurance. Pop's ensemble might cause seizures.

"I'll get there early," I said, thinking, So I can get a spot as far away from the stage as possible. I already had a closetful of imitation Elvis scarves.

Pop nodded, sending his wig slightly off center. I helped him right it and mentioned, "Lionel won't be coming tonight. We broke up."

"What? Why?"

I sighed. "I went over to see Lionel and found Stan coming out of the bathroom in Lionel's robe."

Pop's eyebrows disappeared under his wig. "Lionel's gay? I never would have guessed. He doesn't look gay."

Oops. "He's not gay. Dad needed a place to hide out, and Lionel let him crash in the poker room. Except he forgot to tell me about the arrangement."

"And you're upset about that?"

"Yes." Pop gave me a "You're crazy" look, and I said, "I was worried about Stan. Those guys who came after you were chasing after him this morning. Sean went out looking for Dad, but he couldn't find him. All the while, Lionel knew Dad was safe, and he let me worry for nothing. That sucks."

"I can see how that would set you off. Lionel's a smart guy, but he doesn't have my knack for understanding the opposite sex. That comes with a lot more years of experience."

A half century more. I wasn't willing to wait that long.

Suddenly, I got an idea. If I had to suffer through Pop's gyrations, so did Stan. It was the least he could do for making me worry. Maybe I could make him stand in line for a scarf. That would almost make the evening worthwhile.

"Let's take Stan to your gig," I said with a smile. "He's upstairs watching reruns."

Pop looked like he wanted to ask about Dad's new living arrangements, but he didn't. Pop was right: Years of experience made a difference.

Stan's response to attending the Indian Falls Dinner Dance wasn't enthusiastic, but he reluctantly agreed.

Pop practiced his moves in the living room while I went back to change clothes. I had never attended an Indian Falls Dinner Dance, but I was pretty sure a denim skirt and a polo shirt weren't appropriate attire. I slipped into a black halter dress with a cute flirty skirt and a pair of my highest red heels. After breaking up with Lionel, I felt the need to impress. Problem was, next to the dress, the white bandage on my hand looked conspicuous.

I glanced toward my mom's chest of drawers and took a step toward it. After she passed, Pop packed up a lot of her things and gave them to charity, but a lot remained. After moving in, I'd dusted and straightened this room, but I hadn't been able to bring myself to go through Mom's stuff.

Eureka. The drawer was filled with slips and scarves. Pawing through the silky material, I came up with a black-and-red satin scarf. A little creative wrapping and my arm looked like it was doing a Michael Jackson impersonation. Not great, but better than looking like an unraveled mummy.

In the living room, Stan had changed into his slick salesman look—gray pants, shiny silver dress shirt, and a skinny black tie. He was now giving Pop pointers on how to rotate his hips without dislocating them. Helpful, if not a little strange.

The rink was quiet as our unusual-looking group headed down the stairs and into the warm summer night—and smack into a large group of Spanish dudes.

And they didn't look happy.

Twenty-one

Oh crap. The big guy in front barked something in Spanish at us. Pop looked at me. I looked at Stan. Stan blinked. We were all stumped.

Pop swaggered forward and planted himself in front of the biggest dude. He looked up at him, causing the pompadour wig to slide dangerously backward. He straightened the wig and said, "Get lost or else."

I couldn't help but wonder, *Or else what?* Pop wasn't exactly dressed for street fighting.

A little guy took a step forward and waved a wooden stick in our direction. Another one took a metal ratchet out of his pocket and slapped it against his hand while circling behind us. There were seven of them and only three of us. We were outnumbered and surrounded.

I considered screaming for help, then chucked the idea. Everyone in the rink had gone home or to the dinner dance. I took a step back behind my father. Easing my cell phone out of my purse, I pushed the Sheriff Department's speed-dial number. The beep from the phone made my shoulders tighten as I waited for the men to notice and get really angry.

When they didn't, I asked, "Why do you guys keep coming to my rink?" I hoped my voice was loud enough to reach Roxy or whoever was manning the department's phone. "Please don't hurt my grandfather or Stan. I'll do whatever you want."

At least I would until Sean got here—and that better be soon.

Pop gave me an outraged look and bellowed, "If you want to hurt Rebecca, you'll have to go through me first."

There were seven of them, one of Pop—and he looked like a light breeze would blow him over. Not good for our side.

The Spanish-speaking guys looked at me with a variety of bewildered expressions. Strange. They talked among themselves for a moment, gestured wildly to me, then looked down the street as if worried the cops would arrive.

For the first time, I took a really good look at the group. They were wearing matching red-and-white bowling shirts. My heart rate slowed and I took a deep breath. It was hard to be completely intimidated by a renegade bowling team.

A third guy spoke very slowly, careful to enunciate every word. This time I understood something. "We do not . . . you . . . want—" The rest of the sentence required a Spanish-to-English dictionary. Too bad the library was closed.

I took a step forward and asked, "Does anyone speak English?"

All seven heads shook from side to side. No English here.

Now what?

A blaring siren rang through the warm night. Red and blue lights flashed. A Sheriff's Department cruiser raced down the street and skidded to a stop on the other side of the parking lot.

Under the dim streetlight, we all watched Sean emerge from the car, pull his gun, and run toward us.

"Law-enforcement officer! Everyone put your hands behind your heads."

Pop and Stan complied. The bowling team just blinked.

Sean's eyebrows pulled together, and his hand tightened around the gun handle. "I said—"

"Wait. Wait. Wait." A short, roundish guy sporting a familiar red-and-white shirt raced down the sidewalk, waving his hands over his head. "Don't shoot. My friends will not hurt anyone."

The matching-shirt gang looked relieved. They smiled and hurried over to the newcomer, who was now bent over, panting. There was a shiny bald spot on the top of his head.

"English," one of the men said, pointing to their track star.

"If you speak English," Sean said, gun still at the ready, "tell them they are under arrest for harassment and assault."

The panting guy turned to his friends and rattled something off. They all began talking over one another. Some barked out a few angry words while pointing at Stan.

"Wait," I yelled, stepping in between Sean and the angry red-and-white mob. Looking at the newcomer, I said, "I've been threatened, my grandfather's been knocked over, and my father looks like he's ready to bolt. Can you tell me why?"

The short, pudgy guy sucked in a few deep breaths and nodded. "My friends did not mean to scare you. They came from Moline to find your father. Mr. Robbins said he was coming to see you, so that is where they looked."

All eyes swung to Stan. He was in the process of creeping backward. The minute he spotted us looking at him, he froze and gave his best salesman's smile. None of us smiled back.

"Do you know these guys, Dad?"

My father shrugged. "Could be. I meet a lot of guys on the road. Can't say I remember them all."

"You took our money." The short, pudgy guy stomped his foot and looked ready to launch at Stan. "Now we are here to get what we paid for. If you do not give it to us, I will tell the police officer to arrest you."

Sean lowered his gun a couple of inches and looked back and forth between the angry mob and my father.

"Is this true, Dad?" I crossed my arms.

"Sounds like something Stan would do." Pop stepped away from Stan and aligned himself with his former intimidators. "I should have known he was a thief before my Kay married him. He has shifty eyes."

"I do not," Stan insisted between offended noises. "And I didn't steal their money. I just had to wait a little longer for their order to come in, and Eduardo here wasn't around to tell. The rest of them have some communication problems."

Eduardo didn't look convinced. "You did not answer my messages. After two weeks, my friends decided to come looking for you. We need our order."

Okay, I just had to ask. "What did you order?" Guns? Drugs? Bootlegged DVDs?

"Musical instruments."

That would have been my next guess. "Musical instruments?" I turned to Stan. "Since when do you sell musical instruments?"

My father shrugged. "A friend of mine has a connection in China. He sends me whatever his company has too much of. This time, it was musical instruments—for their mariachi band. But he had trouble with customs, and I wasn't sure the stuff was ever coming."

"You mean you don't have our order?" Eduardo waved his hands in the air. "We need our instruments. We have two gigs next week."

I looked closer at the shirts. On the left shirt pocket there was a picture of maracas. The shirts must be band uniforms, I decided.

My father puffed out his chest. "Don't worry. I got a call this afternoon from my friend and he says the instruments are on their way. You should have them first thing tomorrow morning."

Eduardo translated Stan's words for the rest of the band. The group let up a rowdy cheer and began slapping one another on the back. They were happy. I was confused.

"Wait a minute. You threatened to kill me over a delivery of instruments?"

Eduardo cocked his head to the side. "We did not threaten to kill you."

"Yes, you did. I read the note you left." Sean seized the opportunity to swagger forward and take charge. "You told Rebecca she couldn't run from you. That you were going to kill her."

Eduardo shook his head. "We didn't write that."

Sean stuck out his chest. "I saw it. Whoever wrote the note had terrible handwriting, but I clearly saw the word *muerte*. You're under arrest for threatening Rebecca with death."

Eduardo slapped a hand to his forehead. He turned to the big guy who had threatened me with the wire and began to yell. The big guy hung his head and said something under his breath. I didn't know Spanish, but I recognized embarrassment when I saw it. The big dude looked like he wanted to climb under a rock.

"I am sorry about Miguel's handwriting." Eduardo shot a pitying glance at the slumped-shoulder Miguel. "The word he wrote was not *muerte*. It was *muérgano*. Your father was looking into getting an organ for Miguel's mother. Miguel wanted to cancel the order."

"I wish I would have known that earlier." I turned toward Sean. "All this time, I thought someone was trying to kill me."

Suddenly, Sean developed a rapt interest in his shoes. Go figure.

"Hey, look at the time." Pop lifted his scrawny wrist to display his Timex. "I've gotta get to the center. I go on in ten minutes. You can all come with me if you'd like. It'd be nice to have fellow musicians in the audience."

"Wait." Sean holstered his gun and held up his hand. "There is still the matter of the assault and harassment charges." He turned to me. "Rebecca, you can still have these men arrested."

"No thanks." I shrugged. They had been chasing my father for stiffing them—something I completely understood.

Eduardo smiled at me and translated for the rest of the band. They all nodded. A few said, *"Gracias."*

"You're welcome. But there's one thing I don't understand. If Miguel wasn't threatening me, why did he have a wire in his hands?"

I looked to Eduardo for an answer, but Miguel stepped forward and carefully enunciated, "No wire. Guitar string." Miguel pulled out the same kind of wire I had seen him with before and smiled. Eduardo added, "He carries it in his pocket."

Some people carry keys or loose change. Miguel carted around his guitar strings. Made sense to me. It turned out the other instruments of torture were also musical accessories. Too bad the fiery car case wasn't as easy to solve. These guys were innocent of wrongdoing, but someone in Indian Falls wasn't. I really wanted to find out who.

I turned to Sean. "Guess this was all a big misunderstanding." Sean looked disappointed he wouldn't be making a bust. So I added, "But it might not have been. Thanks for getting here so fast."

Sean shook his head in resignation and headed to his car. We were all free to leave. Since Eduardo and his merry band had nothing better to do, they piled into their car and followed us to the Indian Falls Dinner Dance.

Dinner had already come to an end when we walked into the recreation room. Right now, it looked like a revival of *Grease*. Records dangled from the ceiling. One corner sported a soda fountain, complete with servers wearing white paper hats. The men all looked like they'd combed their hair with a pork chop, and every woman over sixty was sporting a low-cut top and a poodle skirt. I looked out of place in my black cocktail dress and killer stilettos. The mariachi band looked right at home. Go figure.

Pop ditched us at the door to get ready for his set. The band headed for the soda fountain in search of tequila milk shakes, leaving me and Dad alone in the doorway.

He looked at me and sighed. "I made a real mess out of this instrument deal, didn't I?"

"You got out of it," I said. "You always do."

His shoulders slumped. "I didn't intend for things to turn out like this. I meant for the instruments to arrive on time and for my customers to be happy. Things didn't go as planned."

"They never do." Which was how I was back in this town, selling Mom's rink and doing a poor job of solving crimes. "Once the guys get their instruments, everything will be back to normal."

Stan squared his shoulders, took my hand, and said, "Rebecca, I'm really sor—"

"Stan! I've been looking all over for you." A woman I didn't know came scurrying over. Or at least I was pretty sure I didn't know her. What with the poodle skirt, saddle shoes, black beehive hair, and large quantities of blue eye shadow, it was hard to tell. "The music is about to start, and you promised me the first dance."

My father looked at fifties Barbie and back at me with one eyebrow raised. "Go ahead and dance," I told him. We hadn't had a father-daughter chat for almost two decades. What was one more day? The beehive lady squealed and dragged Stan toward the dance floor.

"Well, would you look at that? Your father has moved on to someone else." Doreen stood next to me in her fifties getup and gave a small *tsk*.

"You did, too," I reminded her.

"Had to." She nodded. "Your father is a heartbreaker. Always knows just what a girl wants to hear and says it in the right way. Problem is, he means it when it says it. That's why we all fall for it. He just forgets. Fun for a night, but a lifetime . . . well, you know."

I did know.

Doreen sighed, gave herself a little shake, and said, "I called the rink earlier, but you weren't around."

"I didn't get the message."

"I didn't leave one." Doreen's eyes sparkled along with her glasses. "There is so much bad news in my business. I like to give the good news in person."

"Good news?" After my breakup with Lionel, I could use some.

"I told the buyers you were anxious to complete the sale. Since there is a trained manager in place, they are willing to move back the closing. How does next Friday sound?"

"Next Friday?" The room in front of me spun.

"I knew you'd be delighted. I even made sure they'd give you

252

a couple weeks to move your mother's things out of the apartment. As long as the place is empty by the end of August, there won't be a problem. That's when their renovations begin."

"Renovations?" What renovations?

Doreen nodded. "They're planning on dividing the office/third bedroom into two bedrooms. Oh, and they're going to remove the living room window that overlooks the rink. I can't say I blame them. I like my privacy."

That window was torture as a kid. Mom would watch me like God from above, seeing every mistake in my skating. But the idea of removing it hurt. A lot. My mother had loved it. Maybe, just maybe, I might, too.

"Ladies and gentlemen." A disembodied voice echoed in the hall. "The Indian Falls Senior Center is proud to present . . . Elvis!"

Synthesized music filled the air. Pop strutted out onto the stage in all his glittering glory. A flock of women crowded the front of the stage. Pop gyrated his hips to the right. The women shrieked. He gyrated his hips to the left, and the women went wild. And then he started singing "Can't Help Falling in Love." Next came "Don't Be Cruel," and the hits kept coming.

To say Pop wasn't the greatest singer was an understatement of serious proportions. But what my grandfather lacked in skill, he more than made up for in style. He smiled, he winked, he moved his pelvis in a disturbing manner, and he gave out dozens of scarves. Everyone was so busy fighting over them, they didn't notice that Pop occasionally forgot the words. Pop was a rock star the likes of which Indian Falls had never seen. Who needed talent?

Thirty minutes after Pop started, he strutted off the stage for a break. With my distraction gone, I was left to wonder why I wasn't up dancing with the rest of the female population. The rink was finally selling. My time in Indian Falls was coming to an end. Life was good.

So why did I feel so crappy? Maybe it was like Christmas when I was a kid. I'd get so worked up anticipating the day. Then, when it came, it never lived up to the hype. That had to be it. It wasn't that I wanted to stay in this town and run the rink. No. I'd spent my entire life running from that fate.

Of course, there were the unsolved car thefts and fires. I wanted to know who was behind them. Leaving town before that case was settled felt wrong. Incomplete. Once the thief was put behind bars, I'd be ready to celebrate my return to Chicago. Right?

I smoothed out my dress and started forward, ready to kick up my heels to Frankie Avalon's crooning. Suddenly, my feet stopped moving and my mouth went dry. Standing in the doorway, looking incredibly handsome, was Lionel—and he'd brought a date.

Twenty-two

Lionel scoped the room. His eyes settled on mine as he wrapped his arm around the bottle blonde next to him. No doubt the same blonde my father'd mentioned ogling at Lionel's place. A gray-haired woman near the couple pointed at them. Then at me. A woman next to her clutched her chest and raced over to share the drama with a group near the stage. The Indian Falls gossip train was heading out of the station. Just what I needed to brighten my day.

The blond bimbo smiled up at Lionel and giggled. My stomach clenched. A simmering rage built in my chest. Most women I knew would have wanted to claw out the chick's eyes in this situation. Not me. I wanted to punch Lionel square in the mouth. He had created this drama. The chick was blameless, even if her clothes were tacky. Lionel's date had vacant eyes, big boobs, and a really short skirt. Not his type. Or was she? The way he smiled at her, I wasn't sure.

With the hall buzzing about Lionel's new love interest, I looked around for a safe haven. Jimmy Bakersfield gave me a thumbs-up from across the room. He was surrounded by half a dozen Senior Center women, who were all watching me with knowing smiles.

The mariachi band seemed to be missing in action, but Clayton Zimmerman had sidled up to the soda fountain and was talking to a couple of ladies. Hooking up with the new lawyer in town might help my bruised ego, but the memory of squirrel dust made me think twice.

Bingo. Walking in the door was Sean Holmes. He'd changed clothes since our adventure in the parking lot. Now he was sporting a white T-shirt, jeans, and a black leather jacket. A small bulge under the jacket made me smile. Only Sean would think it necessary to be armed at a dinner dance. I wondered if he'd lend me the gun. Lionel was giving blondie one of his lazy smiles. I decided death was too good for him, so I went with plan B.

Taking a cue from my grandfather's act, I swung my hips into undulating action and crossed the room. I reached Sean, smiled, and pulled his head down for a kiss. It wasn't a great kiss, but I couldn't blame Sean for that. The guy was surprised as hell. So was Lionel. I could see his nostrils flaring when Sean and I came up for air. Score.

"Jailhouse Rock" boomed from the speakers as Pop bopped back out onto the stage. Behind him were three members of the mariachi band, equipped with tambourines, maracas, and castanets. The crowd went wild.

I yanked Sean onto the dance floor and started jiggling, hoping to entice him to play along. Sean gave me a goofy look, shrugged, and cut loose. Wow, could the guy dance. He spun, twirled, and dipped me without causing injury to either of us.

The song ended, and Pop and his backup band began playing "It's Now or Never." I wrapped my arms around Sean before he could bolt. Lionel and his date were still on the sidelines. Lionel looked furious. The girl looked hurt and confused. She was trying to talk to him but was receiving no response.

"So what's the fight about?"

I looked up at Sean. "What fight?"

He laughed. "Doctor Doolittle has his arm around Betsy Moore, and you're coming on to me. I don't mind being used, but I like to know the pertinent facts."

I snuggled closer for the pleasure of our viewing audience. "Lionel and I had a disagreement about my father today. Before we could talk it over, he shows up with what's-her-name draped all over him. He did it to make me jealous. So I decided to return the favor."

Sean cocked his head to the side and nodded. "Sounds about right."

"Really?" I couldn't tell if he was joking. Thank God Sean wasn't in our poker group.

He shrugged. "You don't sit around waiting for situations to resolve themselves. He should know that. Hell, the whole town knows it. It drives me nuts."

"I can't help it."

"I've figured that out." He gave me a half smile. "But that doesn't mean I'm ever going to like you poking into my cases. In fact, I'm surprised to see you here. Aren't you supposed to be staking out nearby fields in case they explode?"

"Tomorrow," I joked. "Tonight I'm doing the supportive family thing."

"Maybe by tomorrow, you won't have anything to stake out."

I peered up at Sean's knowing expression. "What does that mean? Did you find Sinbad's car? Do you have a lead?"

Sean just gave me a smug smile, which I thought was pretty silly, considering my hand was inches from his gun. The song came to an end. Pop's voice disappeared, and Sean pulled me close. He leaned down. His face closed in on mine. I could smell mint. He must have brushed his teeth before coming to the dance. His mouth stopped an inch from my lips, and he said, "I have an arrest to make. Don't follow me, or I'll shoot your tires."

The next thing I knew, the man was across the room and out the door.

Sean had to have known he couldn't drop a bomb like that and expect me to stay put. He'd just finished telling me as much. It had to be a dare. One I accepted.

A few people tried to engage me in conversation as I made my way to the exit, but I was on a mission. Sean thought he'd solved the car theft case before I could. A part of me hoped he hadn't. Call me crazy, but it was my case. If I was finally selling the rink and leaving town, I wanted to do it in a blaze of glory.

My feet hit the hallway as "Viva Las Vegas" blasted through the center. I was almost to the front door when an arm grabbed me.

"Becky, what the hell was that?" Lionel's green eyes blazed in the fluorescent light.

"What was what?" I could see Sean's police cruiser turning from the parking lot onto the street.

"The number you did with Sean Holmes. You hate the guy."

"*Hate* is a strong word." I watched the car turn left and strained to see it as it disappeared out of sight. Drat. Looking up at Lionel, I said, "You're right. Sean and I don't always see eye-to-eye. Today we do."

"What's so different today?"

My first answer was a D-cup blonde in a miniskirt. I went with my second choice. "Until today, I was involved with you. Now that we aren't dating, I thought I'd give Sean a whirl before I leave town."

Lionel dropped my arm as if scalded. "You're really leaving town." It wasn't a question. He was pronouncing a death sentence.

"We close on the rink next Friday," I said, trying to ignore the sick feeling I got when talking about the sale. "As soon as I pack up the apartment, I'm off to Chicago. Then you won't have to worry about my getting in the way of you and your blond girlfriend."

"Well then, I guess I should give you something to remember me by when you're gone."

Lionel moved quickly. One minute, he was standing three feet away; the next, his mouth was on mine. For a minute, I tried to stay uninvolved, but his mouth was deliciously insistent and was causing tiny goose bumps to sprout up and down my spine. So I caved. Yeah, I was pissed at him for trotting out the resident blonde. And I hated that he'd kept my father's whereabouts a secret. But damn, the man could kiss. I wrapped my arms around him as my body tightened and tugged in response while striving for more.

"See, honey, Lionel and Rebecca are still together. I knew you got it wrong."

I blinked as Lionel's warm body stepped away from mine. Beaming at us were Doc Truman and his wife.

"Hi," I said, trying inconspicuously to assess whether my garments were all in the right place. "I didn't see the two of you at the dance."

"You were both busy," Mrs. Truman tittered. She was a birdlike woman with sparkly eyes that matched her disposition. Tittering worked for Mrs. Truman.

Doc smiled down at his tiny blond wife. "Mary came early with the Ladies' Guild. I had to make a trip to the hospital. At least I made it in time for 'Viva Las Vegas.' "

"Hospital?" An image of a trembling Max sprang to mind. "Who's in the hospital?"

Doc waved off my concern. "One of the Finn kids fell off his bike and broke his wrist. He'll be good as new in six weeks."

"You sounded concerned, dear." Mary Truman gave my arm a little pat. "Is there someone you're worried about?"

"My rink manager, Max, went home from work sick. When I stopped to see him earlier today, he was pale and unsteady. I told him to give Doc a call." I turned to the source and asked, "Did he?"

Doc shook his head. "Sinbad's boy? Can't say he did. Eleanor might have answered the phone, but she would have told me about it. I'll drop by his house tomorrow and check on him, if it'll make you feel better."

Small-town hospitality at its finest. It put the big city I loved to shame.

"That's okay. His mother is probably stuffing him with chicken soup and taking his temperature every five minutes."

Doc shrugged. "Well, I'll have Eleanor give his mother a call and see what's what. If the flu is going around, it's best to be prepared. Now, the two of you enjoy your evening and I'll see you both for our game tomorrow."

Hand in hand, Doc and his wife strolled out of the center, leaving Lionel and me alone.

"I should probably get going." I inched closer to the front door.

"And you should get back to your date. She's going to be wondering what happened to you."

A smile tugged at the corner of Lionel's mouth. "I doubt it. When I left, Betsy was flirting with some new lawyer in town. Guess she figured out I was more interested in the floor show than in her."

Something told me Betsy was exactly the welcoming committee Clayton was looking for. I just hoped she had a fondness for stuffed wildlife. Still, as fascinating as Betsy's love life was, I had to get going.

"Look, I'm sorry about tonight. My maturity level hit a new low." Lionel looked ready to delve into deep conversation, so I quickly added, "I really have to go. During my trip through high school behavior, Sean said he was off to arrest someone for the arsons and murder. I don't have an idea where he went, but—"

"You want to find him."

I bit my lip and nodded.

Lionel looked like he was torn between murdering me and giving me a patronizing pat. Before he had to choose, though, his phone buzzed. He looked down at the screen. "Sean is at the firehouse. Come on. I'll drive."

Sure enough, Sean's cruiser, its red and blue lights blazing, was parked behind the building. And chaos was raging inside.

"You are not going to arrest Kevin. If you try, you're going to have to go through me." Fire Chief Chuck was standing in front of an angry-looking surfer guy, whom I vaguely recognized as Kevin. Behind him, rookie Robbie was flexing his muscles and trying to look intimidating.

Sean had his back to us. For the second time tonight, he was brandishing his gun. "Look, let's take this down to the station, where we can talk quietly. I just want to ask Kevin a few questions."

Chuck wasn't buying it. "It's quiet enough here. Ask your questions and Kevin will answer them." Chuck added, "If I think you have cause to arrest Kevin, I'll take him down to the station myself."

That did it. Sean heaved a big sigh and holstered his gun. "We'll do it your way, then."

Chuck stepped aside with a nod. Robbie looked downright disappointed. Kevin ran his hand through his blond mop of hair and asked, "What do you want to know?"

Sean got out his little cop book. He noticed me out of the corner of his eye and smiled. Yep, Sean had wanted me to witness his triumph. "Where were you last Tuesday between seven and nine in the evening?"

Kevin swallowed hard and shot a look at Chuck. He had Guilty stamped across his face, which he was. This was the guy who'd been ditching a night at the in-laws. He was busted.

Sweating, Kevin admitted, "I was at Chuck's house, watching the Cubs game."

Sean's eyebrows rose. He looked at Chuck with a scowl, as if daring him to alibi a guy who was so obviously guilty.

"My wife and son can vouch for him if you need other witnesses." Chuck was all authority. "We got the call about the fire and drove here together."

"Really?" A flush of anger traveled up Sean's neck. "Then why do I have proof that Kevin ordered Safety Zone fire retardant and had it delivered to his house two weeks ago? The same fire retardant used at the site of both car arsons." Sean looked over at me and winked.

I was impressed. This time, Sean had actually done his homework before arresting a suspect. Too bad it was once again the wrong person.

The guilty look left Kevin's face. Now he looked baffled. "You think I bought that stuff so I could set fire to a couple of cars? You're crazy."

"I'm crazy?" Sean's hand reached for his handcuffs. "You're the one who's crazy around here."

"My son had to do a volcano project for summer school, and I wanted to keep my backyard from catching on fire." Kevin's face turned as red as Sean's. "Two jugs of Safety Zone wouldn't have kept those fields from catching. Hell, for the amount the arsonist used, my son and I could have built a volcano like the one in *Dante's Peak*."

Sean said something. Kevin said something else. I didn't hear any of it.

A lightbulb was flickering in my head. A movie. Holy crap! Suddenly, everything made sense. The stolen cars with insurance policies to cover the damage. The care with which the arsonist protected the fields around the fire. The missing rink key. The dead community theater tech guy in a burned-out car. And the tiny gray sponge I'd found in the field. It was a wind protector for a microphone.

I knew who had set the fires. It was someone who had told his crew to look for warehouse space to film scenes. Someone making an action movie. Someone I'd thought was sick, but who was trembling and sad because he had killed a friend. Someone who yelled at a roller derby team about responsibility with stunts because he had failed at one.

Someone named Max.

If I remembered correctly, he was finishing filming his movie this week. My bet was on tonight, which meant Sinbad's car was about to blow. I needed to stop Max before he had the chance.

Sean, Chuck, and Kevin were yelling at one another. Robbie was jumping from foot to foot, as if debating whether to enter the fray. None of them had noticed my Sherlock Holmes moment. I nudged Lionel and hooked my finger toward the door.

We hit the night air, and I started running for Lionel's monster truck.

"What's going on?"

"Sean has the wrong guy, and it's going to take too long to convince him. We don't have the time." I climbed into the truck and strapped in as Lionel swung into the driver's seat. "The right one is going to blow up his father's car tonight. We have to get to the rink. Fast."

"Why the rink?"

"I think Max has been using the rink as a soundstage. The farmers are on the lookout for anything suspicious. So is everyone else. Where is the one place Max can walk around doing whatever he wants without looking out of place?" No one would question why my rink manager was at the rink so late. People would just think he was trying to do a good job. And if he had friends with him, so what? He was a college grad just blowing off steam. It was a perfect cover.

Lionel pulled into the rink's side parking lot, and I hopped down from the truck. All was quiet. Maybe I had misjudged Max. Maybe he wasn't using the rink for his movie.

"All right, everyone. We have only one shot at this. The dance will be over soon. Let's make Kurt proud."

Max.

I took off toward the front of the rink. I could hear Lionel running beside me. Nobody was in the front lot, but I could see some kind of lights glowing on the other side. My heel caught in a pothole, and I stumbled. Lionel's quick hands saved my butt from meeting the ground, and we kept running.

"Action."

We turned the corner and ran into a blinding wave of light coming from the vacant lot between the rink and the neighboring antiques store down the road.

"Stop, Willard. Don't make me shoot you," a chick's voice yelled.

My eyes adjusted to the light. A brunette woman wearing black leather pants, a T-shirt, and a black leather vest was brandishing a gun. A scruffy guy with something clutched in his fist was yelling back. Next to the scruffy guy, looking bright and shiny, was Sinbad's car. A couple of other people scurried around the fringes of the scene, doing God only knows what.

"I can't stop now. I've sacrificed everything for this. My family. My friends. You won't take this from me, too."

"Please, Willard. Don't throw what we have away. I'll make sure you get a fair shake."

Hello, melodrama. I looked around for Max. Squinting, I spotted him far in the distance. He was way in the back of the vacant lot, stationed next to a guy holding a camera.

"Come on." I grabbed Lionel and circled around the now-embracing actors. Either Max had a camera with a great zoom lens or this was a really wide-angle shot. I'd never made a movie, but it seemed to me he should really be closer to the action to be able to hear what was going on. We had to be well over a hundred feet away.

I stepped behind Max and tapped him on the shoulder. He turned.

"Rebecca," Max whispered, casting a nervous look at the camera. "I thought you'd be at the dance with everyone else in town. You're not supposed to be here."

"I thought you were home sick," I said, not caring if my annoyance was recorded for posterity. "I guess both of us were wrong. You need to turn yourself in to the police. They'll go easier on you that way." I pulled my phone out of my purse and hit Sean's speed-dial number.

"And now!" someone to our right yelled.

Now what?

A car door slammed. I looked back to the set, where a guy was frantically sprinting away from Sinbad's car. The next thing I knew, I was flat on my butt. The car had exploded.

Flames lit the sky. Tires exploded, sending sparks and flaming rubber everywhere. *Kaboom.* Another explosion hit, louder and brighter than the first one. Set lights blew, the crew started screaming, and smoke filled the air.

"Cut and print," Max yelled.

Lionel helped me off the ground. I took a step forward as I peered through the flame-lit haze. Sinbad's car was toast. I hoped he had good insurance.

I took a couple of steps toward the fire, and then I saw it. I couldn't breathe. It was as if someone had just sucker punched me.

Max had blown a hole in my rink.

Twenty-three

I sat up in bed and hoped it had all been a bad dream. Nope. I was in Pop's house. That meant everything was horribly real. Crap.

Fire trucks and Sean's cruiser had arrived moments after the explosion. By the time Pop and the folks at the center had tromped over to see the excitement, the fire had been extinguished. After several real fires, our firefighters really knew what they were doing. Practice really does make perfect.

I pulled off the cocktail dress I'd slept in and grabbed the robe hanging on the back of the door. The fake satin had faded to barely pink and the lace trim was coming off, but it did the trick.

Barefoot, I headed to the bathroom. Flipping on the light switch, I choked back a scream. My face had a gray, smoky quality to it. My hair looked like it had been styled with a blender. Rolling up my sleeves, I noticed the faded outline of a sooty handprint. It was from Max.

Max had grabbed my arm the minute Sean and Sheriff Jackson

arrived at the scene. It took me a minute to realize he'd been talking to me. I was having a hard time focusing on anything other than the hole in the side of my mother's beloved rink.

"My film. I need to finish my film. You understand that. You'll take care of the film until I have a chance to come get it. This movie needs to be seen."

Sean raced over with his gun drawn. Finally, it was pointed at a bad guy. A very confused bad guy. He pushed a couple of DVDs into my hands just as Sean grabbed him. A few minutes later, he was trussed up in handcuffs.

"Making a movie isn't a crime," Max cried as Sean dragged him to the cruiser and stuffed him in. "Once the movie is edited and the right people see it, I'll be famous. Even my father will see it. He'll understand how important this is to me. Wait. This is a mistake."

A mistake that had landed me at Pop's for the night. Now that I was scrubbed clean, I went back to my bedroom and pulled on the shorts and tank top that had magically appeared in my absence. Then I followed my nose downstairs in search of coffee.

"There she is." Pop gave me a toothy grin. "I wanted to wake you up, but Lionel said we should let you sleep off the excitement. Last night was a real humdinger."

Lionel stood next to the kitchen sink, holding out a mug. I grabbed it and sucked the contents down. I held out the empty mug and Lionel refilled it.

"Okay, what happened while I slept?"

Pop's eyes danced. "The phone has been ringing off the hook. Your insurance agent is going to meet us at the rink in a half hour to do an assessment of the damage and start your claim. Then Sean Holmes called."

"Is he pissed at me?"

Pop cocked his head to the side. "Why would he be? I thought the two of you put away your differences. It looked that way from the stage."

"Last night wasn't what it looked like."

"It looked like Lionel here tried to make you jealous with Betsy Moore. You decided to get even with him by making a spectacle of yourself with Sean."

Okay, it was exactly what it looked like.

"If Sean doesn't want to arrest me, what does he want?"

"Your statement," Lionel said, passing over a DiBekla Bakery box. "You were a little overwrought about the rink last night. He thought it'd be best to wait until you got some rest. I can give him a call and ask him to meet us at the rink." His eyes told me he would also tell Sean to go to hell if I needed more time.

I blew a lock of hair out of my eyes. "Go ahead and call him." I armed myself with two chocolate croissants from the box. "Let's get this over with."

"Well, you were lucky the blast didn't do any structural damage." Aaron, my insurance agent, wrote something down on his clipboard and gave me a smile.

I tried to smile back. I was finding it hard to think I was lucky while looking at a seven-by-five-foot hole in the back side of my rink. Bricks, assorted car and lighting parts, and a bunch of other odds and ends were scattered all over the asphalt.

The sounds of kids laughing during their morning skating lessons made me smile for real. George had taken one look at the hole and grabbed some police tape and a couple of folding chairs.

He then blocked off what he considered an appropriate amount of rink space to ensure patron safety and plastered a big OPEN sign outside. It was probably a huge safety-code violation, but the three-piece-suit-wearing Aaron hadn't shut us down. If he didn't, no one else would.

"I'll send in my assessment, along with the police report about the explosion and about the break-in last week."

"Why the break-in?" Pop asked. He had added a hard hat to his ensemble of a tight white T-shirt and jeans. I thought he looked like a member of the Village People. He thought he looked macho.

Agent Aaron jotted a few more notes. "Oh, insurance companies are famous for holding things up if a member of the staff was involved in the claim." My stomach rolled. Aaron must have noticed my discomfort, because he added, "Don't worry. Deputy Holmes told me your manager already confessed to stealing the key from your grandfather."

I thanked the agent, watched him walk away, and heard a throat clear behind me. Sean.

Lionel was leaning against a holeless part of the rink, a small smile on his face. Perfect.

"I know you're tired, but I need to get your statement. Do you want to do this inside?"

Sean was back to his nice-cop routine today.

"Here is fine." Getting it over with was better. I walked Sean through the events of the week, finishing with last night's explosion. He asked a couple of questions but mainly let me do the talking. When I was done, I asked, "Was Max in the diner the night my father came to town? None of the people I talked to mentioned having seen him."

"He was there to order takeout but never got around to it. Your dad started talking about his car, and Max headed for the door."

Made sense. Clayton had mentioned a guy waiting behind him for takeout. It must have been Max. I didn't know why, but I felt better tying up that loose end. I also learned the rest of the crew had been camping out ten miles outside of town, which was why none of the gossips had reported seeing them.

"How's Max holding up?" Pop asked. "The kid is completely unhinged, but he was fun to hang out with."

Sean shrugged. "Max is fine. He's made a full confession, and his dad is talking to some new lawyer in town, hoping the guy will represent him. The fact that Max verified that all cars were insured before he blew them up might help him get a lighter sentence. You never know."

"Will you charge him with Kurt Bachman's murder? I heard Doc thought Kurt was knocked unconscious before the car was engulfed in flames." I left Eleanor's name out of it. Protecting my sources was important to me.

"It wasn't murder. Turned out the guy had a bad heart. According to Max, Kurt was supposed to light a fuse, then get out, so he could be filmed running away from the car as the car exploded. The fuse must have been shorter than the one that Max and Kurt used for the practice explosion."

Ah, that explained the dummy in the car. They'd only been practicing the first time. Too bad for everyone that practice in this case didn't make perfect.

"Doc figures Kurt panicked when the car exploded early. His blood pressure shot up and he knocked his head on the steering wheel when he lost consciousness. Max and his two cameramen might have figured that out if they'd actually checked the car, but they panicked when Kurt didn't get out of the car as planned."

Made sense. Except for one thing. "I never saw Max and the crew."

"You were probably too busy looking at the fire to notice them driving off in the vans they had parked at the other end of the field. Max said they parked far away from the site to keep the scene free of unnecessary obstructions. He didn't want to take the chance of ruining the shot, since they had only one take to get it right."

A man was still dead, but hearing it was an accident made me feel better. It was nice to know I hadn't hired a murderer.

"Oh, Max wanted me to remind you to keep his film safe until he gets out." Sean snapped his book shut and shot a strange, almost confrontational look at Lionel. "I'll drop by a copy of this later after Roxy types it up. Let me know if you need anything. I'd be happy to keep an eye on the place tonight. Don't want looters to take advantage."

"Already got that covered." Pop gave me a big grin. "Jimmy and a couple of the guys are bringing their lawn chairs and a cooler. They'll keep an eye out until the hole gets boarded up. Jimmy figures he owes you for finding his car."

If Pop was looking for another explosion, he was going to be disappointed. Sean didn't take the bait. He just gave my arm a squeeze and said a pleasant good-bye.

Pop slapped his hands together. "Well, I gotta get going. I promised to drop by the center. The talent agent from last night is stopping by to talk to me and the band about setting up some gigs."

I winced. "You're taking the band from your garage?"

"God no. They were awful. No, I'm playing with Hermanos Mariachi now. Their instruments arrived COD this morning.

Stan moved heaven and earth to get them here and then didn't have the cash to foot the bill. Since they're my band now, I fronted the money."

I groaned. "Are you sure that was a good idea? How do you know Stan isn't going to skip town?"

"He doesn't have a car." Pop flashed a big grin. "I made him agree to be the band's tour manager. I get his cut of the profits for as long as it takes to get the loan paid off. Then he'll start making money. He's a pretty good salesman, and he's motivated. Oh, and he's moving back in with me so I can keep an eye on him. That man needs supervision."

Pop strutted away singing "Viva Las Vegas," leaving me staring after him, stunned.

Lionel pushed away from the wall. He crossed over to me, leaned down, and lightly touched his lips to mine. I had unresolved anger issues with him, but right now there were too many other problems for those to really matter. Tomorrow would be another story.

Hand in hand, we walked to the front of the rink.

"Rebecca!" Danielle's voice rang out. "I just heard about the rink."

The minute I spotted her walking down the sidewalk, I knew why she hadn't heard the explosion last night. Danielle was wearing a lovely summer dress with a modest neckline and calf-length hem, along with tiny heels. A large diamond ring sparkled on her left hand.

"You and Rich got engaged?"

She nodded, and I gave her an enthusiastic hug.

"What happened? You were getting ready to break up with him."

Her cheeks colored. She shot a look at Lionel, as if assessing how much to say. "Right. Well, last night I finally asked Rich if he was attracted to me. I said I didn't want to be in a relationship where the attraction was only one-sided. That's when he popped the question and begged me to marry him before he burned in hell for impure thoughts! Getting close to me was making it hard for him to feel virtuous on Sundays. So he was keeping me at arm's length until he could make a romantic proposal. Guess I blew that."

Danielle looked so proud, I had to laugh. "When's the wedding?"

"Soon. Very soon."

"Rebecca! Yoo hoo!"

Crap. I turned to see Doreen getting out of her car.

"Your grandfather told me I'd find you here. I'm so sorry about the rink, dear. To think your rink manager was to blame for the damage. It's such a shame."

Shame wasn't the word I'd have used. "Did you need to talk about something?"

"Well, I don't know how to say this, but I talked to the buyer this morning. I had to tell him about the little problem you had last night. I felt terrible because my loyalty is to you and your mother, but . . ."

A dull ache began to build behind my eyes. "I understand, Doreen. You were doing your job."

Doreen sighed. "There's no good way to say this. With a hole in the rink and your manager in jail, well, the buyer has pulled out of the deal. I tried to talk him out of it, but there was nothing I could do."

I waited for a wave of panic to hit, for that feeling like the walls were closing in. Nothing. Huh. Maybe I'd been expecting the news. Then again, it could just be that I was on overload. I was sure I'd hit the roof and start cursing the fates when the shock wore off.

"Rebecca?" Danielle said softly. "This might not be the right thing for me to say. But since you're going to be in town awhile longer, would you be my maid of honor?"

I looked at the rink. A family of five came out of the front doors, smiling. Because of the rink's new window, I could hear the sounds of the Hokey Pokey playing from inside. I looked at Danielle, who was oozing happiness out of every pore. Lionel stood behind her, studying me with look that said he'd be happy to forget our fight and get right to the making-up part.

Maybe the explosion had been a message. Maybe I was supposed to think about keeping the rink and staying in Indian Falls.

I shook off the thought with a laugh. "Sure, I'd love to be your maid of honor."

Danielle was a great friend. Besides, until the rink got fixed and I could sell it, what else was I going to do?